OBLIGED TO BEND

by

B. A. BRADBURY

Published by **CHIMERA**
ISBN 9781780806709

Chapter 1

It was shortly after noon on a bitterly cold February day, the coldest yet in this winter of 1892, that I first set eyes on Irene Hammond.

Alice, the housemaid, announced her. I say 'announced' - Alice's anxious face appeared around the study door and she stammered a few words to the effect that my visitor had arrived. For some reason the girl always seemed dreadfully nervous in my presence.

'Show her in,' I said.

I rose from my desk as my visitor came into the room. I took one look at the new arrival and promptly offered up a silent prayer of thanks: for Irene Hammond, in the flesh, was everything I had hoped for.

I knew a great deal about her already - far more than she could ever guess. I knew she was thirty-two, five feet four, with chestnut brown hair and grey eyes. I knew also that she had been a widow for a year and a half, that her late husband had left her with substantial debts, and that she lodged in a rundown boarding house in Newbury in consequence.

I'd been assured that she was attractive, with a splendid figure to boot - needless to say I had been eager to judge these latter claims for myself (a second-hand description being no substitute for the evidence of one's own eyes).

That she was attractive was beyond question, even though her face was dreadfully pale and pinched with cold. As to her figure, there was an impressive fullness of breast and buttock clearly evident despite the thick woollen coat and muffler she sported. It was apparent too that the poor woman was frozen half to death. That she had chosen to walk the three miles from the railway station on such a day, rather than pay the local man to bring her by pony and trap, confirmed what I knew of her financial situation.

'Mrs Hammond,' I said, full of concern, 'please, come and sit by the fire. Kindly allow me to take your coat. May I get you a warming drink? Some tea, perhaps; or would you prefer a hot toddy?'

My concern was genuine. It had taken many months of searching and some considerable expense to find precisely the right individual for my needs. The last thing I wanted was to lose her immediately to pneumonia. She agreed to tea and I rang for Alice. I fussed and pampered my visitor, eventually she thawed sufficiently to stop her teeth chattering, and smiled, thanking me for my kindness.

'Think nothing of it,' I said. 'I'm happy to be of service. Just as I hope you may be of service to me.' A weak joke, but she smiled dutifully. If she could have guessed that the service I had in mind involved presenting her bare behind to cane, tawse and paddle she would have fled the house shrieking, not stopping until she was back in Newbury. Without, I suspect, pausing long enough even to put her coat on.

I discovered my true nature at an early age. I was just a boy when my father passed away. My mother had died when I was born and it was her father who assumed responsibility for my upbringing.

On the day in question I had wandered unannounced into my grandfather's study and found him disciplining one of the maids. She was kneeling on a stool, shoulders forward and head down, her elbows resting on the stool's edge, her hands clasped as though in prayer. Her skirts had been hiked up to her waist and her drawers pulled down. My grandfather was standing behind her, arm raised, a thin cane grasped in his strong bony hand.

As I entered the room my grandfather froze. I stood there in the doorway, transfixed by the sight of the girl's pale round buttocks raised in the air. They were striped with pink weals, a fact that excited and intrigued me beyond all reason. I often think it was at that precise moment that certain feelings surfaced from deep within me and have remained with me ever since.

My grandfather regarded me for several long moments, then he beamed. 'Come in, Jamie!' he cried. 'Do come in, my boy.'

His manner was jovial, and this, together with his cheery countenance, dismissed any uncertainty or awkwardness I might have felt. I've often wondered since whether he recognised, in those few brief seconds, a kindred spirit, and that's why I was invited into his inner sanctum.

I went closer. The unfortunate girl was a recent arrival, new to service, being fresh from one of the estate farms. I assume she had done something to earn my grandfather's displeasure and was now paying the price.

She was a pretty young thing, as I recall, with as trim a figure as one could wish for. Kneeling there in the study, however, in her present distressed state she was not looking her best. Her face was white, she was trembling uncontrollably, and her blue eyes were brim full of tears, I watched entranced as they rolled slowly down her cheeks to drop from her chin onto the rug.

'Why's she crying, grandfather?' I asked naïvely. 'Has *her* rabbit died, too?'

'Crying?' the old man said. 'Stuff and nonsense - she's putting it on. Here, I'll show you. We'll perform a little experiment, you and I, and you'll soon see the truth of it.'

He came around in front of the girl and tipped up her chin, forcing her to look him in the eye.

'Now listen to me, Fanny,' he said sternly, 'you must cease with this nonsense instantly, do you hear? Stop crying, and you can go back to the servants' hall. Any more blubbering, you know what to expect.'

He waved the cane under her nose in an ominous fashion. 'One stroke for every tear; is that understood?'

She nodded miserably.

'Good. Now then, Jamie, you wipe her face. Dry her off properly, then keep watch for any waterworks. Sing out if you spot a tear run down her cheek.'

He handed me a spotlessly clean white handkerchief. Strands of Fanny's pale blonde hair had come adrift from her cap and were hanging in her face. I carefully brushed them aside and proceeded to dry her eyes and cheeks. She regarded me mournfully throughout but I was at that age when another person's suffering is of little consequence.

At last it was done and I stood back. 'Ready, grandfather.'

'That's fine, my boy. You keep a sharp lookout, now.'

I waited, and watched. The pain in her well-thrashed bottom must have been considerable, for fresh tears welled up in her eyes. She bit her lip, presumably trying to hold them back, and blinked - but this proved disastrous. A large tear coursed down her left cheek, followed immediately by its twin on the right.

'Two, grandfather!' I cried happily.

I heard a swish, then a snick - not overly loud, but full of portent. Fanny flinched mightily, her eyes opening wide in pain and shock. Her mouth gaped, and she gave a shuddering cry. A second stroke followed quickly, which, to judge from her reaction, was even worse than the first.

'Mop her again, Jamie-lad,' my grandfather said.

I dried her face once more, then waited, barely able to stand still in my eagerness. I could see her trying desperately to fight back the tears, but a single large drop escaped the pale lashes. 'There's another!' I yelped excitedly.

The merciless stroke landed, and Fanny's head snapped up as she howled like a banshee. I clapped my hands with joy. This was definitely the best game I had ever played in my whole life.

The ritual with the handkerchief was repeated once more, and once more I stood back to await the inevitable. This time, however, through some Herculean effort on her part, Fanny somehow managed to stem the tide. Her eyes brimmed, I opened my mouth to shout out, but the tears never fell. I was tempted to pinch her nose to force the issue but wasn't sure this was in the rules. After another full minute I was forced to speak out.

'She's stopped, grandfather,' I said in dismay.

He chuckled at my reaction then dismissed the unfortunate girl. She pulled up her drawers, rearranged her skirts, and was out of that room in a flash.

'You see, Jamie?' my grandfather said in a kindly tone. 'Take no notice of a female's tears, no matter how great the flood. They can turn 'em on and off like a tap.'

Truly wise man, my grandfather. His words are a constant source of comfort and inspiration to me.

For the interview proper we moved from the couch to my desk. Irene Hammond sat across from me, her hands folded in her lap.

As usual a cane rested on the polished walnut top before me. I kept it there purely for effect, as I'd found in the past that the mere sight of a naked cane was enough to induce a fit of the shakes in most penitents. Irene Hammond's eyes rested briefly on the object, her face thoughtful, but I did not comment on it; any question in her mind remained unasked.

I enquired about her previous employment, and after a slight hesitation she launched into her story. She told me how, following the death of her husband some eighteen months previously (an unfortunate accident involving a runaway carriage), she had taken up a position as helper and companion to an elderly lady. She recounted how this lady had expired quite suddenly - so suddenly and unexpectedly that no provision had been made for her - and finally how she, Mrs Hammond, had been quite unable to obtain another post due to her lack of references.

'Ah, yes,' I said, 'remind me again about the references.'

Some of this I had learnt from the letter she wrote me, following an approach from a trusted intermediary with a provisional offer of a position: namely, that of governess. Now, however, I wished to hear it from her own lips - not because I found her account especially enthralling, rather that I liked listening to her voice. It was soft and mellow, with just a hint of the West Country to betray her origins. A very pleasing voice, a voice I looked forward to hearing under other, very different, circumstances.

While she was speaking I opened the folder before me, the folder containing Charlie Spikeman's report, and read again about Irene Hammond. The *real* Irene Hammond.

The part about her husband's death was almost true: it had been a coal wagon, not a coach that had ushered him from the mortal realm. Perhaps she thought being run over by a coal wagon was somehow demeaning. However, the elderly lady and the conflagration that cruelly devoured her references... these were pure fiction, and it was a lie that could well come back to haunt her.

In reality Mrs Hammond had actually been a governess, employed by a Hampshire bishop. The Right Reverend Bailey and his good lady were often abroad ministering to the heathen, leaving the welfare of their two sons in the hands of the governess. The abrupt termination of one of their trips due to an outbreak of cholera had caused them to return home unexpectedly, where they discovered, to their mortification, precisely how she discharged her duties. For Irene Hammond had been beating the tender young behinds of their offspring - and beating them till they glowed.

I made no attempt to challenge her account at this point, being content for now just to listen to that melodious voice and watch the play of firelight on her cheek. Indeed, I wanted her to commit herself fully to this fiction - the fuller the better, as far as I was concerned, as all this was part of my plan, carefully worked out and refined over the past few weeks.

I waited until she reached the end of her story and fell silent. I nodded slowly, sat back in my chair, folded my hands together then delivered the deathblow.

'Mrs Hammond,' I said solemnly, 'I feel you should know that the Right Reverend Bailey is a close personal friend of mine.'

That was, in fact, a lie almost on a par with hers. I'd never even met the man; but that was neither here nor there. My words achieved the desired effect, for her face became as pale as when she'd first arrived. Her mouth opened to speak, then closed again as her mind failed her. The play of expression across her features was wondrous to behold - bewilderment, shock, dismay, and back to bewilderment once more.

'But... but why then...?'

'Why did I agree to see you, knowing your history?' I smiled. 'To understand that, Mrs Hammond, it's best that you hear *my* history.'

Chapter 2

It is often said that boyhood is the happiest time of a man's life; and for me that was certainly true. Growing up in my grandfather's house, watching him (and in later years helping him) discipline maids, housekeepers and cooks galore was a magical time indeed.

Though my grandfather was undoubtedly the centre of my universe, he did not have sole claim on my affections, but shared them rather with Grace Forsyth, his lifelong friend and companion. Grace, as she always insisted I call her, was a genteel lady who had fallen on hard times, my grandfather had taken her in and given her a home. I was most fond of her, and she was always kind to me and smiled a great deal. Her eyes were brilliant blue, her hair silver-grey and she was invariably most elegantly dressed, for my grandfather was never mean with his money.

I became aware of the hidden side to their relationship one Christmas morning. I went along to Grace's sitting room, wishing to thank her for my present. Finding the door closed I opened it and ran in - a gross invasion of her privacy and inexcusable, I realise that now, even for a youngster carried away by the excitement of the season. It was certainly ill mannered of me but I had no ulterior motive for entering the lady's domain uninvited, being innocent in the ways of the world.

Prior to this I had watched my grandfather discipline one or other of the female staff on numerous occasions, but it never occurred to me that Grace also might be obliged to bend. The spectacle that met my eyes came as a considerable shock therefore, though not necessarily an unpleasant one.

Grace was standing before the fire, hands clasped behind her head, leaning forward from the hips. She wore nothing but a thin silken shift, pale blue in colour and trimmed with white fur. The hem was raised to her waist and pinned there so that her broad bottom, plump thighs and calves were fully displayed. Her limbs were white as milk though her buttocks were a deep pink with darker red patches. My grandfather was standing behind her, a tawse in his right hand. With his left hand he stroked her buttocks, as though assessing the damage caused by the strap.

Grace's eyes were closed, and for a moment or two she was oblivious to my presence. My grandfather looked over at me, however, and straightened, a broad smile spreading slowly across his whiskered face.

'Jamie,' he said cheerfully, 'there you are. Come closer and don't be shy. Mrs

Forsyth doesn't mind, do you, my dear?'

Grace opened her eyes and regarded me. She appeared less than comfortable at my presence, but murmured that I was welcome always.

'Come, Jamie-lad,' my grandfather said. 'You haven't seen Mrs Forsyth take her medicine, have you?'

I went further into the room. Though I loved Grace dearly, and would never wish to hurt her, a part of me tingled with excitement at the prospect of seeing her spanked.

'Since Jamie's here,' my grandfather said to her, 'we'll have another dozen.'

'Gerald,' she protested gently, 'he's just a lad.'

'Damn it, Grace,' came the reply, 'he has to learn sometime. In any case, he's seen a good few thrashings already, haven't you, lad? Didn't upset him a bit. A man after my own heart, our Jamie.'

Pride surged through me. This man that I so revered was speaking of me as an ally and *confidante*. I felt closer to him at that moment than I'd ever been to anyone in my life.

Grace made no protest thereafter, though I could tell she was not entirely happy at having me there. My grandfather told her to adopt the position once more as she had straightened and lowered her arms during the exchange. She complied, leaning forward once more clasping her hands behind her head.

'A dozen, then,' my grandfather reminded her. 'Count them, if you please.'

He raised his arm and gave her a hard stroke full on the curve of her buttocks. He was using a long, heavy, three-tailed tawse - though at the time I thought of it simply as a strap, being unaware of the distinction - and the crack as this fearsome article contacted her skin was astonishingly loud.

Grace let out a cry, and her shoulders rose.

'Down,' my grandfather warned her. 'Bend lower.'

It was clear that the force of the blow had caught her out. Slowly she reassumed the stance, leaning forward so that her torso was almost horizontal.

'One, sir,' she said, in a voice that was far from steady.

My grandfather looked at me, deadly serious, and winked. It was as though we shared a secret known to no one else in the world. I grinned at him as his stern expression cracked into a smile.

His second stroke was even harder but this time Grace bit back her cry, presumably to keep from upsetting me. 'Two, sir.'

My grandfather raised his arm. I was facing the same dilemma now that I had encountered at those previous sessions, watching Fanny, Sylvie and Nell under the rod. I wanted to look at her bottom, to see the strap bounce off her quivering flesh and observe the change in colour - from pink to red, and red to purple - as tender flesh protested this terrible mistreatment. But I also wanted to watch her face as the blows landed, to see her mouth gape and her eyes mist with pain. In short, I was in the classic flogger's predicament.

I resolved it now as I had before, by watching the first half dozen from the back, then moving forward to witness the rest from the front. This tactic clearly amused my grandfather, though he made no comment at the time.

Stroke number seven was brutally hard, and Grace's face showed extreme distress. Her posterior had been well drubbed even before this dozen started, as evidenced by the substantial bruising, so these fierce strokes must have been agonising for her.

The punishment proceeded slowly, my grandfather clearly in no hurry. At one point she tried valiantly to smile at me, wanting, I suppose, to reassure me that everything was all right, but pain turned her smile into a grimace.

The twelfth stroke came at last, hardest of all. Grace Forsyth took it with immense courage, remaining in position as a dutiful penitent should. 'Twelve, sir.'

My grandfather turned and treated me to another wink. 'What do you say, Jamie? Shall we give her a few more for luck?'

I stole a glance at Grace and saw her face fall. That the beating should continue when she thought it over was a cruel reversal, and dreadfully hard on her.

'How many more should we give her, do you think?' my grandfather asked. 'Six? Twelve?'

This landed me with another dilemma. As Grace's friend I wished to spare her more suffering, but the spanker in me was caught up in the excitement, wanting the punishment to go on forever. I was in a quandary, and unable to decide I stared at my grandfather in confusion. He must have perceived my difficulty, for he posed the same question to the lady herself.

'Six or twelve, Grace dear?'

'Twelve, sir,' she replied promptly.

'Hard strokes or medium?'

'Hard strokes, please sir.'

It was with the utmost lack of enthusiasm that she spoke these words, yet there was no hesitation or uncertainty. I was astonished that she could ask for such a thing, given her present distressed state.

'Well, Jamie?' my grandfather said. 'Do we do what Grace wants? Is it to be another dozen sizzlers?'

He was smiling, but I knew it was a serious question. It was as if this were a test. The quandary remained, but I knew I must answer without delay. Knowing no better, I said what was in my heart. 'No grandfather, I think she's had enough.'

His smile broadened, and he nodded. 'So do I, my boy... so do I. You may stand up straight, Grace. This punishment is concluded.'

At the time it seemed not so very different from the several other thrashings I had witnessed, except that the recipient was someone dear to me. But looking back on it now I understand that my grandfather was furthering my education, making me aware of new aspects of this noble art of spanking. I now knew that a strong, courageous woman could endure a hard punishment with fortitude and spirit... that affection for the victim was no bar to beating them... that the victim should never beg for leniency, rather she should ask for more. And, finally (and most importantly of all, perhaps), that it was sometimes appropriate and just for a flogger to show mercy and restraint - a valuable lesson.

Exciting and novel though my boyhood experiences had been, I refrained from relating any of this to Irene Hammond, confining myself solely to recent events.

'Some four months ago,' I said, 'a relative of mine and his wife met with an unfortunate and somewhat bizarre boating accident on the River Thames and were drowned.' (Unfortunate for them, that is, but remarkably fortunate for me, marking as it did a significant upturn in my fortunes. I kept this observation to myself however, as it could easily be misconstrued as avarice).

'Bertram and I were only distantly related,' I went on, 'through the husband of a cousin of my mother's - a tenuous link, yet I remain the closest living male relative, and Bertram had named me his heir. Naturally my main concern was the welfare of their three daughters, so tragically orphaned. Upon inheriting the estate I appointed myself their guardian - a role, Mrs Hammond, I do not take lightly. For a confirmed bachelor such as myself it is a heavy responsibility, as I'm sure you appreciate.'

'Indeed, sir,' she murmured.

It was clear from her face that she was perplexed. Baffled, no doubt, as to what all this had to do with her.

'A *heavy* responsibility, Mrs Hammond,' I repeated, 'and one I feel keenly. Young people need constant attention and guidance if they are not to stray from the straight and narrow, tender young souls in peril and all that. Wickedness is all around us, don't you agree?'

'I... of course, sir...' she stammered.

'Naturally you do,' I said. 'We adults can see the dangers that they often cannot. If my wards are to grow into fine upstanding women they need considerable... considerable...' I waved my hand, searching for the right word.

'Help?' she suggested.

I shook my head sadly. 'Discipline, Mrs Hammond. Considerable *discipline.*'

There was a pause, then her mouth curved in a faint smile. At last she understood what all this was about - or thought she did.

I became suddenly very brisk and businesslike, explaining that she would have to reside here at the hall, naturally, and that a sitting room and bedchamber had been made ready on the upper floor for that purpose.

'As to the remuneration,' I said, 'I'm prepared to offer one hundred pounds per annum.'

Her face registered utter astonishment. It was a huge amount, three times as much as she could have hoped for. With such a large income she could no doubt envisage a time, just a few years hence, when she would be free from debt.

'Are you able to start immediately?' I enquired. 'Today?'

'Why... yes of course, sir. Yes indeed!'

'Excellent! I must tell you, Mrs Hammond, how delighted I am that you'll be joining us. Having someone I can rely on will be a great relief. In addition to my wards, there's the staff to consider.'

'The staff, sir?'

'Just so, I had to dismiss most of them; they were quite unsuitable. I allowed a few to stay on - two of the maids, Alice and Rose, and Willie the hall-boy. All three require constant supervision, I'm afraid. They seem incapable of completing even the simplest of tasks to my satisfaction and I find myself having to punish them constantly. I've made some small progress with Rose and Alice, so I intend to continue disciplining them myself. The boy, though, is another matter. I wish you to take him under your wing, as it were. I only hope that you might succeed where I've failed.'

She smiled, feeling firmer ground beneath her feet, no doubt. 'I'll certainly try, sir.'

'Excellent. Possibly I should have dismissed Willy too, but Christian charity prevented me. He's a pitiful creature, with not a single friend or relative in the whole wide world, no one to confide in, no one to share his troubles with. All, all alone.'

Her smile became almost predatory.

'We also have a gardener, groom and stable boy,' I said. 'They generally keep their own company, and rarely need to enter the house. You may wish to seek them out and look into their little ways. The gardener and groom are elderly and probably beyond redemption, but Jack the stable boy is a different kettle of fish. He seems a spirited enough lad, though perhaps a little lazy at times. Please feel free to deal with him as you see fit. It may be you can make something of him, should, of course, your other duties allow you the time - and should you feel so inclined.'

'I think it is my bounden duty to try, sir,' she said, 'for the good of the boy.'

'A noble sentiment, Mrs Hammond,' I said, 'and one that does you credit.'

'Thank you, sir.'

'The only other person here,' I said, 'is Mrs Morgan, our cook. I couldn't very well have dismissed her or we should have starved. Nevertheless, she will have to go. I wish you to seek out a replacement as soon as it may be arranged. Someone who is more suited to our situation here. I leave all that to your good judgment, Mrs Hammond.'

She inclined her head at the compliment and the display of trust.

'There may be other services I require of you,' I went on after a moment. 'Services of a more... personal nature.'

I gave her a very direct look as I spoke these words, a look no grown woman - especially one who had been married - could fail to understand. The smile faltered and she became quite still. She hadn't had relations with a man since her husband died - Spikeman's report was quite clear on that; servants' halls are full of gossip and crafty Charlie, I was confident, could sniff out the least whiff of scandal.

Irene Hammond seemed to gather herself. She took a deep breath, lifted her chin bravely, and returned my look measure for measure. 'That will be perfectly satisfactory, sir,' she said in a quiet but determined voice.

I was, I have to say, intrigued, for I couldn't tell whether or not she was pleased at the prospect. Though it may be immodest of me to say so, I believe I am a tolerably handsome man; or so I have been assured by women of my acquaintance. Unquestionably I am tall, and dark of hair and beard. It is true that grooming sessions of late had revealed an increasing number of grey hairs, particularly in my beard, which I habitually keep short and neatly trimmed, but this should not in itself render me instantaneously hideous. It seemed reasonable to hope, therefore, that my physical appearance would prove help rather than hindrance in furthering my suit.

Though her precise opinion was not easily determined, it was clear that Mrs Hammond was not dismayed or shocked by my proposition. It was with considerable eagerness therefore that I looked forward to exploring that particular aspect of our relationship.

Now I deliberately lightened the mood, smiling expansively to show I was really quite a jolly fellow after all.

'That's settled, then,' I said. 'Splendid. My wards will... but wait; I don't believe I've told you about the girls yet, have I? How remiss of me.'

There were three, as I said: Catherine, known to everyone as Cathy, was the youngest. She was a sweet enough thing to look upon, blonde-haired, blue-eyed, and exceedingly pretty. Her figure was starting to fill out and I judged she would make a very striking young woman in a year or two's time. At present she was still at that coltish stage, with a propensity to run rather than walk, and speak too loudly and too often. Cathy was not over-endowed with intelligence, I have to say, although I know many who consider that a positive advantage in a woman.

Victoria came next. Less frivolous and more intelligent than Cathy, her most striking physical feature was her copper-red hair. She was not as pretty as her younger sister though her features were regular enough, although she was a little unfortunate in the matter of freckles, of which there were many. Her figure spoke of a definite liking for pastries and cakes, and though 'fat' is perhaps too unkind a word she could certainly be described as plump. And yet, strangely, though each of these aspects left something to be desired, the whole was decidedly appealing. I had contemplated this conundrum many times without ever reaching a satisfactory conclusion.

The eldest of my wards was Elizabeth. She was, to put it simply, a beauty. She was tall and elegant with hair as dark and lustrous as polished ebony, and had astonishingly lovely hazel eyes. Her complexion was creamy and flawless. To watch her coming down the stairs, head erect, back straight, breasts jutting proudly... well, it was enough to bring a tear of joy to the eye of even the most jaded and cynical of bachelors. It certainly made *me* happy.

Three young women then, each with a very different disposition, and not a scrap of family resemblance between them. Most odd. It was tempting to conclude that their mother must have entertained officers from the county regiment in her husband's absence.

Not that I burdened Irene Hammond with such conjectures at this time. I described the nature and manner of each of the girls, and explained that the younger ones had been growing somewhat wayward of late. 'Let me give you an example,' I said.

The story that followed was the purest poppycock, invented by myself that very morning for reasons that will shortly become clear. One thing I have learned, however, is that provided one maintains an earnest expression, even the most outrageous tale has every chance of being believed.

'A few days ago,' I said, 'late in the morning, I had cause to go up to my bedchamber. As I was about to mount the staircase I happened to see Cathy coming from her room dressed as though for a summer fair. She was playing some fanciful game, twirling her parasol and singing a little song - something about a pixie and a porcupine, as I recall. Do you know the tune, Mrs Hammond?'

She replied that she did not.

'The song is of no consequence,' I said. 'What matters is what happened next. The girl's spinning parasol caught one of the pictures on the wall and knocked it to the floor. I decided to observe her behaviour at this point, and concealed myself behind the aspidistra. I heard the door to her room close, and went up to investigate. The picture had been replaced on its hook, but the frame was badly split, obviously from the fall. Later that same evening I advised my wards that the maid had reported the damaged picture frame to me, and asked if any of them knew how it might have happened. Each of them, in turn, said that they did not.'

I paused briefly to let the full import of this sink in.

'Cathy lied, Mrs Hammond,' I said gravely. 'She stared me straight in the eye, and denied all knowledge of it.'

Irene Hammond looked suitably shocked.

'I was tempted to thrash her then and there,' I went on, 'though I did not. Weakness; pure weakness on my part. I felt pity for the girl and neglected my duty. I must not allow that to happen again. Sins must be punished, for the good of the sinner; do you not agree?'

'Indeed I do, sir.'

'We must not flinch from our duty. We must flog them, if necessary - flog them till they scream for mercy, no matter how distasteful we find it. Their posteriors may suffer, but think of the benefit to their souls. A good whipping is worth a thousand sermons, as my old grandfather used to say.'

'Oh quite, sir,' Mrs Hammond said enthusiastically. 'I do so agree!'

Her eyes were bright and her cheeks flushed. I could see that saving souls was a task that appealed to her greatly. I stroked my chin thoughtfully. 'Perhaps,' I said slowly, 'it's not too late after all.'

'Sir?'

'To punish young Cathy. I could send for her this instant. A smartly applied cane on her bare buttocks would soon have her singing a very different tune. No porcupines in *that* one, I'll be bound! How many strokes, would you say, for a lie? A lie deliberately and knowingly told?'

Mrs Hammond started to speak, but then her face changed. She had seen the trap, and I was more pleased than ever at my choice of governess. Quick and intelligent, as well as beautiful. But not quite quick enough. The trap was already sprung and she was caught, with no means of escape. Irene Hammond's own lie had, as predicted, come back to haunt her.

She regarded me with uncertainty and apprehension plain to see in her eyes. Another person might well have left in high dudgeon at this point, and in theory so could Mrs Hammond, though I knew she would not. She was facing ruin unless she could find the means to clear her debts. Lacking references, her chances of securing another position were remote. The very generous wage I was offering sealed her fate, for it was the answer to all her prayers. My position, I knew, could not have been stronger. Irene Hammond was utterly and completely in my power.

'I think it's important we understand one another,' I said pleasantly. 'I couldn't, in fairness to my wards, consider employing someone who took a lenient view of such transgressions. How many strokes then, for a deliberate lie? How many, plainly put, for *you*, Mrs Hammond?'

She swallowed. 'Two dozen...?' she suggested tentatively.

I frowned.

'Three?' she said quickly.

I allowed my face to clear, and nodded. 'Three dozen it is,' I said. 'And no time like the present, as they say.'

I rose and went around the desk, took her arm, and raised her to her feet. There was a momentary hesitation, a second or two of resistance, and then she yielded. Though a woman's mind is a strange and unfathomable thing, as I led Irene Hammond across the room I felt sure I could guess what was in hers. She was wondering what in God's name she had let herself in for.

Chapter 3

Between the tall oak cupboard and the bookcase in my study, directly opposite the door that leads out into the hall, is a second door. It was to this that I led Mrs Hammond.

The key was in the lock, I turned it, opening the door to reveal a medium-sized room. The governess gave a gasp of astonishment, or possibly dismay, for the room housed a collection of whips, lashes, riding crops, straps, paddles and canes that I doubt can be bettered anywhere in England, if not the whole of Europe. There was barely an inch of wall space that was not occupied by some implement of correction.

They hung on pegs, row upon row of them, and beside each piece was a small plaque giving details of its pedigree. Some were antiques, far too precious to be used. Many had travelled from distant and exotic countries. A select few had been owned by famous people and were of considerable historical and sociological interest. Few people would guess, for instance, that a certain government minister was never without a tawse, even when he journeyed abroad, or that a lady within the royal household carried a special folding cane in her handbag.

Many more, perhaps half of the total number, were more commonplace and I had no compunction about using them - as Alice and Rose knew to their cost. But, prestigious or prosaic, every last one of them was imbued with a sense of purpose that was tangible.

Mrs Hammond stared at the display in a sort of hunted fascination. The flogger in her must surely have been awed and enthralled by the sight, but she was seeing the collection from the viewpoint of a recipient, which was a very different kettle of fish.

I allowed her to absorb the spectacle for several seconds longer, and then closed the door. 'We shall not,' I said gently, 'be needing any of these today.'

She looked at me, treating me to another play of expression across those delightful features. Confusion, uncertainty, and finally hope all took their turn at centre stage. Truly, the woman had a most expressive face. 'Shall... shall we not, sir?'

'No indeed, Mrs Hammond. We shall not.'

I locked the door and pocketed the key. She realised then that I had been teasing her all along, or perhaps testing her resolve. Her bottom was to be spared - there was to be no punishment, no three dozen. The relief and gratitude in her eyes was most satisfying, I have to say. No one wishes to be thought an ogre, after all.

I stepped to my left and opened the doors to the oak cupboard. 'One of these,' I said, 'will do perfectly well.'

Irene Hammond's look of relief died in infancy as she surveyed my day collection. Any woman relying on my sense of compassion to deliver her from her ordeal is living in a fool's paradise, and as for being regarded an ogre, or anything else for that matter, any man who cares a jot about what others think of him is a poltroon.

My day collection might be small compared with that in the adjoining room, but all the articles had been carefully selected for their practicability. There were three (one light, one medium and one heavy) of each of the more common types of implement - cane, paddle, ruler and tawse. In addition, there were a couple of multi-thong lashes and a short whip of the style usually referred to as a quirt.

Side by side, the governess and I viewed this modest yet versatile collection. I swept my hand across in a grand gesture. 'Please select one, Mrs Hammond,' I said.

Now, it was not at all my usual practice to allow the penitent the luxury of choice at this point. This was a special occasion however, and I was interested to observe her reaction. She stood there for a full minute, her hand hovering first over one item then another. Finally she chose the medium cane. I suspect it was a case of 'better the devil you know...', but it was not a wise choice, and spoke to me of a lack of appreciation of the finer points of flogging.

A cane, particularly one of the heavier varieties, can inflict a monumental amount of pain in the right hands. She would have done better to have picked the lightest ruler or paddle. These can certainly sting fiercely when wielded enthusiastically, but cannot replicate the searing, white-hot pain of a hard cane stroke.

But no, a cane it was to be, she held it out to me, handling it somewhat gingerly as though the thing might bite her. I accepted it graciously, took her arm once more, and led her to the centre of the room.

'We shall have three sets of twelve,' I announced, 'with a change of position following each set. Is that agreeable?'

'Yes, sir.'

I didn't give a fig what she thought of the proposal and she knew it. She was obliged to accept whatever I chose to hand out. I was tormenting her, pretending she had some say in all this.

'Then kindly raise your skirts,' I said, 'at the back.'

She gave me one last unhappy glance then lifted her skirts to her waist. I squatted behind her and pulled her drawers down to her ankles, and she murmured as I did so, clearly ill at ease. I guessed she had hoped to retain these for modesty's sake, but there was not the slightest chance I would allow that, out of respect for my grandfather's memory if nothing else. I can still hear him now, spluttering with indignation at one of the maids who'd had the temerity to make such a request prior to a caning.

'Keep your bloomers on?' he cried, his eyes almost popping out of his head. 'Why, I never heard of such a thing! Next you'll be asking me to eat a pheasant with the feathers on. An extra dozen for you, young lady, for impertinence!'

So I drew down Irene Hammond's drawers, then stepped back to admire the view. Charlie Spikeman, I thought, you prince among men; you've earned yourself a sizeable bonus for this day's work, for our new governess was utterly magnificent. Her broad, full buttocks were creamy-white, smooth, and beautifully rounded. I challenge any man alive, be he butler or bishop, lord or labourer, to regard those buttocks and not wish to bestow upon them a smack or two at the very least. Without a doubt, Irene Hammond possessed the finest pair of cheeks I had ever clapped eyes on - and I've seen a good few in my time.

I was tempted to smack her myself, there and then, for there's nothing quite like the feel of a firm bottom bouncing under your palm; but I refrained, not wishing to set my dignity at risk by appearing frivolous or flighty. A punishment is a serious matter, and must be conducted accordingly. A few playful slaps might be great fun (for me, at least) but could easily give the impression this was all just a game, which it most certainly was not.

So now Mrs Hammond waited, eyes shut fast, breast rising and falling rapidly; yet I delayed, savouring the moment. Pleasure of anticipation for myself, trepidation for our new governess. A few precious seconds of this, then I raised the cane and tapped it lightly against her buttocks three times - tap-tap-tap.

'Oh!' she gasped, buttocks clenching and back arching as she rose up onto her toes.

She had no way of knowing it, but she had just been introduced to my famous Triple-Tap-Tester. And much it had revealed to me, for I was convinced now she was a virgin. I'm not suggesting that her maidenly portals had never been breached, you understand. George Reginald Hammond may have been remiss in the matter of road safety, but that was no reason to suspect he was neglectful of his duties in the marital bed. Indeed, only a fool of the first order would fail to avail himself of Irene Hammond's abundant charms.

No, the virginity I allude to is of a different kind altogether - the woman had never been caned before. Her reaction to the gentle tap was that of a complete novice, out of all proportion to the mere tickle she received. She was a spanking virgin, which made all this doubly pleasurable for me. Like footprints across a field of freshly fallen snow, the stripes I was about to leave on her posterior would be all mine, with no one there before me. The marks would fade in a few days, but no matter what befell her after, James Montague esquire would always be the man who gave Irene Hammond her first caning.

And I could delay no longer. I drew back my arm and struck her. This was no light tap, but a lively stroke that whistled on its way. Not desperately hard, yet crisp enough to give her something to think about, it contacted Irene Hammond's behind with a satisfying *thwick*. She yelped and her hips jerked forward, mimicking the coital thrust.

Mrs Hammond; dear Mrs Hammond, I thought - if only the Right Reverend Bailey's boys could see you now. Would they not jump for joy and clap their hands with glee? Possibly they would snatch the cane from me in their eagerness for revenge. And I would snatch it right back. I'd worked and schemed for this moment, and no one was going to take it from me.

A second stroke followed, then a third, and a fourth. Once she realised it wasn't quite as bad as she'd feared, Mrs Hammond seemed to settle a little. I made the fifth stroke somewhat harder, both to undermine her confidence and to set her twitching again.

After the next I stopped to examine her. Six narrow pink tramlines, marks typical of a cane, showed against her white skin. Evenly spaced and virtually identical, they were weals to be proud of. An excellent start, I thought, to what promised to be a most enjoyable session.

'May I rub, sir?' she asked, once she realised this was more than just a longer pause between strokes. I was pleased that she understood a penitent must ask permission before rubbing her bottom. There are some, I know, who consider this old-fashioned but I was taught by a master of the old school and take pride in these ancient traditions.

While Irene Hammond rubbed her tingling behind, I watched her face. She looked very thoughtful, and I imagined she must be wondering how much worse it would get. An experienced flogger herself, she would be familiar with the principle of escalation. 'Start easy, finish hard,' as my grandfather used to say. 'That's the way to let 'em know they've had their bums whipped.'

'Thank you, sir,' Mrs Hammond said, with a respectful glance in my direction. She hitched her skirts up a little higher, then became still once more, closing her eyes to await the remaining strokes.

I had to smile, for I recognised these actions of hers - thanking me, and adopting the position in this way - for what they were. She was attempting to dictate the pace of the proceedings. It was understandable that she wanted her punishment over and done with as quickly as possible, but the penitent must never be allowed to take control in this manner. It was of the utmost importance that I establish my authority at this early stage in our relationship. Mrs Hammond must be left in no doubt as to who was master. She wished to hurry things along, so I would delay matters.

I left her standing there, stoically awaiting the remaining two and a half dozen, while I strolled to the bell-pull and rang for Alice. The maid appeared in a trice, I asked her to pour me a brandy, and I saw her eyes register astonishment as she took in the scene before her as she scuttled across to the cabinet by the window.

'Tell me, Mrs Hammond,' I said, 'do you think you will like our Oxfordshire countryside?'

'Why... yes, sir, I... I believe I will,' she stammered.

'We have some fine elms in the neighbourhood. Did you notice them on your way from the railway station?'

'I... no, sir... I can't say that I did.'

'Particularly fine,' I said, 'though we will have to wait till summer to see them at their best, of course.'

Alice carried the brandy over to me on a small silver tray, curtsied, and then attempted to slip away unnoticed. I had other ideas, however.

'Alice,' I said, the poor girl almost jumping out of her skin, 'you're a native of these parts, I'm sure you'd agree the countryside hereabouts is beautiful.'

'Yes sir, thank you, sir,' she said, glancing at the door with a look of desperate longing, curtseying twice more for good measure.

I swirled the brandy in the glass and sampled its nose. Excellent; truly excellent. Bertie was as fine a judge of brandy as any Cornish smuggler.

I strolled back to where Irene Hammond waited. Casually I stroked her buttocks, pretending to examine the marks left by the cane. In reality, of course, I was drawing the maid's attention to them - and more importantly, letting Irene Hammond know that I wished the staff to witness her humiliation.

'England can boast many fine counties,' I said, 'but I challenge anyone to name a prettier valley than our own, eh, Alice?' It was a ridiculous question, of course. The girl had never in her life been more than ten miles from the village where she was born, let alone travelled the country. I expected, and got, the stock reply to almost any question posed to her.

'Yes sir, thank you, sir.'

'Thank *you*, Alice. You may go.'

She curtsied once more and hastily departed. Normally I would have called her back for a lecture on decorum and a quick dozen, but I was in a good mood and let it pass. Her eagerness to be back in the relative safety of the servants' corridor was understandable. Canes and raised skirts were all too familiar to the girl; possibly she believed the combination to be contagious.

I finished my drink at leisure, deposited the glass on the table and sauntered back to my victim. I stood before her and looked directly into her troubled eyes. 'I think,' I said quietly, 'we will now carry on where we left off. Does that meet with your approval, Mrs Hammond?'

Since I had made my point with all the subtlety of a stampeding carthorse, there was little chance she could fail to take my meaning. From the chastened guilty look on her face I knew that she did, indeed, understand. Now that things were back on track I could happily resume the session. I whipped the cane through the air two or three times, partly to loosen my arm, but mostly to unnerve her.

'Count the strokes out loud, if you please,' I said. 'Start at seven.'

I used this common spanker's device routinely. The slow disintegration of control as the punishment proceeds can be heard quite distinctly in the victim's voice, and as such is a most reliable indicator of her suffering. Anyone can exaggerate a flinch, and most can cry out reasonably convincingly, but few can fake the quaver in the voice that results from stress, or make it crack in a plausible manner.

I lifted the cane and whipped across in a firm but controlled manner, somewhat harder than before. Irene Hammond gasped, and flinched very prettily. I waited.

'Seven, sir.'

Simple and to the point. I'm not one of the 'seven-thank-you-very-much-sir' brigade, which to me has a false ring to it. One particular acquaintance of mine goes even further, but 'seven-thank-you-sir-and-pardon-me-for-being-a-bad-girl' turns the whole affair, in my humble opinion, into a farce.

I delivered another stroke of identical weight, but targeted at a slightly different point on her posterior.

'Eight, sir.'

And so we continued, with the strokes perhaps fifteen seconds apart. By the tenth her voice was starting to falter. I made the twelfth the hardest of the lot so far. As the last stroke in this first set she would expect no less.

'Twelve, sir,' she said, her voice quavering in a most enchanting fashion.

I waited; so did she, maintaining her position. Most satisfactory. The temptation here for penitents knowing a change of stance is due, is to rub to ease the sting or abandon the position or lift one leg, or do all three at the same time. Mrs Hammond did none of these things, I nodded in quiet satisfaction.

I stepped up to examine her more closely, stroking my hand over her buttocks. The pink weals were nicely spaced, with little overlap, though naturally there was some slight difference in colour due to the varying stroke strength. A good start, I thought, and decided to share that happy thought with her.

'A good start, Mrs Hammond. Only two dozen more to go.'

Was that a sigh from her lips? I couldn't be sure, though it seemed likely. Her bottom must be stinging considerably by now, and the thought of another two-dozen more to come would not be a welcome one.

'You may lower your skirts,' I said. 'Feel free to stretch, or rub, at your leisure. Should you wish to take a turn about the room, please do so; but pray don't forget your drawers are still around your ankles. I would hate to see you fall flat on your face.'

She took me up on two of these options, rubbing her bottom and lowering her skirts in that order. In the meantime, I helped myself to another brandy.

Chapter 4

I allowed her to rest for five minutes or so. Initially grateful for the respite, she had begun to fidget by the end. She was impatient to see the back of all this, of course; unlike her employer, who could think of no better way to pass a frosty winter's afternoon.

'Very well,' I said. 'For the next dozen you must bend over and grasp your ankles.'

She complied, and I raised her skirts. Though hardly original, this position is both eminently practical and nicely humiliating. And it possesses one further benefit - if the victim's drawers are down, the flogger is afforded a clear view of her slit.

I walked behind the governess, and sure enough, nestling in a tuft of dark hair was that most delightful of organs. Back at my old house, if Polly were to present her rear- end in such a provocative fashion I would most likely dip into her. Family ties had prevented Polly joining me here in my new residence, and I sometimes regretted not having pressed her a little harder. In the end I acquiesced, and secured her a place with the local squire. To judge from her letters she is content enough there. The squire, she informs me, is less severe than I with the cane (which she appreciates) but, being no longer a young man, mounts her far less often (which she doesn't). Then again, as I pointed out in my reply, one cannot have everything.

As I looked at Irene Hammond, bending over for punishment, I decided this was sheer balderdash. A highly attractive woman was presenting her beautifully formed and nicely striped rear end for further treatment. Should I wish to avail myself of her charms they were mine for the taking. In this same household three young women lived in blissful ignorance of my plans for their tender young bottoms, whilst the pair of maids were only too aware of my intentions towards theirs. Maybe one cannot have *absolutely* everything in life, but this came pretty damn close.

Thinking of Polly had set certain carnal notions running through my mind. I resolved not to indulge myself at this time but to stay with my original plan and administer a straight caning. There would be plenty of time for dalliance later, and I had some rather specific intentions for Irene Hammond in that regard. It would be a shame to spoil things by plunging straight in - as it were.

I did allow myself one small treat, however. I stepped close behind her, reached down, and ran the tip of my middle finger against her slit. She made a sound like a startled owl, and shot bolt upright.

'Get back down!' I snapped.

She stared at me in consternation, started to speak, changed her mind, and went down again almost as fast as she had come up.

'And stay down, or by God I'll make you sorry!'

I quickly re-hoisted her skirts and gave her an immediate swipe with the cane. It was a substantial stroke, guaranteed to take her mind off all extraneous matters. She groaned and swayed forward a little. Another advantage of this classic position occurred to me then - the victim cannot diminish the force of the blows by jerking her hips forward at the last second, as she can when standing upright. Whatever is delivered, that is what is felt.

'Thirteen, sir,' Irene Hammond murmured.

I had not rescinded the instruction to count the strokes so she was doing what she had been told and was obeying the last order given. In some aspects of this art, she was remarkably sagacious; in others, surprisingly naïve.

I decided to reward her good behaviour and made the next four somewhat lighter. This change was immediately detected in her voice as she counted. Rewards are all well and good of course, but I would hate her to think I was going soft. The very next stroke, therefore, was once again a firm one.

'Eighteen, sir.'

The quaver was back, and I felt a sense of deep satisfaction. I had practiced this art for many years and prided myself that I was master of both it and myself. I realise I risk being branded a braggart, but this is my honest opinion and false modesty is more reprehensible to me than conceit.

Now, our good vicar tells us frequently that we are all sinners and I don't doubt that he is right. If pride is sinful, then surely unwarranted pride is doubly so; and it was for this reason I resolved to test my skills.

Six more strokes were due Irene Hammond in this second set. The challenge would be to make each stroke harder than the one preceding, and to cause her voice to crack on the final stroke, but not before.

Could I do it? I was confident that I could - and if I did, then I reckoned I could justifiably claim the title of Master Flogger and consider myself a very fine fellow indeed. If I failed, then clearly I needed a great deal more practice, and Mrs Hammond, Alice, Rose, Elizabeth, Victoria and dear Cathy had better resign themselves to taking their meals standing up from now on.

So I composed myself, like a musician about to attempt a difficult piece. I flexed my arm, took a deep breath, and took careful aim.

Swish, went the cane... then *snick!*

'Oh!' went the governess... then, 'Nineteen, sir.'

The swish-snick combination was repeated, and the count climbed slowly. Twenty. Twenty-one. Twenty-two... her voice so very close to breaking now. The next stroke would be critical. Too much and I would have failed; yet my self-imposed rules demanded it be harder than the last.

I drew back the cane, and snapped it forward. It contacted with a solid *thwack!*

'Ah-hhh!' she gasped.

The next few seconds were each about a fortnight long. I realised I was holding my breath. Would the damn woman *never* speak?

'Twenty-three, sir,' she said in a voice that quavered mightily, but did not, quite, break.

After that it was easy. A slight extra impetus to the swing was all that was required. I was confident she would not move. She knew what was expected, and had herself well under control.

I raised the cane and swiped it across the lowest part of her behind, in the crease where buttock meets thigh. It is a particularly sensitive spot and it drew forth an agonised gasp. The wait for the count seemed interminable, but I had no real doubts as to the outcome.

'Twenty-four, sir,' she said, her voice cracking beautifully.

James Montague - flogging supremo. I almost stepped forward and took a bow.

I allowed Irene Hammond a longer rest, fully fifteen minutes, following this second dozen. From the look on her face when I announced this I knew the respite was most welcome. The desire to finish the session was tempered now by her need to recover somewhat, for her behind must be burning exceedingly.

She rubbed vigorously and, having removed her drawers altogether at my behest, proceeded to walk about the room. Every few seconds she would stop and bend her right knee, raising her foot at the back in that curious way women do when their bottoms are on fire. I have never fathomed out why they do this exactly, and can only assume it provides a degree of relief in some fashion.

For the third and final dozen I decided to try her in an unusual and rather difficult position - difficult for both of us, that is. I cleared the top of my desk and had her stand upon it, needing both my assistance and the use of my chair as a step to manage this feat. She seemed somewhat ill at ease ascending to this elevated position, and I held fast to her hand, assuring her I would not let her fall.

I had her stand with her back to me, her heels at the very edge of the desk, and then squat down. At my instruction she gathered up her skirts and pulled the loose material about her waist. Her bare buttocks overhung the edge of the desk, positively inviting a slap.

Mrs Hammond's stance reminded me of Annie Mappleton, many years ago, squatting on a tree stump to take a pee. Taking a stroll about the countryside I came upon Annie, the eldest girl from Lea Farm, obeying a call of nature at the edge of Barley Wood. I carried a stick with me for beating aside brambles and suchlike, and I resolved to fetch her a whack across her white rump to see her jump. But as I was creeping up behind her a twig snapped under my foot, and I was discovered.

At that age I was very quick on my feet, but not quick enough to catch the Mappleton girl that morning. She took one look at me advancing, stick in hand and no doubt grinning evilly, and with a yelp of dismay took off across the fields like a hare.

The image of Annie squatting on the stump stayed with me and inspired me to try this now. It is not, as I said, an easy position, either for punisher or recipient. Blows must be delivered in an upwards direction, which feels most odd and unnatural and requires considerable practice if accuracy and consistency of strength are to be maintained. It is certainly not a position the novice flogger should be contemplating.

The difficulty lies in the strained position. Most women find it uncomfortable after just a few minutes, with thighs and calves tending to cramp. It does have one particular advantage however, that being the easy access it affords to the victim's private parts. A hand slipped underneath will immediately find the slit, soft and inviting - which is precisely what I did to Irene Hammond. As my fingertips located the area in question she gave a muted squeal, and showed signs of rising.

'Stay down, madam!' I warned.

I stroked her slit while she squatted before me. I made no attempt to penetrate her, and paid no special attention to her clitoris as I was not intending sexual gratification at this time. I was merely staking my claim, as it were, and getting her used to the idea of being handled. I fondled her for a while longer then took up the cane once more.

'So... here we are,' I said. 'The final dozen.'

I was standing behind her and somewhat to her left. I rested my left hand lightly on her shoulder to steady her, touched the tip of the cane to the floor directly below her buttocks, and then whipped it upward. I made this a very firm stroke, the hardest yet. She jerked; or rather, bounced on the spot. Her face was buried in the gathered folds of her skirts so that her cry was somewhat muffled, as was her voice when she spoke.

'Twenty-five, sir.'

The caning continued. I paused after every third stroke, rubbing her slit again, and each time I did so she trembled.

I made the final three harder still. I was striking with a fair degree of force and knew the pain must be considerable. She had curled into a tight ball, hugging her knees with her arms, her head and shoulders down. Muffled though her voice was I could hear her distress clearly as she counted. The final stroke was, in accordance with a custom that went back to the dawn of time, hardest of all.

'Thirty-six, sir,' she said.

There was no hint of relief in her voice that I could detect. She waited, a shivering ball, her trembling very pronounced - I presumed from the strain of her position. I sensed apprehension. Possibly she was expecting the return of my finger seeking her cunny. Possibly she feared further punishment. I learned this classic flogger's trick - the allocation of extra strokes just when the victim believed it was all over - at an early age. It can be astonishingly demoralising for them, shattering the last vestiges of control they'd been hoarding so scrupulously. I remember watching one of my grandfather's kitchen maids - Olive, I think her name was - endure an especially fierce four dozen with courage and dignity, yet burst into tears when he announced an additional six strokes.

In fact, I did neither. I told her to get down, taking her hand while she did so.

She was rather unsteady on her feet, her face pale and drawn. I led her to the couch and lay her facedown while I examined her buttocks. They were, I have to say, in something of a state. They were crisscrossed with weals, some greater, some lesser. The last dozen strokes in particular had been especially hard on her. Owing to the stance I couldn't tell precisely where the strokes were landing; and I now saw that three of them were virtually superimposed. I was pleased and most agreeably surprised that she had borne it all so well, for it had not been an easy punishment and had been her very first.

I rubbed her bottom gently, she stiffened, gasping. I considered applying the lotion I possessed, specially formulated to ease the pain of violated flesh, but in the end decided it was appropriate she experience the full aftermath of the caning. It would be an invaluable experience for any aspiring flogger.

I retrieved her drawers, and had her put them on.

'That was very well done, Mrs Hammond,' I said, while she was putting herself in order, straightening hair and garments. 'Well done indeed.'

'Thank you, sir.'

She seemed rather distracted, which was understandable, and I imagined she was keen to retire to her room.

I rang for Alice, and told her to send Willy the hall-boy to me immediately. He arrived, anxious and breathless, and stood before me fidgeting and bobbing about in that irritating way he had.

'Willy,' I said, 'this is Mrs Hammond, who will give you your instructions from now on. Is that clear?'

'Yes, sir,' he said, tugging his forelock. 'Ma'am.'

'Good. Now show Mrs Hammond to her room, and take her bags up. I assume you have luggage, Mrs Hammond?'

'Just a small overnight bag, sir,' she said.

'We can get the rest of your things sent on,' I said. 'Come and see me in the morning and we'll discuss the arrangements.'

I turned back to Willy and fixed him with a purposeful stare. 'You blacked the fire grates this morning, did you not?'

'Yes, sir,' he said, visibly paling and starting to quake.

I pointed to the fire and the ironmongery in question. 'That,' I said, 'is the most slovenly, careless, disgraceful job of blacking I have ever had the misfortune to gaze upon. I am ashamed to have to invite Mrs Hammond into a room with such a grate. I expect she wishes to have a word or two with you about it in private - and more than just a word, I shouldn't wonder.'

I had not relinquished my hold on the cane and held it out to our new governess. She took it automatically as her look of surprise slowly gave way to something else. Something that boded ill for young Willy, I surmised.

They departed and I closed the door and went back to my desk. Later I would write to Charlie Spikeman and tell him of the bonus he had coming. Knowing Charlie as I did, that would certainly bring a smile to his weasel-like face. For now, though, I took out my journal and began to write up the afternoon's events.

All in all, it had been a most encouraging and enjoyable start. And, of course, the best was yet to come.

Chapter 5

My new home, Bleekston Hall, is an impressive residence of some sixty-odd rooms, set in superb countryside but a few hours' ride from the fine city of Oxford.

My predecessor, that most unfortunate and un-seaman-like cousin of mine, maintained a veritable army of servants; Bertie always did have pretensions of grandeur.

As I imparted to Irene Hammond during her interview, on taking up residence I had dismissed those I considered unsuitable. This, in fact, amounted to two thirds of them. The housekeeper, the governess, and several of the maids simply refused outright to submit to discipline. I consider myself a reasonable man, quite prepared to listen to another's point of view, but in this matter I am adamant. There is no place in this house for a female who is not prepared to bend.

I also dismissed the butler and both footmen. I have no objection in principle to having men about the place, but I'll be damned if I will tolerate those who feel the need to disparage the change in circumstances in supercilious tones within my hearing. I do not require servility from my staff but I do insist on a measure of respect.

I had set Irene Hammond the task of finding a replacement for the cook, the recalcitrant Mrs Morgan, and it was also my intention to set on an additional maid or two just as soon as I could find suitable replacements.

Whilst I'm a firm believer in working staff hard to keep them out of mischief, there is a limit. Rose and Alice had to manage everything between them, with the somewhat dubious assistance of the hall-boy, and were in danger of working themselves into an early grave. That wouldn't do at all. Maids who will accept a thrashing cheerfully - or even not so cheerfully - do not grow on trees.

My interview with Irene Hammond had left me in a highly exuberant mood. I was pleased with myself for steering matters to such a satisfactory conclusion, and more pleased still with our new governess. Physically she was everything I could have hoped for, and she had taken her punishment remarkably well, especially for a beginner. It had been a most enjoyable session indeed.

Thinking about Irene Hammond's three dozen led to other thoughts, I put away my journal and rang the bell-pull for Rose, the kitchen maid. Rose arrived promptly, which robbed me of the perfect excuse to warm her behind with a quick dozen or so. An excuse was not absolutely essential, I should add, but such pretences made the game all the more enjoyable.

Rose was a slim young woman, dark-haired and dark-eyed. Too slender for my tastes, she was also rather gawky and lacking in grace. What was even worse, she had a habit of straight speaking that was positively insolent at times, a trait that had earned her many a thrashing these past few months. Not, you might think, the ideal choice for a servant - yet, for reasons that will shortly become clear, I wouldn't be without her for the world.

She entered the room and stood before me, her face calm and devoid of expression. I moved the spanking chair out to the middle of the room and sat down.

Spanking chairs, I should perhaps explain, come in a variety of forms and sizes, and can be used in a number of different ways. Mine is sturdily built of good English oak, and looks like a heavier version of a common straight-backed chair, though the backrest is not so high, and the top rail is padded. This protects the victim's stomach when the chair is used as a support, with the victim standing behind the chair bending over and grasping the seat, so allowing the position to be maintained for lengthy periods. Now, however, I was using the chair simply as a chair, with the intention of delivering an over-the-knee spanking.

'Take your drawers off and come here,' I said. My choice of seat made my intentions all too clear of course, and her expression changed subtlety.

'Have I done something wrong?' she asked.

No thought of appending a 'sir' to that, you'll note. Her lack of respect for her betters, for those infinitely above her in the grand scheme of things, was astounding.

'You have now,' I said. 'What have I told you about addressing me?'

'You must be a mind reader, then,' she said, 'to know what I was going to say before I even opened my mouth.'

There are times, I swear, when I could cheerfully throttle the wench. What my dear old grandfather would make of it, looking down from heaven, I dread to think. Disown me, probably, for allowing such familiarity in a servant.

As an alternative to strangling Rose, however, I settled for growling menacingly, which appeared to intimidate her not in the least. She did however condescend to remove her drawers as instructed and approach me. I seized her wrist, none too gently, and drew her facedown across my lap. I then whipped up her skirts and gave her rump a hearty slap. I don't know what it felt like from her side of things, but it certainly made my palm sting.

'Owww!' she cried. 'That hurt!'

'That's fortunate,' I said, 'since that was my clear intention.'

I laid on another three or four, equally hard, and she began to squirm in my lap. I held her down with my left arm and spanked her soundly, barely pausing for breath.

'Oooo, sir,' she wailed, 'that's enough!'

'So it's "sir" now, is it?' I said, gasping somewhat from my exertions. 'It would seem I've found the secret to getting a little respect from you, wouldn't you say?'

'But sir, I... ahhh! I always give you... ohhh! The respect you deserve... owww!'

'You impudent hussy!' I cried, delivering a veritable flurry of blows to her bottom, her writhing growing more fevered still. Her posterior was turning a most attractive shade of pink, inspiring me to even greater efforts.

After a while I paused, I was growing decidedly breathless, and slipped my hand between her thighs. Up to this point she had kept her legs pressed tightly together, but now they parted slightly and my fingers, seeking her slit, encountered moisture. 'Wanton trollop,' I said. 'You've been having lascivious thoughts!'

I rubbed her, and the sounds she made took on an altogether different tone. I worked on her clitoris and she ground her pubis against my thigh, trapping my hand in her eagerness for more pressure. My manipulations slowed, not from wilful cruelty, rather that Rose's gyrations restricted access to those very parts she wished fondled.

'Don't stop,' she groaned.

It was a tempting thought - a lady friend of mine had told me once that stopping halfway was crueller by far than even the hardest of floggings. To leave Rose in this aroused state might teach her a lesson. Unfortunately it would mean denying myself also, and my need was rapidly becoming as urgent as Rose's.

'Greedy, selfish girl,' I chided. 'Isn't it about time you started thinking about others, and not just yourself?' I gave her clitoris a quick nip by way of reprimand, causing her to yelp. 'Up,' I said. 'Stand up, trollop. Sit on the edge of the desk.'

She needed no second bidding, jumping to her feet and perching on the desk as ordered. Rose had one quality that more than compensated for all her other failings - she enjoyed a romp as much as any woman I have ever known.

Without a word from me she dragged her skirts up about her waist, then leaned back on her elbows. She lifted her feet off the floor and raised her knees almost to her chest. Now it was I who needed no second bidding. I took out my cock, which came promptly to attention like the good soldier he was, touched it to her cunny and drove hard into her. She tipped back her head and let out a long groan of pleasure.

I began to move in her - slowly at first, then gaining in tempo, and she began panting in a most becoming fashion.

'Oh yes,' she gasped. 'Yes!'

She reached out and clutched my shoulder, bringing her other arm up to clasp her hands behind my neck. Her legs went around my waist, locking to me tightly. She took control, ramming her hips against me, dictating the tempo. Her thrusts became almost frantic as anguished sobs wracked her.

When I was a boy a skewbald pony called Lady once ran away with me. I lost the rein, lost the stirrup, and ended up clinging to her neck for dear life while she galloped off across the park. Then, as now, I could do little but hang on tight and pray for deliverance. With Lady it came in the form of a ditch too wide to jump. With Rose it was our combined shuddering climax, that brief but spectacular explosion when a man and woman are truly one.

And afterwards, as always, came lassitude and long contented sighs from both parties, and a genuine affection for the wench on my part. What she thought of me I could not tell, for already we were two individuals once more, a man and a woman, master and servant, her mind being closed to me.

She retrieved her discarded drawers and put them on, smoothed down her skirts, straightened her cap, and started to leave. She paused at the door and looked back at me. 'When you rang for me, sir,' she said, 'was there something you were wanting?'

'Indeed there was, Rose,' I answered. 'And you provided it in a truly memorable fashion. Thank you.'

She treated me to a rare smile, and departed.

When Rose had gone I sat at my desk, leaned back in the chair, and gave serious thought to the matter of my wards.

When I first took up the role of guardian, I explained to the three of them that family punishments would take place in the study on Friday evenings after tea, at six o'clock precisely - unlike the staff, whose sins were generally dealt with on the spot. They exchanged secret smiles as I made this announcement, clearly believing themselves incapable of any crime or sin whatsoever, and certainly nothing that would merit corporal punishment. I was hard pressed not to smile myself, as I knew better.

Now, whilst it may be perfectly acceptable to subject a servant to a beating for little or no good reason, with Elizabeth and her sisters I felt I needed a valid pretext. It was necessary, therefore, to devise a number of ploys that would give me an excuse to warm their bottoms. This was no chore, you understand - on the contrary, I found the devising and planning of such stratagems almost as enjoyable as enacting them. Pleasure of anticipation, after all, can be intoxicating indeed.

I decided to start with Victoria. On more than one occasion lately I had found myself staring at her copper locks, wondering if she was the same colour all over. A bare bottom spanking invariably provides a glimpse of pubic bush, which would settle the matter once and for all. A somewhat base motive for punishing a young woman, you might think, but then I'm a rather base fellow - as Victoria was about to discover.

Chapter 6

My plan for Victoria's downfall was based on the fictitious tale of the broken picture frame I'd told to Irene Hammond at her interview. The arrangements could hardly have been easier. I bought a cheap but exotic-looking vase and made a point of calling the entire household together to explain that it was a rare and priceless artefact from ancient Persia. It would occupy a place of honour, I said, standing on a small table in the hall - and woe betide anyone who so much as scratched it!

I delivered this warning in my most intimidating voice, and I still recall the look of utter consternation on the face of Alice, who realised she would be the one who would have to dust it. I scowled at her as though her fumbling fingers had already dropped the thing, and she almost swooned on the spot from pure terror.

'Is that understood?' I said sternly, looking at each of them in turn. 'Elizabeth, I include you in this. Victoria? Catherine? Not one scratch, is that clear?'

'Quite clear, Uncle James,' Elizabeth said, speaking for all of them as usual. 'We shall be most careful, I promise.'

The rest of the plan was simplicity itself. I looped a length of fine black silk thread, virtually invisible to the naked eye, around the bottom of the table leg, and ran this along the skirting and under the study door.

Later that day I sent word for my wards to attend me in the study, where I informed them they were to spend a few days in London, seeing the sights and shopping for new clothes. They and their governess, I said, would be catching the train the very next morning.

They were positively beside themselves with joy, the two younger ones especially, jumping up and down and clapping their hands in delight. A trip to the capital is always an exciting prospect in itself, and for young ladies, shopping for clothes verges on a religious experience.

As they hurried out to start packing I followed them to the door and took hold of the silk thread. The three of them went quickly across the hall, skirts billowing, so a tug on the cord at the right moment and table and vase went crashing to the floor.

Victoria, bringing up the rear, had been the nearest (her skirts were a good two feet clear, in fact, but none of them had the wit to realise that) and Elizabeth and Cathy turned to her with a look of horror. There was a stunned silence as they all stared at the shards of pottery scattered across the tiled floor.

'Oh, Victoria,' Elizabeth said. 'Whatever have you done?'

Victoria promptly burst into tears and fled upstairs to her room, with her sisters in close pursuit trying their best to console her. I smiled with satisfaction at a job well done, reeling in the black thread, so removing all evidence of my connivance. Once again, the old adage that simple plans are best was proved true.

The shopping trip to London, it goes without saying, was promptly cancelled. What a shame.

Victoria's 'accident' with the vase occurred on a Monday. A cynical individual might conclude I had arranged it that way deliberately, to give the unfortunate girl the rest of the week to contemplate her fate. My wards had never been beaten in their lives, but they had heard Alice and Rose in full cry on many an occasion and could be in no doubt as to the severity of my punishments.

The house was remarkably subdued over the next few days, the more so as Friday drew near. Victoria was very withdrawn, and even Elizabeth's cool confidence seemed to have taken a knock. Once or twice she appeared on the verge of speaking with me, perhaps to request leniency for her sister, but I hardened my face each time she approached, and her words remained unspoken.

Friday evening came at last. As the clock was striking six Mrs Hammond led Victoria into the study.

The governess, I should explain, had not been made privy to my plan. She had listened to my address to the household on the subject of the vase with suitable gravity, and nothing in her expression at the time suggested she took it at less than face value. And yet, looking at her now, it seemed to me she harboured suspicions. Certainly she would remember the story of Cathy and the broken picture frame, and perhaps the similarities were sufficient to raise doubts in her mind. Although we never discussed the matter, either then or later, I was sure she knew I had contrived the whole affair. She was, as I said before, a very astute woman.

Now, however, we were both concerned with the matter in hand - young Victoria's first (but by no means last, if I had any say in the matter) punishment.

I sat at my desk, my face set in my sternest expression. The cane was there in front of me as usual, but I doubted I would be using it this evening. Other implements, I felt, were more appropriate to a first spanking.

I contemplated the unfortunate young woman before me, who was not, I have to say, looking particularly happy at that moment. Her eyes were downcast, her hands clasped behind her back, her whole demeanour that of someone who would definitely prefer to be elsewhere.

'Victoria,' I said, in a voice like an undertaker, 'do you know why you are here?'

'Yes, Uncle James,' she whispered.

'Speak up, girl. Explain to me why you are here.'

'Because I broke the vase.' This was a little louder, though only a little.

'The *priceless* vase,' I reminded her, exaggerating monstrously; one shilling and three-pence it cost, if memory serves me correctly. 'For breaking a *priceless* vase,' I went on, 'do you think you deserve to be punished?'

She didn't answer, but merely hung her head even lower. I glanced at Irene Hammond and risked a conspiratorial wink. The governess's eyes were bright with anticipation, she was clearly having difficulty maintaining her own suitably stern expression. I wasn't the only one who was relishing this, clearly.

'Come, Victoria,' I said, 'you must answer when I speak. Should I punish you?'

'Yes, uncle,' she murmured.

'Very well,' I said. 'As this is your first offence, I had thought to let you off with a warning, but you've elected to be punished, and I shall respect your wishes. Mrs Hammond, how many strokes has this unhappy person earned by her gross carelessness?'

'I think,' the good woman replied, 'two dozen, sir.'

'Very well - two dozen it is. Kindly prepare the penitent in any way you deem appropriate.'

It was Irene Hammond's own suggestion, made to me the previous day, that I utter these precise words at this point in the proceedings. When I'd asked what particular preparations she had in mind, she had merely smiled and asked if she might keep it a surprise. As I enjoy surprises - particularly pleasant surprises, which this promised to be - I agreed, intrigued as to what she had in mind. Was Victoria to be fitted with harness and bridle, I wondered? Was she wearing red French silk knickers beneath her skirts, and were these now to be revealed in all their glory? After a day of waiting and wondering, I was about to find out.

'Take off your clothes, Victoria,' Mrs Hammond said, in a tone that brooked no argument. 'Every last stitch, now.'

I'm not sure who was the most surprised, my ward or me. Surprised and delighted in my case, needless to say, rather than surprised and horrified as with Victoria. The girl gasped and looked at the governess in shock. I merely gawped, wondering if I had heard correctly. For a young woman to be naked in front of an adult male, even if the male in question was her guardian, was a thing unheard of.

'Quickly now,' Mrs Hammond snapped, 'or I shall be recommending an extra dozen for tardiness. Are you to keep your uncle waiting all day?'

Open-mouthed, Victoria turned to me. Fortunately I was able to compose my own features in time, and now gave a solemn nod. If Irene Hammond believed she could pull this off then she had my wholehearted support.

Victoria's face crumpled. To my utter astonishment her hands went to the back of her neck and she unfastened the top button on her dress. Mrs Hammond undid the rest. Undressing her was hardly a quick operation, but I wasn't complaining. The slow revelation of successive garments - in the knowledge that these, though manifold, were not inexhaustible - was a most stimulating experience.

Victoria remained silent throughout the disrobing, never once voicing her opinion on the proceedings. As each item of clothing was discarded Mrs Hammond folded it neatly and draped it over the back of a chair.

Finally Victoria was naked, with not the merest strip of fabric between her most intimate regions and my gimlet gaze. For a brief moment only her full charms were on display, then her right hand moved to cover her groin, and her left forearm covered her breasts. I was naturally disappointed at this, though her modesty was perfectly understandable. That she had consented to undress at all was nothing short of a miracle. Acutely embarrassed, her cheeks were the colour of strawberries and she was trembling most appealingly.

My dilemma, of course, was how to get a better look at her. 'Kindly move your arms so I can see your tits and cunny' might do it, but would make me sound like a drooling, lecherous old man. 'Stand to attention, girl!' was slightly less obvious, perhaps, but I could think of no credible reason why I should need her to adopt a guardsman's pose at that particular moment.

Fortunately, Mrs Hammond had anticipated this difficulty. She now produced a length of black ribbon from her pocket and instructed Victoria to tie up her hair.

'And carefully, mind,' the governess added. 'I want to see it neatly done.'

There was real authority in her voice. Lots of practice with the bishop's sons, I supposed. Few young women of Victoria's age would find it easy to defy such a voice. This was the first real opportunity I'd had to observe Irene Hammond in action, as it were, and I was most impressed.

At the same time I was not a little surprised at Victoria's early capitulation. True, there had been unhappy looks aplenty, and a general sluggishness when removing her things, but I would have expected more of a show of resistance. Some of this I put down to Mrs Hammond's no-nonsense manner, but still....

A few moments later all such thoughts became academic. Since it is patently impossible to fasten a ribbon one handed, Victoria was obliged to raise both arms to undertake the task. Her delights, no more than glimpsed previously, could now be savoured to the full.

She was plump, certainly, but she possessed a sensual voluptuousness that simply could not be denied. She looked literally good enough to eat. Her breasts were larger than I had expected, tipped with swollen nipples of the palest pink imaginable. Her belly bulged delightfully, and beneath was a nest of curls two shades lighter than the hair on her head.

All too soon the copper locks were trussed up, and my opportunity to gaze on her sadly came to an end - or so I feared. But my spirits were soon lifted when Mrs Hammond chided the girl, saying she had made a poor show of her hair and promptly ordered her do it all over again. My respect for the woman rose even higher.

At last it was done, and in so tidy a fashion even the most critical governess could not object. I went to the cupboard and selected the medium weight ruler. I say 'ruler', but there were no graduations marked upon its surface. It was simply a flat strip of polished ash a little over an inch wide, a quarter of an inch thick, and perhaps eighteen inches long. An inoffensive item compared with many in my collection, yet still capable of inflicting a cruel sting when wielded energetically. An eminently suitable choice, in fact, for a young lady's first punishment.

I approached the pair of them, and saw Victoria staring at the ruler fearfully. Though I thought it unlikely she would bolt, I wanted to take no chances.

'Mrs Hammond,' I said, 'if you would kindly hold Victoria's hands. She may find it a comfort during her ordeal.'

The governess stepped in front of the girl and took hold of her hands as requested. The two of them were now standing face to face, and I stood at Victoria's left side.

'Are you ready, Mrs Hammond?' I asked.

I saw her take a firm grip on Victoria's hands. 'I am, sir.'

'And you, Victoria? Are you quite ready?'

'Yes, uncle.'

'Very well. We will begin.'

I took careful aim and delivered a crisp whack to the upper curve of Victoria's buttocks. She let out a little gasp and her hips pushed forward. I waited for her pale skin to flush - a pink band across the tops of her twin mounds.

I wondered if Victoria grasped the significance of this moment. She had just crossed a major watershed in her life, having moved from the ranks of the un-spanked to those of the spanked. Life for her would never be the same. Never again would she see a leather belt or a cricket bat without a twinge of apprehension. Never again would she look upon walking stick, cane, or any rod-like object without her buttocks clenching involuntarily and a shiver running down her spine.

Did Victoria understand any of this, in fact? Probably not. Probably she was thinking solely about the tingle in her bottom and feeling rather sorry for herself.

Almost sighing with the pathos of it all, I flicked my wrist and laid a second stripe alongside and just below the first. Again she made that most entrancing of sounds, the breathless gasp of a woman under the rod, again her hips jerked in a reflex as old as time. When the first caveman laid an elk-thong lash across the buttocks of the first cavewoman she must have gasped exactly like that, and flinched in precisely that same manner - and it is still as charming now as it was all those aeons ago.

'Try to keep still, Victoria,' Mrs Hammond said. 'You're making it very difficult for your uncle by jumping about in that manner.'

I glanced up at the governess and our eyes met. There was total accord, total understanding. She, at least, would recognise the true import of the situation. I had a sudden urge to carry her off to bed and draw from her gasps of a different nature; but such pleasures would have to wait. Right now there was a bottom in need of a spanking - and I was the very man to see to it.

I proceeded to lay further strokes in the same manner, each alongside the previous one. I was wanting even coverage, the hallmark of an experienced flogger.

In my customary manner, I paused after six. I like to step back and view the scene, and assess how well or how badly the victim is faring. Such observations form an important part of the detailed punishment reports in my journal.

Victoria, I have to say, was doing rather well, despite Mrs Hammond's admonishments. My ward was making surprisingly little fuss and was not fidgeting or crying. Her knees dipped when I paused, but that was not unusual - it was rather endearing, in fact. I said she was not crying, but by this I mean she was not weeping. Certainly her eyes had filled with tears, but this again is a normal response to the sharp sting of the ruler. All in all, it was an admirable performance for a novice.

The sixth stroke, as it happened, had been placed at the lowest point on the curve of her bottom, just above the crease where buttock joins thigh. These first half dozen had achieved nominal coverage, therefore, but some gaps were in evidence. This was inevitable, as even an old hand like myself cannot achieve absolute perfection.

For stroke number seven I went back to the top and started again. This half dozen hurt more than the previous six, as confirmed by Victoria's reaction, since the ruler was now contacting areas already sore. Her whole body stiffened as wood met flesh, and her gasps were louder and more distressed. Tears were now rolling freely down her cheeks, but I paid little heed. As I explained before, I was taught at a very early age that a woman's tears are a poor indicator of her true feelings.

Eventually the twelfth stroke was duly delivered to the very underside of Victoria's bottom. I stepped back taking a moment to enjoy the sight of my ward standing there, trembling as she held fast to the governess's hands, her red bottom telling clearly of her ordeal. It was a perfectly delightful vision that made me regret my limited artistic skills. I would attempt later to capture the scene in pen and ink in the pages of my journal, but I knew I could never do it full justice.

I went to the cupboard and put away the ruler, taking out instead the light tawse.

I then brought the spanking chair out from its place by the wall, and sat down facing my ward.

I had a fancy to administer an over-the-knee spanking, but using a strap rather than my hand, as is the normal practice. I asked Mrs Hammond to bring her charge to me and she laid Victoria facedown across my knee, with her head to my left. The feel of the girl's soft plumpness pressing against my thighs was most agreeable. This is the chief advantage of over-the-knee in my view - the contact between the punisher and the punished lends a particular intimacy to the proceedings.

Tactile pleasures are all well and good, but now I had a spanking to administer. Without further ado I raised the tawse and proceeded to swipe her smartly across her rump. She gave a little squeal of dismay and jerked on my knee. A second stroke followed, then a third.

When I paused after the sixth, Mrs Hammond cleared her throat. 'If I may make a request, sir,' she said, 'perhaps I might administer the remaining strokes personally.'

I was about to damn her for her impertinence, but something in her look stopped me. She was trying to tell me something, that much was plain, though I couldn't imagine what it might be. Intrigued, I told Victoria to stand up and Mrs Hammond took my place. With Victoria now draped across her knee instead of my own, the strapping got underway once more.

The first five were routine, if a little faster than I would have liked. They were somewhat harder than my own strokes too, each one drawing from Victoria a shrill warble. Just before the sixth and final stroke Mrs Hammond paused, and shot me a significant glance as she deliberately shortened her grip on the tawse. She took careful aim, and struck forcibly.

Victoria shrieked. The stroke had landed badly off target, catching her left buttock alone, but very low down, half onto her thigh. The end had curled around inside Victoria's leg and caught her vulva. Mrs Hammond gave a satisfied smile and I realised I was wrong - the stroke had not been off target, rather very much *on* target. I assumed I was about to find out why.

'I'm terribly sorry, sir,' the governess said, 'but I'm afraid that last stroke was poorly placed. I seem to have injured the poor girl's tantalus region. Hopefully it isn't serious, but may I suggest you examine it, just to be on the safe side.'

'The... *tantalus* region?' I said.

'Just so, sir. Perhaps we should change places again.'

The *tantalus* region? I thought, as we played our own unique version of musical chairs come pass-the-parcel once more with a sobbing Victoria. I'd never even heard of the deuced thing. She was making it up, surely?

I ceased worrying about the authenticity or otherwise of anatomical terms, for Mrs Hammond did something quite sublime. Victoria was facedown across my lap, her rosy pink bottom sticking up in the air. What the governess did was place her hands inside Victoria's knees, and part the girl's legs. Victoria's slit, that most secret and private of parts, came fully into view. I sat staring at it, quite, quite entranced, every detail crystal clear. I saw the delicate folds of the labia, enticing and delightful; and her clitoris beneath its hood-like sheath. I saw the way her maidenhair sprouted all about it, and further back, her tightly puckered anal sphincter.

Mrs Hammond took hold of my right hand, and straightened out my fingers. I wondered what on earth she was up to. She looked at me in that significant way once more, and guided my hand between Victoria's thighs. Then to my astonishment and everlasting delight, she laid the edge of my forefinger against Victoria's slit.

Victoria moaned and her legs closed. Undeterred, Mrs Hammond parted them once more. She used no force to speak of that I could tell, just a gentle insistent pressure on the girl's knees. The governess then placed her hand on mine once more and pressed lightly so that Victoria's labia partially enveloped my finger. Then, while I was still gawping incredulously at my own hand, she began to move it up and down so that my finger slid back and forth against Victoria's slit. The girl groaned, her buttocks clenched. Mrs Hammond continued to work my hand for another full minute before, with another of those glances that spoke volumes, she took her own away. I continued alone, knowing that was what she wished me to do.

The next few minutes were sheer bliss. Victoria began to wriggle on my lap as I looked to Mrs Hammond for affirmation that all was well. I duly received it in the form of a reassuring nod, so I carried on with a clear conscience. I would dearly have liked to rub the girl's clitoris but I dare try nothing new without a sign from the governess. She had complete charge of this situation, without a doubt. She was the tutor here, I the pupil.

Victoria's wriggling suddenly took on a new dimension, and her legs closed again. Mrs Hammond immediately put her hand on my wrist and shook her head quickly. I desisted instantly, for it was clear something had changed, though I didn't know what.

'Stand up now, Victoria,' Mrs Hammond said. 'Let's get you dressed. We don't want to be late for dinner, do we? I understand cook has some special treat for us.'

She continued to chatter genially to Victoria as all the while she was helping the girl dress. Her tone of voice and indeed her whole demeanour were entirely the reverse of what they were at the start of the session, as she fussed and praised the girl repeatedly.

'You behaved quite wonderfully, Victoria,' she said, for the third time in as many minutes, 'and I'm very proud of you. I just wish *all* young ladies were as obedient as you, I do indeed. I'm sure your uncle must be proud of you too.'

Mrs Hammond glanced at me as she spoke these words, I hastily concurred. It was true, in fact - I couldn't have been more pleased with the girl - but I was still at a loss to explain the change in Mrs Hammond's disposition. Her harsh, unyielding manner was magically transformed, so that she now seemed amiable and sympathetic. Victoria brightened visibly under this cheery onslaught and when the time came for Mrs Hammond to take her out the girl actually smiled at the pair of us. It was all very, very odd, and I wondered how on earth I was to make sense of it when I wrote up my journal.

Understandable or not, I was more impressed than I can say with Irene Hammond; and later, as we talked in the study, I told her so.

'I'm most pleased, *most* pleased, with your performance this evening, Mrs Hammond,' I said. 'Your handling of the girl was exemplary.'

'Thank you, sir,' she said, smiling graciously at the compliment.

'But I'm still not sure how you managed it. How did you know Victoria would be willing to strip naked in front of me? And, what's even more remarkable, how did you know she would submit to being fondled in so intimate a fashion?'

'Well, sir... there's often more to young women than meets the eye. It's simply a matter of recognising the signs. Men tend to see only what's on the surface, whereas we women look deeper.'

She was being just a little smug, perhaps, but I didn't feel any resentment. She had earned her moment of triumph so I indulged her. In any case, I was already planning her downfall, so I could afford to be smug too. The difference between us was, I didn't let it show.

'At the end, though, when you stopped me, I thought the girl was enjoying it, but something changed, didn't it? Did I do something wrong?'

'Not at all, sir. She did enjoy it, but you have to understand what Victoria is going through. These are new feelings for her - powerful, even frightening feelings. All I ask is that you are patient for just a little while longer. I think I can promise you a great deal more from your ward. A few weeks hence I doubt you will recognise her for the same young woman. As I said, there's more to Victoria than meets the eye.'

That had a nice ring to it; 'more than meets the eye'. A man could imagine scrutinising her most closely in search of this elusive quality, peering deep into every nook and cranny; indeed he could.

I nodded. 'And the tantalus region? I have to confess, the expression had me baffled for a moment. You *did* use the term for a reason, I take it?'

'Yes, sir. All the real words for that particular place sound so sordid, I always think.'

'Vagina?' I said. 'Or crack? Cunt? Cunny?'

'Just so,' she said.

I was surprised to note her look of distaste as I spoke these words. It was all the more remarkable considering what had just taken place, and what was taking place at this very moment. For we were seated side by side on the couch, my trousers were undone, my penis out, and Mrs Hammond was masturbating me.

She had been doing this for ten minutes or so and I was finding it increasingly difficult to concentrate on our conversation. Soon, I knew, the time for talking would be over.

Irene Hammond was far from adept at this, I have to say. When first I made the request of her, upon her return to the study after escorting Victoria back to her room, she was quite taken aback. She agreed, however, and proved a willing student as I explained what she must do. And, in a perverse way, her very inexperience added to my pleasure rather than diminishing it. This was another form of virginity, in a way, and I took considerable satisfaction from knowing she had never in her life done this to a man.

I watched her as she worked me, her eyes on my cock, the tip of her tongue peeping out from between her lips as she concentrated on the job in hand, as it were. She really was a most attractive creature. I saw how tightly the material of her dress stretched across her breasts. I remembered the perfection of her behind as she stood with her skirts raised and her drawers around her ankles.

'Oh God!' I muttered, feeling my climax build.

Her look of concentration turned to one of alarm. 'What shall I do?' she asked, in a little girl's voice.

'Get the glass,' I said through clenched teeth, and with her left hand she picked up the brandy glass I had set between us for this very purpose.

'Catch it!' I cried, and it was to be my last utterance, for the next second the climax took me, and with a loud groan I ejaculated. Mrs Hammond's reactions were just quick enough, fortunately, and she managed to collect my semen in the glass, so avoiding an unholy mess on the floor.

Chapter 7

A few days after Victoria's punishment, I went into the library to search out a book on horticulture. I had a mind to attempt the cultivation of certain exotic varieties of cane, in my never-ending search for perfection. Alice was in the room, standing on a stool, dusting the books on the topmost shelf. I had made it plain to both her and Rose that I expected the house to be spotlessly clean at all times, even in those hard-to-reach places, and doubly plain what the penalty would be should I discover otherwise.

When I saw her there I decided to have some sport, for I was in a somewhat frivolous mood. Consequently I went over and stood close beside her. She pretended not to notice me, no doubt hoping that I would do whatever I had come to do and then leave. Sadly, it was not to be.

'Alice,' I said sternly, and she started so violently I thought she would fall off the stool. It wobbled precariously for a second or two, but then she regained her balance, glancing down at me fearfully.

'Alice,' I repeated, in a somewhat gentler tone, 'hand me down your duster.'

With trembling hands she passed the thing down to me. I had intended merely to rid her of the encumbrance so she could hitch up her skirts, but now I examined the utensil, for I had the spark of an idea.

It was a simple enough affair - a clump of feathers bound with thin wire to the end of a cane. I flicked it idly over my palm, feeling the feathers' soft caress.

Perfect, I thought, as the idea solidified in my mind.

'Right then, girl,' I said, raising my head, 'let's have those skirts up and drawers down.'

She complied instantly, having learned through hard experience that any reticence or tardiness would only prolong the misery, and would probably earn her extra strokes into the bargain. I began to walk slowly around the stool.

She was a little mouse of a girl, but she did have some redeeming features. Hard work and long hours accounted for the trimness of her figure. Her buttocks, thighs and calves were smooth and firm. Her cunny, never before observed from this angle, was delightful, peeping tantalisingly from a neat little bush.

All throughout my unhurried inspection Alice's eyes followed me as the rabbit watches the stoat. The cane I held may have borne a feathery adornment at one end, but it was still a cane. Alice had an almost pathological fear of that particular implement, stemming, I think, from the very first beating I ever gave her. It was a hard first punishment, certainly - possibly too hard, for poor Alice was quite unnerved and had never really recovered from it.

In fact, beating her was the last thing on my mind at that moment. I intended instead to conduct an experiment in arousal. 'Spread your knees,' I said.

Again she obeyed immediately. I put the feather end of the duster between her legs and began to tickle her there. She looked startled, but knew better than to protest. I didn't stop, neither did I pause in my endeavours, but rather kept up a steady flick-flick-flick with the feathers, my eyes never leaving her face as I watched for a reaction.

After a minute or two I got one. A flush appeared on her pale cheeks and her breathing quickened. Her hips began to twitch, just a little at first, but with increasing frequency and vigour as the seconds and minutes passed. I genuinely hadn't known whether I could arouse a young woman who so feared me. I had my answer now, and the logical thing would be to halt the experiment; but something made me go on.

Alice's eyes were closed, and she was panting now. The twitching of her hips had become a rapid back and forth coital thrust. The tips of the feathers glistened with her juices, and I sensed she was just minutes away from her orgasm.

Deliberately, and with a certain malicious glee, I began to slow my movements - slower and still slower, till she opened her eyes and looked at me in dismay.

'Oh sir...' she moaned softly. 'Please, sir.'

Now this was remarkable. In the few months I had known Alice she'd barely had the courage to answer when I spoke, yet here she was pleading with me on her own initiative. A true demonstration of the power of sex, I thought. But perhaps an even more powerful demonstration was possible.

'I have a proposition for you, Alice,' I said. 'I shall continue tickling you if you agree to a caning. Say, a dozen strokes.'

Considering Alice's fear of the cane, I thought it highly unlikely she would accept; but I felt obliged to try anyway in the interests of science.

'The choice is entirely yours,' I said, to make sure she understood. 'You may climb down from the stool now and leave, or you may stay and enjoy a good feathering - provided you pay the price.'

I was certain she would depart, but speeded up my hand movements anyway, just for the fun of it, and soon had her gasping and squirming once more. She truly was a brazen little creature.

'I'll take the dozen, sir,' she said breathlessly.

If I had been surprised before, I was now astonished. I would have wagered a hundred guineas she would sooner forfeit her orgasm than receive twelve strokes of the cane. And I would have lost.

Alice made her decision, however, so now I honoured it. I took hold of the cane in my right hand, grasped the feathers in my left, then twisted and pulled. The two halves came apart, leaving me with a pair of implements, one for pleasure, one for pain.

Even this brief cessation had her whimpering in frustration and looking round for her toy. I obliged her, and soon she was lost in her reverie once more, eyes closed, mouth partly open, her breath coming quick and fast.

Without breaking the rhythm of my hand, I took a step to the right to see if I might successfully wield the cane whilst simultaneously tickling her. I soon realised this would not be easy. Her bulky skirts did not help, though she was holding them just as high as she was able.

'You will have to take off your dress,' I said. 'Quickly, now.'

She needed no urging, slipping out of her dress and underskirt, and casting them to one side in a trice. She kicked off her drawers, too, leaving her clad - most appealingly, I have to say - in shoes, stockings, cap, vest and corset.

'Down you go,' I said. 'Squat right down now, Alice.'

She did as I commanded, so that her head was barely higher than my own, placing her hands upon her knees. I took up my tickling duties once more, but this time from the side. It would not be easy maintaining this throughout the caning, but I intended to try. Shortening my grip on the cane, I judged that I would now be able to deliver a proper stroke, albeit of limited power. Since the infliction of pain was not the prime objective, I considered this perfectly satisfactory.

I gave her another minute or so to settle, then flicked the cane in a rising stroke to the under-curve of her buttocks. It made solid contact and Alice yelped and straightened, her body rising slightly. I was about to caution her when she sank back down of her own accord, her cunny seeking the silken caress.

'One, sir,' she murmured, unasked, so well ingrained was the habit.

The remaining strokes followed quickly, each one a fraction harder than the last. Alice barely moved, even though they must have been hurting considerably towards the end, and I guessed her reaction to the first stroke was mostly surprise. She had taken the beating with less fuss, less noise, and far less jumping about than usual; and the reason was plain enough.

Following the twelfth stroke I set down the cane, and stepped back in front of her. I changed hands, taking the feathers in my right, for my left wrist was aching abominably from the unaccustomed effort.

I now felt more in control, and better able to service the little trollop. I began to increase the tempo, building slowly to a crescendo. Her hips jerked violently and her head went back, the expression on her face almost agonised.

Without warning she fell forward, wrapping her arms around me and burying her face in my neck. Alarmed, I tried to step back, thinking myself under attack, but she held fast to me, panting in my ear and whimpering. I realised then it was no murderous attack, rather that her climax was almost upon her. I smiled ruefully at my own reaction. To be afraid of Miss Mouse was not a thing to be proud of.

I reached around with my left hand and grasped her buttocks, sinking my fingers into her firm flesh. She did not react - I doubt she even noticed.

The feathers were doing sterling service, going ten to the dozen. Alice squealed and her whole body convulsed, once, twice. She clasped me so tight I struggled to breathe. And then - surely the most unlikely and impossible thing of all - she kissed me on the cheek.

There was no question, of course, that this was out of affection; she was in the throes of passion, when we all do and say things that later astonish us. I understood this, and so said nothing, but continued to hold her in the aftermath of her climax. My left hand rubbed her buttocks, while my right stroked the feathers - now thoroughly wet - against her cunny in a languorous manner.

I felt her shiver and she let out a long, sated sigh. And then she went rigid and pulled away from me, her face frozen in horror and disbelief. Obviously she had just remembered what she had done. She had kissed the master, without his permission, and it was clear from her expression that she now expected the most savage of beatings imaginable.

She was not an especially pretty girl, Miss Mouse; and yet, as she crouched there with her cap askew, her cheeks flushed from her exertions, and her dainty mouth in a perfect O, I considered her the most adorable creature imaginable. Without a thought, I leaned forward and popped a kiss on her red lips.

I cannot claim to be clear on my motives for this, though I suspect mischievousness played a large part. Her lips tasted of honey, and I guessed she had been working in the larder before starting on this room. Under normal circumstances, raiding the honey pot would earn her a couple of dozen at least, but nothing that had happened here was normal. I wasn't so much of a cad that I could bring her to climax in one breath, and beat her in the next.

The effect of my kiss on Alice was startling. A sly girl might have smiled knowingly, and scolded me in that teasing, shallow way they have, thinking she had found a weakness she could turn to her advantage. A crafty, ambitious girl might have attempted to insinuate herself in my affections, and elevate her status within the household accordingly. Alice, on the other hand, just looked as though I'd informed her she was to be hanged in the morning - and I liked her all the better for it.

To say that she was disturbed was an understatement of monumental proportions. Almost I think she would have preferred the beating to this. Her world had turned upside down, and nothing made any sense. She had hugged the master, and kissed him, and instead of thundering at her and thrashing her unmercifully, he had kissed her back.

I was, I have to say, hard pressed not to smile. I refrained, however, thinking this might push her over the edge into total insanity. God knows, she must be close to that already. So I merely dismissed her, and she jumped off the stool, snatched up her discarded clothes in a bundle, and scurried away.

Or perhaps, after all, I *was* such a cad.

'Alice!' I snapped, as she reached the door.

She froze.

'How many times have you been warned about pilfering honey? Report to my study in an hour's time, and by God you'll smart for it!'

'Sir,' she piped, bobbing, and dashed out.

I did allow myself to smile then. Without a doubt this had been a most unusual experience. Unusual, and also instructive. For in that last brief moment before she disappeared through the door, Alice looked relieved. The world was spinning on its axis once again, and she was in her rightful place. Everything, in other words, was back to normal.

I laughed softly at the frailty of females, and went to look for my book.

Chapter 8

My plan for Cathy was considerably more complicated than Victoria's vase, due to the need for special equipment. I intended to have the governess cart secretly modified in such a way that Cathy's dress would end up in shreds in the wheel. My main concern, it goes without saying, was how to ensure Cathy wasn't shredded along with it.

After many hours spent sketching possible designs, only to reject them on the grounds of risk or impracticability, I believed I now had a viable solution. Soon, I was confident, I would be watching Cathy strip, fearful and sulky, whilst I stood glowering, slapping a paddle menacingly against my palm.

I was contemplating this happy prospect one morning when I happened to look out of my study window, and saw my three wards run out onto the lawn. It was a fine bright day, unseasonably mild for March, and I guessed Mrs Hammond had allowed them a break from their lessons to take a breath of fresh air. There were women in the village little older than Cathy with children of their own, yet here were my two younger wards, skipping along with their skirts held out to the side, frolicking and cavorting like lambs. Watching Cathy now, and knowing what was in store for her, I almost felt like rushing out and cavorting with them.

I was about to turn away when the accident occurred. The two girls ran close by one another, and Victoria inadvertently stepped on the hem of Cathy's dress. There was a loud tearing sound and Cathy, in full flight at the time, went sprawling.

Her sisters rushed to her aid and helped her to her feet. She wasn't injured, fortunately, but her dress was badly torn.

'Oh, Elizabeth,' Cathy wailed after they had assessed the damage, 'whatever shall I do? I'll be punished, indeed I shall! Uncle James will punish me, won't he?'

It was fate, of course, calling out in the clearest of voices; and the irony of the situation was not lost on me. Victoria's single careless step had, at a stroke, achieved the precise result I'd been seeking for weeks. Fate, it seemed, was not without a sense of humour.

'Don't be a silly moose,' Elizabeth was saying soothingly. 'It was an accident; no one will blame you.'

So should I now abandon the *Catherine Wheel*, as I had already dubbed my current ruse? Had all my efforts on the dress-shredding cart design been for naught? I ruefully concluded that indeed they had. Fate had called, and it would be positively churlish to turn a deaf ear.

'Anyway,' Elizabeth added, 'I'm sure we can mend it. Victoria's stitching is neat as can be - perhaps it won't be noticed.'

'I wouldn't bank on it,' I murmured softly, already heading for the door, and a quiet word with the governess.

An hour later Irene Hammond brought Cathy to the study to report the damaged dress. The stitching was indeed neat, but still clearly visible if one knew where to look.

I scowled at the girl, and condemned her to a flogging. That was the precise word I used, in fact. Cathy, needless to say, promptly dissolved into tears.

All this took place on a Wednesday, which meant she had just two days to contemplate her misfortune and think about how much it was going to hurt. I would have preferred this to be longer, naturally, but *c'est la vie*.

On Friday, at the appointed time, a knock on the study door preceded the appearance of both victim and governess. Cathy's misdemeanour was reviewed in suitably funereal tones, after which Mrs Hammond pronounced sentence - one dozen strokes. A paltry amount, true, but she could hardly have done otherwise. Victoria had received just two dozen for breaking a 'priceless' vase. To condemn Cathy to the same for damaging a ten-guinea dress would be patently unjust.

'Take off your things,' the governess said to my youngest ward. 'Hurry, now.'

Cathy looked just as appalled as Victoria had done at this point. Unlike her sister, however, who had borne it stoically and in silence, Cathy objected volubly.

'Oh uncle,' she said, turning to me in appeal, 'I cannot. It is wicked! I must not... tell her I must not!'

The source of this Puritan mentality was clear to me. I put the blame firmly on the vicar, Reverend Wilkins, and those interminable, narrow-minded sermons of his.

'Catherine, you will obey me,' the governess said, in a voice that would freeze water in a pail. 'If one dozen is not sufficient I can soon recommend a higher figure to your uncle.'

'You must do as your governess commands, girl,' I added for good measure. 'I will not countenance disobedience.'

'But Uncle James... it is wicked. I shall die of shame. Truly, I shall swoon...'

On and on she went, melodramatic and tedious in the extreme, but through a combination of threats and cajoling, assisted by a further stern rebuke from myself, Mrs Hammond finally persuaded my ward to cease her protestations and undress. Even then, the removal of every item of clothing was a minor battle in its own right, and after twenty minutes of this I was sighing with impatience and thinking that Cathy's dozen wouldn't be quite so gentle as originally planned.

At long last perseverance triumphed, and the wayward girl was naked. As with her sister Victoria, Cathy immediately covered her breasts and groin; and Mrs Hammond again produced a length of ribbon and instructed her to tie her hair. Even this proved frustrating in the extreme, however, as the girl twisted sideways in an attempt to evade my gaze. Mrs Hammond was obliged to seize her shoulders and force her to face me square on, and so - finally - I was able to get a good look at her.

My bad temper simply melted clean away. Despite all the fuss and delay, it had been worth the wait.

For Cathy was at that magical stage. She was in bloom. Her breasts were firm, her belly flat, and her legs long and slender. Her hips, though not quite wide enough for my tastes, were shapely, the subtle curves emphasised by the extreme narrowness of her waist. Without a doubt she would be a sight to take a man's breath away when she was Elizabeth's age.

When her hair was duly secured, I rose from my desk and walked slowly around the girl. The view from the rear, I was happy to discover, was equally as pleasing as that from the front. Her buttocks were delightfully round and firm. A virgin bottom, which had never before felt the hot kiss of cane or strap - nor even, to my knowledge, a smack, playful or otherwise. Cathy's behind had waited patiently for this moment from the day she was born, and now its destiny was about to be fulfilled.

I continued my tour of inspection, and came to a halt in front of her. 'Do you have any last words, Cathy, before we begin?' I enquired.

She murmured that she was truly very sorry, and I snorted. 'Sorry? I expect you are, and I'm certain you'll be even sorrier in just a few seconds' time. Mrs Hammond, the chair, if you please.'

The governess brought me the spanking chair, and I sat down and drew Cathy across my lap. I used my hand, the least severe 'implement' of all. The nature of Cathy's crime did not warrant more, and neither, I thought, would she willingly submit to a harsh punishment. The thought of a three-way wrestling match with a rebellious youngster held no appeal whatsoever. And I had another reason, a purely selfish one, for using my hand - it is the most intimate of all methods. To have a firm young bottom under the palm, to feel the muscles clench under the blows, and the skin warm as the spanking proceeds, these are pleasures not to be missed.

And so the spanking got underway. Cathy, as feared, did not behave well, twisting and squirming excessively and bawling quite unnecessarily. A very poor performance, I have to say. She was in no great pain, yet to hear Cathy screech one would think she was under the cat aboard a three-decker.

So unsatisfactory was it, I ended up rushing the whole affair, delivering the twelve slaps in less than half a minute. I cannot imagine what my grandfather would have said about such a poor showing, or what he would think of the present generation. If young people today cannot take a thrashing steadfastly and in good spirit, it makes one despair for the future.

The one bright spot in this whole sorry affair, in fact, was about to happen. I looked up at Mrs Hammond and advised her that I would now check Cathy's tantalus region. She hesitated slightly before replying.

'As you wish, sir,' she said quietly. 'I'm sure a very brief examination will be acceptable.'

What was this? If she was intimating I couldn't or shouldn't do this, I would most certainly *not* be pleased. Ever since Victoria, I had looked forward with eager anticipation to repeating it with both Cathy and Elizabeth. I could think of no good reason why I should be denied.

Whatever her reservations, Mrs Hammond duly parted Cathy's legs, and I was treated to a view of her most intimate region, totally delightful, and just the sight of it restored much of my good humour.

I laid my finger against her slit and proceeded to rub her gently, but from the very first moment I knew something was amiss. Cathy went rigid as she lay across my lap, and her legs snapped shut, trapping my hand. She let out a distressed cry, and I looked up at Mrs Hammond in some alarm. Victoria's legs had closed too, but not violently. This seemed very different, and I wasn't surprised to see the governess shake her head. The expression of concern in her eyes confirmed what I already suspected - this was not to be.

Needless to say, I immediately slid my hand out from the clamp of her thighs. To see a female squirm under the sting of crop or cane is one thing - to have her writhing with revulsion at your touch is quite another.

Mrs Hammond once more took charge, chatting cheerfully as she had with Victoria while helping the girl dress. She appeared to manage the same miracle as before, and Cathy departed in tolerably good spirits, or so I judged - which is more than I could claim for myself, as I sat on the couch awaiting the governess's return. I had much to say to her, for I was not a happy man.

It was Irene Hammond who did most of the talking, in fact, as we sat together some time later. My cock was out, but she was not holding it this time, rather stroking it with a feather. She had been teasing me thus for the past five minutes or so, and I had an erection any man would be proud of.

'Cathy isn't the same as Victoria, sir,' she said. 'They have very different temperaments. I've had some concern from the start that this might happen.'

She seemed somewhat anxious, as though fearing I would blame her for this disappointment. I did not, though I dearly wished to know what was happening, and precisely what had gone amiss.

'I don't understand,' I said. 'It is pleasurable to be touched there, surely, for a woman?'

'It is supremely pleasurable, sir,' she confirmed. 'I'm sure one day Cathy will come to appreciate that.'

I was somewhat mollified, though Irene Hammond was clearly making no hard and fast promises. It might be years before Cathy delivered up her charms. And then a most terrible thought struck me.

'And Elizabeth?' I said. 'What of her?'

'Yes,' the governess said thoughtfully. 'Elizabeth might well be a problem too.'

'A problem?' I snapped. 'A *problem*, you say? I sincerely hope not, Mrs Hammond, or *your* very next problem will be ascertaining the times of the trains back to Newbury!'

It was shabby of me to take it out on her, perhaps, when it was through her good endeavours this whole new world had opened up for me, but she'd given me a fright. I'd had lustful designs on beautiful Elizabeth since the very first moment I set eyes on her, and the thought that she might be physically out of reach was simply intolerable.

Irene Hammond looked shocked at my outburst, and stammered reassurances, saying she was sure it would turn out all right in the end. I'd given her a fright too, which was no bad thing if it achieved the desired result - namely a naked Elizabeth in my clutches.

I indicated to Mrs Hammond that she should continue. The erection I'd been so proud of had wilted somewhat (a shock will do that to a man) but I felt sure she could restore it to its former glory.

She proceeded to do those things I had taught her: drawing the feather up my shaft, flicking it around the glans, and - best of all - putting the tip to my urethra and tickling that sensitive spot. As predicted, my erection soon returned with a vengeance.

'Shall I get the glass, sir?' she asked, when my movements were becoming more pressing.

'I have a better idea,' I said. 'Have you ever tasted semen, Mrs Hammond?'

'I... no, sir,' she stammered.

'I'm told it is not exactly pleasant, but neither is it harmful, even when swallowed. You understand what I require of you, Irene?'

It was the first time I had addressed her by her given name, and I did it quite deliberately - an intimacy to pave the way for other intimacies.

'Yes, sir,' she murmured. She looked none too happy at the prospect, but I knew she would do as I asked.

'Very well,' I said. 'You may begin.'

She leaned over me, but this felt a little strained and awkward. I suggested she kneel on the floor, and she complied while I removed my trousers altogether. She rested her hands on my bare thighs and leaned forward to suck me. Needless to say, she was most inexperienced at this; but as before, that actually increased my pleasure. No man's cock had been there before me. It was an undefiled mouth that I breached, and as desirable a thing, surely, as any cunny.

I encouraged her in small ways, praising her softly when she gave me especial pleasure, cautioning her when teeth caught engorged, sensitive flesh. It was no more than a word now and then, to help her understand the way of things.

Gradually she settled into a sort of rhythm, and I could lay back and enjoy the experience. I watched her face as she serviced me, seeing her slowly gain in confidence. Without a doubt, having your cock sucked by a beautiful but inexperienced woman has to rank as one of life's greatest pleasures.

All too soon I felt a particular urge rising within me. I thought about the rosy glow on Cathy's bottom following that all-too-quick dozen. I remembered her slit, pink and vulnerable and chaste, and imagined what it would feel like to enter that warm, moist opening. I imagined my cock inside her, and Cathy bucking beneath me, her legs around my waist, crying out as the orgasm took her.

I squirted and felt Irene Hammond recoil. I held her head, drawing her down on me to keep my cock in her mouth as I emptied myself into her. She gagged, a natural reflex when a foreign object enters the throat, and tried to pull back. I held on, partly out of selfish need, partly to help her understand that this was normal, and that there was nothing to fear. She became still at last, and finally I withdrew. She took a deep breath, and I saw her shudder.

'There now,' I said. 'That wasn't so bad, was it?'

She made no reply, but simply knelt there, her head down, breathing rapidly.

'Mrs Hammond?' I said, and she raised her head. I feared to see anger in her face, or revulsion, or misery, but it was none of these. She looked a little overwhelmed, perhaps, as though it was all rather too much for her.

I pulled on my rapidly softening penis, and a thick blob of semen appeared at the end.

'One last drop,' I said, and she leaned forward to lick it off.

Chapter 9

Almost from the start I realised that Mrs Morgan, our cook, would have to go. This was not for want of culinary skills on the woman's part, but for her outright refusal to submit to discipline.

Harriet Morgan was a thin, sharp-faced, sharp-tongued woman who, in Bertie's time, had ruled below stairs with an iron hand. Never an easy woman to deal with, her temper was not improved when I dismissed the scullery maid along with all the others, and allotted some of Rose's time to general duties, so causing a significant increase in the cook's own workload.

Now, I have to say that bringing stiff, unpleasant women to brook, though often a challenge, can be most rewarding. I remember one of my grandfather's housekeepers, a Mrs Young, who had started out the most arrogant, unyielding woman imaginable. From the day of her arrival she dominated the rest of the staff, and even attempted to dominate my grandfather. In that contest, however, she was seriously outmatched, and within a month or two she could hardly be recognised as the same person. She still held sway below stairs - though she was noticeably more reasonable in her dealings with the other servants - but above stairs, and especially in my grandfather's presence, she was positively meek.

The reason for this transformation was not hard to divine, of course, even for a youth such as myself. I understood my grandfather's ways only too well, and by lurking around the study I was eventually presented with the fine sight of Mrs Young having to endure a lengthy corporal punishment session involving a wide range of implements and positions.

I had thought, at one time, to attempt a similar 'conversion' with Harriet Morgan, but it soon became clear that it was not to be. My several efforts met with outrage and threats of resignation, and I came to the conclusion that Mrs Morgan was one of those women who would never yield. Dismissal, therefore, was the only option. It was regrettable, and I would certainly miss her steamed puddings, but there was simply no choice. Having made this decision, I set Mrs Hammond the task of finding a suitable replacement.

As the days and weeks went by she interviewed a number of women, but without immediate success. It was clear that the right person was not easily to be found, and Irene Hammond, evidently worried I might hold her personally responsible for the delay, grew increasingly uncomfortable when I asked how the search was progressing. Perhaps she even feared a chastisement, and I confess it was a tempting thought. It was over a month since our first and only session, and I was keen to see those magnificent buttocks of hers again, and keener still to lay a few stripes across them.

In the end, however, my sense of fair play ruled. It had taken me three months to find the right person for the position of governess, and that with the assistance of Charlie Spikeman and his extensive network of underworld contacts. It would be churlish to punish her for failing to produce, unaided, a suitable cook in just a few weeks.

At all events, the governess persevered, and eventually her efforts bore fruit in the person of Mrs Smith, a widow who had been in service at a large country house in neighbouring Warwickshire.

Winifred Smith, it was immediately apparent, was the very opposite of our present cook in almost every respect. She was a matronly, middle-aged woman whose brown eyes looked out anxiously from a round, honest face. Her clothes were decidedly shabby, though clean, and it was plain to see she had fallen on hard times.

Irene Hammond had already explained to me in private that the good woman had been dismissed from her previous post, having been caught *in flagrante delicto* with one of the footmen. Without references, of course, it was impossible for her to obtain another situation, and her future looked bleak indeed. The only real alternatives facing a woman in her position, dismissed in disgrace and lacking references, were the workhouse and prostitution. A simple soul like Mrs Smith would not cope well with the latter, which meant the workhouse loomed ever closer.

She appeared nervous when I interviewed her in the study, which was understandable considering her circumstances. In a voice that quavered a little she assured me she was an excellent cook, able to make clear as well as thick soups, serve fish and poultry in a variety of ways, and make creams and jellies. Her whole demeanour was most encouraging, I have to say. Her physical appearance, too, was promising in the extreme - her ample backside was simply begging for a good whacking, and I looked forward to seeing her un-harness those heavy mammaries.

'Very well, Mrs Smith,' I said. 'You appear eminently suitable, and I'm happy to offer you the position of cook. Were the wages discussed, at all?'

'No, sir.'

I guessed her plight was such she would settle for anything, even roof and board alone, but meanness has never been a fault of mine - though some would say I have no lack of others to make up for it. Also, as with Irene Hammond, a financial dependence helps guarantee compliance. When the cane was biting and she wished herself elsewhere, that could well be an important factor.

'Then I can offer you eighty pounds per annum,' I said, 'payable quarterly. I trust you find that satisfactory?'

Her mouth fell open and her eyes almost popped out of her head. It was a substantial wage, especially for a cook who was in disgrace and virtually unemployable.

'Why... thank you, sir,' she gasped. 'Thank you. You are most generous... most kind. Thank you!'

'Kindness, dear lady,' I assured her solemnly, 'has absolutely nothing to do with it.'

I had not specifically agreed with Irene Hammond which of us would 'take charge' of our new cook, as it were. Of the three indoor staff presently under discipline, I owned two and she the third - and from the stiff-legged walk Willy tended to adopt these days, I knew she was not neglecting her duties in that direction. It seemed to me that Mrs Smith, being female, should logically be mine. Nevertheless, I felt the governess deserved some reward for having found her, and so I sent for her the minute Winifred Smith departed.

'Is everything in order, sir?' Mrs Hammond asked upon her arrival. She looked a little apprehensive. Being summoned to the study, it seemed, was not something any female in this household relished - which was exactly as it should be.

I informed her that we now had a new cook, and thanked her for her sterling efforts in securing Mrs Smith's services.

'I wish you to take charge of our new arrival for the first month,' I went on. 'See that she settles in, and so forth - explain our little ways. Being new, of course, it's likely she will err. Should it prove necessary to discipline her, I'm sure you won't fail in your duty.'

'That I won't, sir,' she assured me with a smile.

'Good,' I said. 'I knew I could rely on you, Mrs Hammond. I should like to watch you deliver a punishment, purely out of professional interest, you understand. Who knows, perhaps one day I might look forward to an invitation to the show?'

The household quickly adjusted to the change, as households do, and we settled into our new routine. Mrs Smith's culinary skills soon proved the equal of her predecessor's, which removed any lingering concerns I might have felt about the shrew's departure.

One afternoon there came a furtive tapping at the study door. Alice, I thought. Would a dozen for failing to knock properly be excessive? Possibly it would.

'Come!' I bellowed.

The door opened a fraction, and Alice's disembodied head appeared. 'Mrs Hammond sends—'

'Desist!' I roared, and the head shot out and back in again like a startled ghost. 'Come forward,' I said, in slightly modified tones. 'Stand before me.'

Alice crept in and stood by my desk, eyes downcast, shaking like a leaf in a November gale.

'Do you believe,' I enquired, 'that by leaving your bottom outside this room it is safe from punishment?'

'Sir?' she whispered. 'N-n-no, sir.'

'That is good. Because it is *never* safe, do you understand? No matter where you are, or what you are doing, I can find you. *This* can find you.'

I tapped the cane that lay across my desk, the one I kept there for effect - and it certainly had the appropriate effect on Alice.

'Now then,' I said, 'repeat your message.' But the damage was done. Alice stammered and stuttered, positively incoherent with fear. It was my own fault, of course, for terrorising the girl. I resolved never to do so again. In future I would get the message first and terrorise her afterwards.

It took a while, but eventually I managed to tease it from her a syllable at a time. 'Mrs Hammond sends her respects, and the show is about to start.'

Needless to say, I lost no time in making my way upstairs. The door to Irene Hammond's sitting room was open, and as I stepped inside a most delightful spectacle met my eyes. Winifred Smith was kneeling on the chaise longue, her calves overhanging the edge. She was fully clothed, but her skirts had been drawn up to her waist and her bloomers pulled down to expose large, white buttocks. These were unmarked, confirming that the punishment had not yet begun. Beside her stood Mrs Hammond, cane in hand.

'Mr Montague, sir,' the governess said, 'I'm sorry to trouble you, but I am obliged to rebuke Mrs Smith for a serious error of judgment. Perhaps you'd care to witness the punishment?'

I replied that I would indeed, and stepped closer for a better view. Straight away

I knew this was the first such punishment the cook had ever experienced. There was a look of fearful uncertainty on her face as she glanced back over her shoulder at me; a look I had seen many times before in the uninitiated.

'Oh...' Mrs Smith stammered, '...but the m-master...'

'You will remain silent,' Mrs Hammond said severely. 'Mr Montague's presence is no concern of yours. Face forward this instant, and lower your shoulders.'

The unfortunate Mrs Smith did not understand, and had to be pushed into position with a firm hand. With her buttocks elevated in this fashion I was afforded an excellent view of her slit and dense bush. The cook whimpered but remained dutifully in position, shaking as though she had the ague.

Irene Hammond raised the cane and swished it through the air once, then twice.

I am, it has to be said, a connoisseur of the art of corporal punishment. For me a great deal of the pleasure derives from the subtle nuances, the variations possible with regard to implement and position. And yet there is much satisfaction to be had also from a plain beating, using a single implement with the victim in a fixed position.

Mrs Hammond subjected the unfortunate cook to such a beating. Her timing was irregular, and deliberately so. Three or four quick strokes might be followed by a pause, anything from a few seconds to half a minute or more. Strokes fell singly, or in pairs, or as many as eight or ten in rapid succession, either to the right buttock or the left, or sometimes to both simultaneously. The victim had no idea what to expect - which was the whole idea, of course.

Mrs Hammond also used a variation on my 'counting' device. She would ask a question, and as soon as Mrs Smith began to answer, the cane would fall. The poor cook's pain and humiliation could be heard clearly in her voice - and the nature of Winifred Smith's 'sin' soon became abundantly clear.

'You admit, then,' Irene Hammond said, 'the decision to purchase the eggs was yours and yours alone?'

'Yes, ma'am, I... oh! But I did ask the boy... ah! Ah! I did ask if they were fresh... ohh!'

She had bought two dozen eggs, and it later transpired that over half were bad. It was a serious offence, at least in Irene Hammond's eyes, judging from the number of strokes administered. The punishment simply went on, and on, and on.

'Can we be assured, then,' the governess asked, 'that this transgression will not be repeated?'

'Oh yes, ma'am... ahh! I promise... oh! Ohh! I'll be more careful... ahh! In future... ooh! Oooh! Agghhhh!'

This latter, louder yelp was due to a particularly keen swipe from Mrs Hammond's cane.

And so it continued. I stood in silence, watching angry red weals materialise across Mrs Smith's white behind. Irene Hammond fell silent after a while too. This did not mean the punishment was over, however, for her arm continued to rise and fall relentlessly. The only sounds in the room were the swish of the cane, the snick as wood contacted bare flesh, and anguished gasps from a distraught Winifred

Smith.

After many long minutes she could contain herself no longer. 'No more, ma'am, I beg,' she said hoarsely. 'Please, no more.'

Irene Hammond immediately desisted, to Mrs Smith's obvious relief. The woman let out a long sigh and rose stiffly to her feet, evidently thinking her troubles were over. I suspected her judgment was a little premature, and was soon proved correct.

'Mrs Smith,' the governess said calmly, 'it is forbidden to speak unless you are spoken to, and most especially you must not beg for clemency as you have just done. Nor must you abandon the position until given express permission to do so. These are serious offences, and will invariably earn you extra strokes. Do you understand?'

'Yes, ma'am.'

'Good. I was about to allow you to return to the kitchens, but in view of your behaviour we will have to continue a while longer. Is your bottom very sore, Mrs Smith?'

'Yes, ma'am, it is.' There was a catch in the cook's voice, and I knew she was on the verge of tears.

'Very well. As you are new to this, and aren't familiar with the rules, I shall strike a different area. Take off your clothes.'

Winifred Smith glanced at me unhappily but made no protest; new to all this she may be, but evidently she was a quick learner. She disrobed, glancing in my direction every few seconds, her cheeks flushing scarlet with embarrassment. When she was naked, Irene Hammond fetched a low stool from the closet and had Winifred Smith stand upon it.

'Remain there,' the governess said. 'Keep your arms by your sides, do not move, and do not address either myself or Mr Montague unless we speak to you first, is that clear?'

'Yes, ma'am.'

Now it was Irene Hammond's turn to glance at me, but not in apprehension - rather it was an invitation. With a subtle inclination of her head she directed me to inspect the unfortunate woman shivering on her pedestal. Needing no second bidding I proceeded to walk slowly around the victim, looking her up and down.

It would be difficult, I think, to find a single word to describe Winifred Smith's physique. 'Plump', 'chubby' and 'well-covered' all fall somewhat short of the mark, I fear, yet 'obese' and even 'fat' stray too far in the opposite direction. But despite the linguistic difficulty, one incontrovertible fact remains - Mrs Smith was an impressively large lady.

Her most striking feature, without a doubt, was her bosom. Indeed, her breasts were impossible to ignore, for they were huge, hanging almost to her waist, with aureolae so big I think my palm would not cover them. Large mammaries, I freely admit, are a weakness of mine, on a par, in fact, with broad, well-rounded buttocks. Though I would dearly have liked to get my hands on both these regions, I was obliged to control my urges. This was Irene Hammond's show, and it would be most ill mannered to leap in and grope the victim without a clear invitation to do so.

My inspection completed, I nodded to Irene Hammond and took a step back. The governess came forward, cane at the ready.

She had intimated that she would spare the cook's tender behind further abuse, and in this she was as good as her word. If Mrs Smith imagined this meant the worst was now over, however, she was in for a rude awakening, for the governess now targeted the back of her thighs.

'I trust you have learned your lesson, Mrs Smith,' Irene Hammond said coolly, 'both in the matter of diligence when dealing with tradesmen, and as regards the behaviour expected of you when submitting to punishment.'

'Yes, ma'am, I shall be... aagghhh!' The cane whipped across, striking her midway between buttock and knee. The backs of the thighs are more sensitive than the buttocks, and Winifred Smith's reaction confirmed that the stroke was keenly felt. Her knees buckled and she slumped, both hands moving to guard the threatened area. Her tears, so long choked back, now poured forth.

'I insist that you stand still to receive punishment,' Irene Hammond told the sobbing woman sternly. 'Most especially you will not cover up, but keep your hands by your sides at all times, is that clear?'

'Yes, ma'am.'

'Good. We will now continue.'

As indeed we did, for another ten minutes at least, at the end of which time Winifred Smith was wailing loudly and unceasingly. Her thighs were simply a mass of purple welts, and she was shaking so badly it was a miracle she managed to retain her footing on the stool.

Finally it was over, and she was instructed to step down and put on her clothes - an order she seemed more than happy to obey.

Chapter 10

'I'm almost certain we have the Romans to thank for it,' I said, 'though I don't doubt you are right, Mrs Hammond - probably all ancient civilisations practiced medicine in one form or another.'

I couldn't recall precisely how we had arrived at this topic of conversation. I think we started out discussing Winifred Smith's sore bottom and thighs, and speculating how long it would take for the bruising to disappear; some few weeks, we concluded. I said I'd heard there were ointments to speed up the process, and this somehow broadened into a discourse on medicines in general. I contended the Romans gave us the art as we know it today, whereas Irene Hammond said she was sure it was the Greeks.

'Take the evidence of language,' I went on. 'Many of our anatomical terms have a Latin root, as I'm sure you'll agree.'

'I... perhaps so, sir.' She was hesitant, as though unconvinced. I pressed on regardless, positive I was right in this.

'Testicles!' I exclaimed.

'Sir?' she said, somewhat taken aback.

'The word - "testicles". Latin origin, I'm sure of it. As are "penis" and "vagina", I think. "Anus" too, and "rectum", from *rectus*, masculine.'

It was all coming back to me. As a schoolboy I'd searched through the dictionary looking for rude words. It was significant, perhaps, that this was the only Latin I could remember. That, and the school motto: *Scopum Cerne, Cito Caede*: 'See thy target, and strike swiftly'.

'Or is *rectus* neuter?' I mused.

'I'm afraid the gender escapes me, sir,' she said. She seemed a little distracted, though perhaps this was understandable given her present situation. We were in the study, sitting together on the couch, as was our wont following a punishment. The couch was drawn up close to the hearth, for the evening air was chill. Alice had built up the fire some time before at my request, and the flames had taken hold with a vengeance. The logs crackled and sparked, and the fire roared in the chimney.

Irene Hammond was no doubt grateful for the heat of the flames, for she was naked. She sat back on the couch, her arms by her sides and her knees parted. I sat close beside her, on her right, with my hand between her legs. I'd been fondling her cunny for some ten or fifteen minutes, and for the past five I'd concentrated exclusively on her clitoris. This might explain the difficulty she was experiencing gathering her thoughts.

I had the very tip of the middle finger of my right hand on that sensitive nub, and I rubbed it round and round in tiny circles. Irene Hammond murmured, her wonderful breasts rising and falling rapidly. I watched her face as I worked her slowly, taking delight in the preoccupied expression in those beautiful grey eyes, and the flush that had blossomed on her cheeks, and the way her ruby lips parted as she sighed. It was an altogether different visage from that of half an hour before, when dealing with a wretched, hapless cook over the matter of the eggs.

Following her arduous and lengthy punishment, Beatrice Smith had been dismissed below stairs. She dressed with great deliberation, drawing up her bloomers with the utmost care. She was obliged to sit to put on her stockings and shoes, and though she lowered herself most gingerly, as her buttocks made contact with the chaise longue she squealed like a piglet that has sat on a thistle.

Eventually it was done and she hobbled away, the very picture of dejection.

'Well, if nothing else,' I said to Irene Hammond cheerfully, 'I imagine we can all look forward to fresh eggs from now on.'

I invited the governess to join me in the study, and she inclined her head graciously, favouring me with a knowing smile. As I had made that selfsame request following both Victoria's and Catherine's spankings, she would naturally assume I wished her to perform the same service as on those prior occasions. In fact, my intentions were rather different.

When we reached the study, instead of unfastening my trousers I asked her to undress. This was her first intimation that she was in new territory, and her eyes told me she was not quite so composed as her easy smile suggested. She complied with my wish, however, and began to disrobe.

There is something quite delightful in watching a woman undress, especially when the purpose of the disrobing is to make her body available to you. Garments are shed one by one till pale, soft skin is revealed, then curves, and finally the whole woman in all her glory.

I have heard men speak of 'hourglass figures', and have known women so described, but they all paled into insignificance compared to the woman standing before me, for Irene Hammond, naked, was simply breathtaking. The fullness of her breasts was emphasised by her commendably narrow waist, which curved out into broad hips and sturdy thighs. She was truly spectacular, and I was quite at a loss for words.

Few women, no matter how beautiful, can stand naked and immobile whilst a man looks them over. The urge to cover breasts and groin is almost irresistible. Irene Hammond knew very well what was required of her, but knowing it and doing it are two different things. A woman's arms have a mind of their own at times like these, and the governess was presently engaged in a battle of wills with her own limbs. It was most entertaining to observe this struggle, and to try to guess who would win. I would have wagered on Irene Hammond - and sure enough, she seemed to find some inner reserve of willpower, and her arms finally settled at her sides.

I approached and stood before her, and she regarded me with a certain apprehension.

'You seem just a trifle nervous, Mrs Hammond,' I said gently.

'I confess I am, sir, a little.'

'That is understandable. Indeed, it would be strange if it were otherwise. You should know, however, that I have the very highest regard for you, and would not wish to cause you even a moment's disquiet.'

'Thank you, sir.'

Perhaps my words offered some small degree of comfort. The kindest thing of all, of course, given that waiting can be almost unbearable in circumstances such as these, would have been to cease the shilly-shallying and take her straight to bed. Kind to her, that is - not so kind to myself. I had made myself wait four long weeks for the pleasure of seeing her naked, and it would be positively criminal to spoil things by rushing now.

'Has anyone ever told you, Mrs Hammond,' I said, 'that you have the most superb breasts?'

As I spoke I reached out and cupped them. I use the word 'cupped', but it would take the hands of a veritable Goliath to manage such a feat. I simply put my hands beneath them and lifted, taking their weight.

'My late husband... often would admire them, sir,' she said haltingly, shivering at my touch.

Spouses, deceased or otherwise, was not a topic of conversation I welcomed at this point, and I chided myself for asking so tactless and ill-advised a question.

'As do I,' I said. 'Very much indeed.' I thumbed her nipples and felt them harden. Her breathing had quickened, I noticed, and there was a flush on her cheeks. Embarrassment, or ardour? It was difficult to be sure, but most likely it was a little of each. At least, I sincerely *hoped* it was not embarrassment alone. Making love to a woman who has no interest in the proceedings is a thankless undertaking that demeans both parties.

I began to knead her breasts, gently at first, then with a little more vigour, and found them agreeably firm. I squeezed harder still, for some women desire a degree of pain, and the governess gasped and closed her eyes. She made no protest, however, and her arms remained by her sides.

With my left hand still engaged in kneading her breasts, my right moved lower, tracing lightly over her ribs and down across her belly to her groin. I stirred my fingers in her pubic hair, and her hands, obedient to her will till this moment, rose in faint protest.

'Sir,' she murmured.

'Madam,' I countered softly. 'Remain still, if you please.' I stroked her labia, caressing the soft lips yet making no attempt to penetrate her - that delight would come later. My touch elicited a gasp, and she shivered again. Though I was almost sure this was in no way due to the chill of the air, I thought she would be more comfortable if we moved closer to the fire - and it did occur to me also that sitting on the couch would grant me better access to her. I released her and stood back, whereupon her eyes opened.

'Time to have a proper look at you, I think,' I informed her. 'Come, Mrs Hammond.' I led her to the couch, sat her down and parted her knees. This latter accomplishment is easier in the telling than it was in the doing, as there was considerable resistance. I felt sure this was unintentional on her part, however, being a purely instinctive reflex.

Gentle but insistent pressure eventually yielded the desired result, and those alabaster portals parted, revealing her cunny in all its glory. And what a wonderful sight it was. Her outer lips were full and fleshy, whilst the delicate folds of her inner lips formed a prominent, rippled double ridge. This delightful combination was crowned with a bush of dark hair so neat it might have been clipped.

I began to finger her and her knees drew together. There was a certain predictability to this, yet it was rather disappointing even so. She knew very well she should keep her legs open, no matter how strong the urge to close them. Irene Hammond must learn to control herself better than this.

Training in the form of constant repetition would help. Her legs closed, so I put my hands on her knees and opened them. I said nothing by way of reprimand, and there was no disapproval in my glance. I merely parted her thighs and resumed fingering her.

This whole cycle was repeated three or four times, and finally she was able to master her natural instincts and keep her legs apart, though they shook with the effort and her hands were clenched into fists by her sides.

A minor victory, then - no more than a skirmish in a larger war - but a victory still. And now I could concentrate on the task in hand and work her in earnest, seeing the tension drain slowly from her as apprehension, and perhaps even shame, gave way to other feelings.

Some fifteen minutes of this had achieved an accord of sorts, and now here we were, my fingertip rubbing her clitoris and Irene Hammond sighing, staring beyond my shoulder with a glazed look in her eyes. Little wonder her Latin grammar escaped her.

'Tell me, Mrs Hammond,' I said, breaking into her reverie, 'have you ever heard the word "cunnilingus"?' She replied that she had not, and I proceeded to describe the activity in considerable detail. I spared her nothing, and her flush deepened. 'Can you guess where this is leading?' I asked with a wicked smile.

'No, sir,' she murmured, avoiding my eyes.

'Oh, but I think you can.' Without further ado I knelt and began running my tongue along the inside of her thigh, starting just above the knee and moving upwards. I stopped just before I reached her cunny, and promptly subjected her other thigh to the same treatment.

Her legs were quaking as I leaned forward, nuzzling my face between her thighs. Ignoring her murmured protestations I flicked the tip of my tongue rapidly over her clitoris, licking for some time until I felt I could delay no longer. I simply had to have her.

'Let us change places,' I said.

I stood up and helped her to her feet, then lay on the couch. She knelt down and leaned over me, thinking I wished her to suck me in turn, and I was obliged to explain that I wished her to mount me instead.

'I... I don't know what... to do, sir,' she stammered.

I was not entirely surprised. Even in this day and age, poised as we are on the brink of the twentieth century, there are some who consider that anything other than the missionary position (preferably in the dark and under the bedclothes) is degenerate. Those ancient Romans and Greeks were more imaginative and more liberated by far. George Reginald Hammond, I surmised, had not been an adventurous man when it came to activities of the amorous kind.

The same accusation, I am happy to say, cannot be directed at me. There is no coital position I will not attempt, no practice I will eschew. And since thirty-odd years of debauchery have done me no visible harm, I feel I can confidently declare that imaginative, spirited sex is not detrimental to one's health.

I decided then and there that I would take it upon myself to educate Irene Hammond in the art of lovemaking. No matter how arduous the task, no matter how long it might take, I would not stint till she was thoroughly versed in all the myriad aspects of this most marvellous of subjects. In fact, this process had already started. I had coached her in male masturbation and fellatio, I had demonstrated cunnilingus, and now it was time for lesson number four: how to ride a man.

'Come,' I said. 'Kneel astride me.'

She dutifully moved over me, her knees close against my ribs, and I took hold of my cock and aimed him at her slit.

'Down, now,' I said. 'Lower yourself slowly.'

She did so, and came to rest on the tip of my erect cock. She seemed reluctant to impale herself, but I said nothing and simply waited. I saw her gather herself, take a deep breath, and then push down.

Entering a woman for the first time is a truly wonderful experience. As my cock slid into Irene Hammond I gave a groan of sheer delight. For her part she warbled in consternation, but made no attempt to rise and free herself of the thing that had penetrated her.

As the minutes passed, aided by my quiet instruction, she seemed to find her rhythm. Her hips moved more confidently and she appeared somewhat easier in her mind. My hands went to her breasts and she sighed, and put her own hands behind her head, allowing me unimpeded access.

'My dear, dear girl,' I said, as I began to knead her once more, '...my sweet Irene. Truly you are the most delightful, most beautiful creature imaginable.'

Such declarations, made when passions are high, are all too often shallow and fail to abide once those same passions are spent, but my words were from the heart, honestly spoken - and my tone must surely have convinced her of my sincerity. The expression in her eyes softened, and she smiled and put her palm against my cheek.

'I am most happy to please you, sir,' she murmured.

And please me she did, for a good long while.

Chapter 11

'Elizabeth,' I said the following Thursday morning over breakfast, 'there is something I wish to discuss with you - something of a most important nature. Do I have your very fullest attention, my dear?'

'Of course, Uncle James,' she said.

There were just three of us at the table: Elizabeth, Irene Hammond, and myself. My two younger wards had gobbled down their breakfast and rushed off on business of their own - something about needing Rose to help fix their hair.

'It is essential,' I said, 'that this package be delivered to the offices of Jenkinson and Shuttlebottom, our solicitors in Oxford, on Monday morning.'

I held up the package in question. It was the size of a smallish book, wrapped in brown paper and sealed.

'I would take it myself,' I explained, 'but I leave for the south on urgent estate business tomorrow, and won't be back till Tuesday. You see my dilemma, Elizabeth?'

'I do, uncle. And you wish me to deliver the package?'

'That would be a great weight off my mind, my dear,' I confessed, 'though I'm reluctant to burden you with such a heavy responsibility. I can't stress enough how important it is that the package be delivered before noon. It must be placed directly into the hands of Walter Jenkinson, and no other. Do you understand?'

'It seems plain enough,' she said. 'Foster can take me in the brougham. If I leave straight after breakfast on Monday morning I shall have ample time.'

'And you're prepared to take on this responsibility, Elizabeth? I wish you to consider most carefully. The future well-being of each and every one of us will depend on you.'

'There's nothing to consider. I shall deliver the package, uncle; trust me.'

I gave her a wistful smile. 'I do trust you, my dear - I trust you implicitly. But providence can play cruel tricks when we least expect it. The horse might lose a shoe... or you might oversleep.'

She smiled and shook her head. 'The farrier's skills I cannot vouch for; but as for me, I have never overslept in my whole life. Please set your mind at ease on that score.'

The following morning was fine, if a little cool, and I had a ken to undertake my journey on horseback rather than by carriage. I therefore had Foster bring out Whiplash, the black stallion I bought from Lord Newburn just a couple of months previously. Before mounting, I took Irene Hammond aside for a private word.

'Is Elizabeth quite clear on her instructions, would you say?' I asked.

'I believe so, Mr Montague. She's a most prudent young woman - I'm sure you can rely on her good sense.'

'It's not her sense I'm concerned about, rather her health. She's been looking a little fatigued of late, I thought.'

'Fatigued, sir?' the governess said with a puzzled frown.

'Precisely. Worryingly so, in my opinion. What she needs is a good night's rest. Does Rose still bring the girls a mug of hot milk at bedtime, to help them sleep?'

'Yes indeed, sir. Every night without fail.'

'Excellent,' I murmured. 'Should this find its way into Elizabeth's drink, she will sleep like the proverbial log.' I handed her a glass vial containing a colourless liquid. 'It is entirely safe,' I said, 'and odourless and tasteless to boot. I was thinking that Sunday night would be best. You take my meaning, Mrs Hammond?'

I saw comprehension dawn in the governess's eyes, and her lips curved in an appreciative smile as the deviousness of my plan became clear to her - or should I say, almost clear. It always pays to keep an ace up one's sleeve.

'Yes, sir,' she said, 'I believe I do. A sound night's sleep for Miss Elizabeth... and quite possibly a long lie-in on Monday morning?'

'No doubt of that at all.'

Irene Hammond nodded. 'Then the package to be delivered...?'

'Contains an illustrated treatise on the flora and fauna of Peru,' I said. 'Pocket edition. I'm sure the redoubtable Mr Jenkinson would have found it fascinating, had he the opportunity to read it. Alas, we shall never know - always providing Elizabeth drinks her milk, that is.'

'I'll make sure she does, sir,' the governess said. 'You can certainly rely on *me*.'

My plan for Elizabeth's undoing obviously required my absence from the house, to explain my inability to deliver the package personally, hence the 'urgent estate business' I had eluded to. Actually I was off to spend the weekend with an old friend, Humphrey Porton-Jones, at his house in Beckton Measby, a village some fifteen miles to the south east.

Humphrey, a fellow member of Spankers Seven, a group of likeminded individuals devoted to the noble art of spanking, had written to me some time ago to ask if I was free to join him for a few days. He was in the process of training a girl as a 'slave' - a highly specialised role quite different from that of a maid under discipline, such as Alice or Rose. I had owned slaves in the past, but had no plans to acquire one at the present time. To be perfectly honest, I find their unremitting subservience somewhat tiresome - though many floggers would consider this positively seditious - and much prefer my present arrangements.

The girl in question, Humphrey informed me, was a fairly recent arrival by the name of Donnett, who was ready to progress to the next stage in her training, namely public performance. As she was of a timid disposition, Humphrey planned to break her in gradually. Very gradually, in fact, for I was to be the only spectator - and not just a spectator. Humphrey was offering me the chance to spank her as a means of further broadening her experience.

Donnett turned out to be a quiet girl, not very tall, and slimly built. She was a pretty thing, though most painfully shy. She was not, as I had assumed, a servant, but rather the daughter of the village baker. She had been ejected from the family home following a scandal involving a local lad, and Humphrey had taken her in rather than see her dispatched to the workhouse.

His motives for this were not entirely altruistic, of course. He made it plain to Donnett what was expected of her in exchange for roof and board, demonstrating on his longsuffering housekeeper, Queenie Bryce. The choice, in the end, was Donnett's; and she elected to stay.

Within an hour of my arrival Donnett was experiencing her first public punishment. Her face flushed scarlet as she undressed, even though Humphrey told her she could retain her under-things. It was not an especially hard spanking - a dozen with his hand followed by a second dozen with a light-ish strap. I sat quietly at the side of the room and watched, remembering similar training sessions I had conducted. A first showing is always a significant occasion, for audience and participants alike, and this one brought back many pleasant memories.

Donnett was very aware of my presence, of course, but looked at me just once, at the start, and afterwards avoided my gaze. She took her punishment without undue fuss, and I thought she had all the makings of an excellent slave.

The following day, Saturday, I had my first opportunity to try her myself. I told her I would be administering her punishment that morning, at which she paled and started to tremble, looking at Humphrey much as a maiden facing the dragon looks to her knight in shining armour. Donnett's 'Sir Galahad' merely nodded, however, his face grave; at which her own countenance fell.

'I want you to take off all your clothes now, Donnett,' I said. 'Your master will assist with your corset stays and suchlike, should you require it.'

I had agreed with Humphrey beforehand how I should proceed with this, down to the last detail. Enjoyable though this might be for me, that was not the purpose of these proceedings. Slave training is a serious matter requiring thought and care. The slave must be brought on by degrees, in a controlled fashion.

Donnett undressed, though her disrobing was not achieved expeditiously. Considering how badly her hands were shaking it's a miracle she could manage the fastenings at all. Humphrey murmured the odd word of encouragement, and eventually the last of her garments was discarded. Inevitably, her arms moved to shield her.

'Now then, Donnett,' Humphrey chided, 'you know better than that. Let the dog see the rabbit, there's a good girl.'

As he spoke he took hold of her arms and steered them to her sides, allowing me to scrutinise her without hindrance. I did this quite openly, and even went so far as to comment on her figure.

'As comely a form as I've seen for some time, Mr Porton-Jones. Such pert breasts, and such a pretty cunny. You must be pleased with this sweet girl.'

'Indeed I am, Mr Montague,' Humphrey replied, patting her bottom affectionately. 'Very pleased indeed. Donnett is an absolute angel.'

All highly contrived, of course, though Donnett did indeed possess a trim figure. The aim was to break down her natural inhibitions and help her grow used to being gazed upon. Shyness in a slave is natural, some might even say desirable, but excessive modesty often leads to a reluctance to undress, particularly in front of strangers, and this is to be avoided.

When it comes to handing out a punishment my own style is noticeably different to Humphrey's. He is quietly authoritative, gentle but firm, whereas I am sterner and stricter. My somewhat more forceful approach was one of the reasons - friendship aside - Humphrey asked me to participate in this particular phase of Donnett's training.

I made no attempt to soften my manner, therefore, when I instructed Donnett to take up her position. With a final woeful glance at her lord and master, she complied, kneeling on the chair as instructed, head erect, shoulders straight, hands gripping the chair back.

Humphrey handed me a cane, and I gave Donnett a tolerably hard swipe across the buttocks - harder, probably, than she had ever experienced. She gasped, her face registering shock and some alarm.

'Sir...' she said in a voice that quavered, turning once again to Humphrey.

'Face me, Donnett,' I said sternly. 'You must always look to the man who is punishing you.' The next stroke was harder still, to reinforce the message. Erroneous behaviour would not be tolerated.

A further ten strokes followed, during which Donnett said not a word, though she did indeed look at me from time to time, her soulful eyes brimming with tears.

I told her to dress and Humphrey led her away, talking quietly to her. She turned at the door, presumably at Humphrey's prompting.

'Thank you for my punishment, sir,' she murmured.

'You're most welcome, Donnett,' I said.

Giving thanks for her spanking in this way was not something I required of my own servants, as it sounds, to my ear, somewhat artificial. I know a good few floggers who insist on it, however, so Humphrey is by no means unique in this.

This was the only beating Donnett received on Saturday, but over the next two days she had five more, of which Humphrey delivered two and I three. All in all it was a most pleasant vacation, and it was in high spirits that I mounted Whiplash on Tuesday morning and set off home, arriving shortly before noon.

The moment I walked through the door I knew something was wrong. The house had an uncanny stillness, and Alice seemed even more nervous than usual as she took my hat and cloak.

Elizabeth and Mrs Hammond were waiting for me in the drawing room, and one glance at their unhappy faces confirmed my suspicions. In my absence something had gone badly amiss.

They regarded me with anxious eyes, and then looked at each other, neither wishing to be the first to speak up. Possibly we would be standing there still had I not forced the issue.

'Elizabeth?' I said. 'Is there something you wish to impart to me? Not bad tidings, I hope.'

'I fear so, Uncle James,' she said quietly. 'I... I have lost the package.'

I thought that I had never seen Elizabeth so discomposed. Gone was the confident young woman of a week before, and in her place stood a pale-faced, unhappy, troubled girl.

'Lost?' I said. '*Lost?*'

Elizabeth nodded and cast her eyes down in shame. 'It was stolen. By a ragged man in the street outside Mr Jenkinson's office.'

'A ragged...' I shook my head in bewilderment. 'So you journeyed to Oxford as planned?' I glanced at Irene Hammond. Now it was her turn to hang her head in shame.

'Yes uncle,' Elizabeth said, oblivious to the by-play. 'Foster drove me and we reached the city just before eleven. I had the package in my bag. I looked to see that it was safe when I stepped down onto the pavement. I suppose that's when he must have seen it.'

'He?'

'The ragged man. He seized... he seized my bag and ran off up the street. Foster gave chase, but couldn't catch him. I didn't... I...'

Her voice faltered and she fell silent, overcome by remorse and shame. I had to coax the rest from her - how she hurried into the solicitor's office and reported the theft to Walter Jenkinson. How that gentleman promptly escorted her to the police station where she had to tell her story all over again, and sign a statement. And how, after all that, the police sergeant said there was little chance of ever seeing the package again.

I regarded my ward as she stood before me, silent and dejected. It was hard to imagine a sorrier looking young woman.

'This is far more serious,' I said gravely, 'than you can possibly imagine. You have failed me, Elizabeth. You have failed all of us, your sisters included. I take much of the blame upon myself for allowing you to accept such a heavy responsibility. I thought I could trust you. Clearly I was wrong.'

Tears welled up in her eyes and rolled slowly down her cheeks.

'Elizabeth,' I said sternly, 'you must be punished, and punished most severely. Do you accept this?'

She nodded miserably.

'Very well. Friday, six o'clock, in the study. You will now go to your room, where you will contemplate the consequences of failing in your duty.'

'Yes, uncle. I'm very sorry, uncle.'

With that, Elizabeth left. And now it was Irene Hammond's turn to stand there and explain her failure to me.

Chapter 12

If anything the governess was an even sorrier sight than my ward. Her whole demeanour spoke of guilt and anxiety, not to say fear.

'I seem to remember,' I said quietly, 'someone telling me I could rely on her. Do you recall such a conversation, Hammond?'

It was not 'Mrs Hammond' now, for she was in disgrace. Now it was cold formality, and all-too-obvious displeasure. 'Tell me what happened.'

She shrugged helplessly. 'Truly, sir, I don't know. I went down to the kitchen while the girls were preparing for bed. Mrs Smith was warming their milk, and I distracted her and put the sleeping potion in Elizabeth's drink.

At least, I thought I did.

They each have their own special mugs with their names on, that their mother bought them at Brighton.'

There was a slight tremor in her voice, and her hands clasped and unclasped nervously.

'After Rose had taken the tray up, I went to Elizabeth's room on a pretext and watched her drink it. In the morning I went back, thinking to find her sound asleep, but she was already up and dressed and about to depart. I couldn't think of any way to stop her. Then a little later Alice came running to say Victoria was still in bed, and wouldn't wake up properly.'

'Victoria?'

'I'm afraid so, sir. The girl slept till midday, and was still a little drowsy in the afternoon. I think... I can only assume... I put the potion in the wrong mug. It seems the only possible explanation.'

I gave her a long, long stare, and she wilted under the onslaught. When I spoke it was in the grimmest of tones.

'You led me to believe you were someone I could have full confidence in,' I said. 'The truth is, I cannot trust you with even so simple a task as this.'

She looked thoroughly crestfallen standing there, head down. 'But it turned out well enough in the end...' she started to say.

'For which I have a ragged man to thank, it seems,' I snapped, 'and not you. It is simply not good enough, Hammond. I made it plain at the start that I need someone I can depend upon, and quite clearly you do not fit the bill.'

She could see what was coming, for she started to tremble and her face took on a look of desperation.

'It pains me to say this,' I went on, 'for I had high hopes of you - but I shall have to let you go. Given the unfortunate circumstances I am not in a position to supply you with a reference, but your wages will be paid till the end of the month. I shall arrange for Foster to take you to the station in the morning. Good day.'

I started to turn away, but she put her hand on my arm. 'Please, sir,' she begged in a stricken voice, 'don't dismiss me. Punish me, but don't dismiss me!'

'It has gone beyond punishment,' I said. 'How can a mere beating atone for a betrayal of trust of this magnitude? No, no, my mind is quite made up. Good day.'

'Please, sir, no!' she cried. 'Punish me severely!'

I frowned and shook my head, as though further discussion was futile. 'Severely?' I said. 'I expect you think two or three dozen an appropriate punishment for a failure such as this, yet even four would not suffice, I think.'

'Five dozen, sir! It is no more than I deserve.'

'Five, you say?' I pretended to consider this, but then sighed and shook my head. 'I think not. No doubt you would expect gentle treatment to compensate for the sheer number of strokes—'

'Oh no, sir!' she interjected. 'It should be a severe punishment, with hard strokes. Very hard indeed!'

'Possibly,' I said. 'Possibly. But you would wish to retain your drawers, I imagine, as a way of diminishing the blows.'

'Not at all. Whatever you deem appropriate, sir. In underwear, or naked, entirely as you see fit.'

'Yes,' I said, 'but still...'

I shook my head doubtfully. It was growing harder by the second to appear diffident, as the prospect of giving Irene Hammond sixty strokes was a happy one indeed.

As for the governess herself, her customary astuteness had deserted her completely. The threat of dismissal and all that went with it had robbed her of her wits, seemingly.

It was not just the money, I knew. Her life at Bleekston Hall was everything she could wish for - which was precisely why she was pleading with me to subject her to five dozen rather than dismiss her.

Still I prevaricated, however, pretending ambivalence.

'And afterwards,' I said, 'the checking of the tantalus region... that would be of a cursory nature, would it?'

'Oh, no indeed, sir,' she said. 'A thorough check, probing most deeply...'

It was a measure of her agitation that it was only at this point did she pause and look at me, realising I was far more amenable to the idea than my words and tone suggested.

'So,' I said, 'let me be quite clear on what you are proposing. Sixty hard strokes, on the bare if I so choose, following which you will submit to a most thorough inspection. Do I have it right, Mrs Hammond?'

She nodded gravely, perhaps not trusting herself to speak. I stared at her for several long seconds, keeping her on tenterhooks, then sighed theatrically.

'Very well,' I said, 'I accept your proposal. Possibly I am being unwise, but time will tell.'

'Thank you, sir,' she whispered, looking relieved beyond measure. 'Thank you.'

I stroked my beard. 'I intend to punish Elizabeth this coming Friday for losing the package, together with Victoria for oversleeping. Your own punishment will therefore have to take place on Thursday. Is three o'clock convenient?'

'Yes, sir.'

There was, of course, no other answer she could give.

When the governess had departed I poured myself a glass of brandy and toasted my success. It was a little early in the day for hard liquor, perhaps, but I felt I had earned it. My plan had worked to perfection.

Irene Hammond's downfall had been easy to contrive. The mix-up over the bedtime drinks was no accident - I had instructed Rose to swap the contents of Elizabeth's and Victoria's mugs prior to delivering them to the young ladies in question (an extra, empty mug had been secreted in the landing cupboard to enable this transfer to take place). Naturally I had sworn the maid to secrecy, and threatened her with a thrashing to end all thrashings should the truth ever leak out.

Some might think that trusting any female to keep a secret is optimistic in the extreme, not to say foolhardy. Possibly I was courting disaster by relying on Rose's discretion, but I think not.

I have a theory that a girl's resolve is strengthened considerably by bending her over a stool and directing three dozen firm strokes to her bare posterior. It certainly seemed to do the trick with Rose.

The theft of the package was almost as easy to arrange, for Elizabeth's 'ragged man' was none other than the infamous Charlie Spikeman himself, suitably attired.

A week before I sent him his instructions, along with a photograph of my eldest ward for identification purposes. He had simply waited on the pavement outside Jenkinson's office for Elizabeth's arrival. A quick snatch and grab (child's play for a scoundrel like Charlie) had sealed Elizabeth's fate.

With two beautiful females now censured and awaiting chastisement, everything had worked out perfectly.

Chapter 13

For Irene Hammond's punishment I planned to use a different implement for each set of twelve, and to have her adopt positions that were somewhat out of the ordinary.

As the hour of the flogging drew near I spent some time perusing my special collection, and carefully selected five suitable implements. I laid them out on the sideboard; and what an inspiring and noble sight they made!

I swept my gaze over the room. Everything I would need - implements, spanking chair, spanking stool - was in place. Alice had polished the full-length mirror on the wall that very morning at my request. The only thing missing was the governess herself, and that would be remedied shortly.

She arrived promptly, looking composed if a little pale. These past three days must have seemed very long indeed to Irene Hammond. She had gone about her duties with a troubled, preoccupied air that was quite out of character. Not that I thought any the less of her for this, you understand - she would know better than most that sixty hard strokes is a daunting prospect.

'Mrs Hammond,' I said, 'good afternoon to you. Can I offer you some refreshment before we start? A glass of Madeira, perhaps?'

'No thank you, sir,' she said quietly.

No doubt she was keen to make a start - and keener still to get it over with - but I had absolutely no intention of hurrying things. Indeed, I intended to make this session last a good long while, and to savour every single second.

'No?' I said, rising and crossing to the cabinet to pour myself a drink. 'Something a little stronger, perhaps? Brandy? Gin?'

She shook her head. Her eyes followed me across the room, and I knew she could not fail to notice the five implements lying in a neat row on the sideboard.

'Kindly take off your clothes,' I said, as I poured myself a brandy. 'All of them.'

I leaned against the cabinet to observe the disrobing, sipping my drink. She undressed without delay, then stood up straight, feet together, arms by her sides, eyes straight ahead. I set my glass down and went up to her.

'You look like a naked guardsman on parade, Mrs Hammond,' I said. I poked her breasts with a rigid index finger, right then left. 'With some significant differences,' I conceded.

She made no reply, though her cheeks did lose a little of their pallor.

I crossed to the sideboard and picked up the first implement, a spanking mitten. This was of the usual form - a flat pouch of thick leather into which one slipped one's hand - though a little more refined than some in possessing a separate compartment for the thumb, much in the same fashion as a normal woollen mitten. It was of no great antiquity, in fact, being a token of gratitude from Humphrey for some small service I did him a year or two back.

Thus armed I drew up the spanking stool, placing it to Irene Hammond's left.

'Raise your arms,' I said. 'Straight up in the air.' She did so and I sat on the stool, facing her. My left hand went to her groin and I grasped her maidenhair firmly. She gave a faint murmur of dismay and flinched, but her hands remained elevated, to her credit.

'There is no need to count,' I advised her. 'Are you ready, Mrs Hammond?'

'Yes, sir,'

'Then let us begin.'

I began to spank her, alternating left buttock then right. The slaps were not especially fearsome, as a human hand - even with the aid of a spanking mitten - can never compare with strap or cane for sheer power. Though relatively modest in nature, these first strokes were certainly firm enough to see her buttocks pinking nicely by the end of the set.

'That's twelve gone,' I said, rising from the stool. 'Forty-eight to go.' Stating the obvious at times like these was a habit of mine - one that afforded me considerable pleasure, though I am utterly at a loss to explain why. Those I addressed possibly found it irritating, though I cannot recall anyone ever complaining about it - then again, no doubt they had more pressing matters on their minds.

I told Mrs Hammond to lower her arms and she did so, favouring me with a quick smile. Expecting hard strokes, she must have been surprised and not a little relieved at what she received. Possibly she entertained hopes that I'd had a change of heart, and that her punishment was to be less severe than promised. I made no attempt to rectify this misconception. The truth would dawn on her soon enough, as I had decided that the remaining strokes would fully merit the description 'hard'.

My grandfather's definition of a hard stroke was that it tested to the limit the victim's resolve to remain in the designated position. Any harder (he referred to these as 'severe') and the victim would simply not be able to hold her position, necessitating some form of restraint. Though straps, ropes, and even chains are commonly employed for such purposes, my grandfather considered all such devices crude and lacking in finesse. On such occasions as he felt the need to administer severe strokes, he would enlist the help of a third party (a manservant, generally, until such time as I was old enough to fulfil this role) to hold the unfortunate woman or girl's wrists. Since it was hard strokes rather than severe that we had agreed upon for Irene Hammond's five dozen, restraint should not, in theory, be necessary.

I walked to the sideboard to exchange mitten for strap. It was somewhat unusual in form - a two-foot long, heavy strip of leather attached to a short wooden handle. Reputedly it had once belonged to a former president of the United States of America, though I had no documentary evidence to support the claim.

'For this next dozen,' I said, 'I require you on the table, lying facedown, if you please.'

She duly complied, and I took her wrists and proceeded to slide her forward until her torso from the hips upward overhung the table edge, obliging her to bend at the waist and rest her hands on the floor. I took up my position, and swung the strap with vigour. It landed with a resounding crack and Irene Hammond, who had taken the first twelve with barely a murmur, let out a heartfelt gasp and jerked mightily. Eleven identical strokes followed, after which I helped her regain the floor once more. I was interested to note that her smile had quite vanished, and that her eyes were now moist.

For the third dozen I had decided upon a riding crop, and another slightly awkward position. I told her to lie on her back on the floor and raise her legs straight up in the air. I then took her ankles and eased them back, all the way over till her toes touched the rug above her head. The position involved a fair degree of strain, and it was necessary for the governess to prop her hips with her forearms in order to sustain it.

'I appreciate that this is an uncomfortable position,' I said. 'Should you find it difficult to catch your breath, please speak up immediately.'

I pulled up the chair - I saw no good reason I should not be comfortable, even if the governess could not - sat down, and delivered a hard whack to her proffered bottom. Irene Hammond's cry was constricted by her doubled-up stance, which similarly limited her movement. She could not easily wriggle to mitigate the pain or alleviate her discomfort without first lowering her legs to the floor.

At the next stroke her toes came off the carpet as though that was precisely what she intended - but I was ready for it. I put my left hand at the back of her knees and pushed her legs down, then held her there whilst I delivered further strokes.

I paused after six.

'Halfway, Mrs Hammond,' I pointed out, in case the significance of the moment had eluded her. 'Just thirty to go.'

'Indeed, sir.'

I judged from her tone that she was not a happy woman. I, on the other hand, was positively euphoric. I can think of no better pastime than raising weals on a bare female bottom, especially when the female in question is as beautiful as Irene Hammond, and the bottom as spectacular as the one before me.

More strokes duly followed. The governess was suffering considerably now, as evidenced by her anguished sobs of pain and the way she shuddered at each fierce stroke. I could not see her face clearly, which was a pity, but I planned to rectify this with the very next set.

She climbed stiffly to her feet, and in a voice that quavered, asked permission to rub. I nodded, and she proceeded to massage her buttocks most gingerly.

I had chosen a tawse for this penultimate dozen - and one that held great sentimental value for me, being none other than the three-tailed beauty my grandfather had used on Grace Forsyth that first time I saw her spanked. I picked it up and stroked the smooth leather. Though old and somewhat stained, it was a fearsome weapon still, having lost none of its resilience over the years.

I led the governess to the full-length mirror on the wall and told her to stand facing it with her feet apart. I then had her lean forward and place her hands on the wall on either side. I myself took up a position behind and to her left, so that I was able to observe her face reflected in the glass. I then proceeded to beat her.

I had guessed that she was suffering exceedingly, and the sight of her contorted face as the tawse sent streaks of fire across her much abused posterior confirmed this. She was having great difficulty keeping still, twisting sideways and dipping her knees after each stroke, and I was frequently obliged to wait while she composed herself. I cautioned her about this errant behaviour, and she gave a guilty nod, but it was clear she had almost reached the end of her tether.

When I paused at six she glanced over her shoulder at me, plainly wishing to say something, but presumably afraid to speak.

'I do not require you to be dumb, Mrs Hammond,' I said, 'merely respectful. Please say what's on your mind.'

She took a deep breath. 'Sir...'

That single word was followed by a pause so lengthy I began to think she had decided to hold her peace after all. Then she took another breath.

'Sir... is there any way... is there anything I can say...' Her voice was unsteady, which was understandable in view of what she had suffered. Though she did not finish her question I thought I could easily guess the rest. She wished to be excused the remainder of her punishment; and that was also understandable. Her buttocks were in a dreadful state - purple and swollen; and sore, I expected, almost beyond bearing. The thought of a further eighteen strokes must be bitter indeed, and it was only natural she would wish it to end. Natural, but utterly impossible, and normally I would have awarded an extra dozen for even daring to ask such a thing. But since I had invited her to speak, that was clearly inappropriate.

'Is there anything you can say to be excused the rest, do you mean?' I ventured. 'I very much doubt it. However, nothing ventured nothing gained, as they say. Speak up, please do.'

She tried, but the words simply would not come.

'No doubt,' I suggested, 'you would wish to say that you are truly sorry for failing me in this matter. Perhaps you would promise to strive most diligently never again to disappoint me.'

She nodded earnestly, and I studied the tear-streaked face before me, wondering at the thoughts passing through her mind. Perhaps she felt genuine contrition, perhaps not - it was immaterial either way. I could not go back on my word. To terminate a punishment simply because the recipient is suffering would be patently absurd. No self-respecting spanker could possibly entertain such a notion.

'I sympathise with your predicament,' I said, 'but I cannot grant you this. You must bear the full five dozen.'

She nodded as though expecting this, her expression baleful but resigned. I took this to mean she was able, however unwillingly, to proceed, and instructed her to resume the stance.

The second six were inordinately arduous on her. Her legs shook - indeed, her whole body was trembling - and she seemed to take an age coming back to the required position each time. I considered awarding additional strokes, but decided against it. It would be touch and go whether she could manage the five dozen.

The set was finished at last, and she could rub once again and take a step or two. I allowed her five minutes or so to gather herself, then went to collect the last of the five implements - a heavy cane.

And so we had arrived at this, the final dozen. I had Irene Hammond lie on her back on the table with her buttocks overhanging the edge, and her legs raised in the air and spread wide apart. I did rub her cunny briefly, but such a diversion seemed out of place in view of her tribulations. I had already decided to forego the 'tantalus' exploration we had agreed would conclude this session. There is a time and place for everything, dalliance included, and this was not it.

The set got underway, and it was evident that each stroke was the sheerest purgatory for the governess, who uttered a most pitiful cry each time the cane struck her ravaged posterior. I felt sorry for her, naturally, but was powerless to help. Any let up in force during this, the final dozen, was clearly out of the question. Irene Hammond must find her own salvation.

The final stroke of any punishment is traditionally the hardest, and I made no exception. I suspect the governess had lost count, for she seemed unprepared for it, but I used the full power of my arm, sparing her nothing. She screamed, rolling onto her side and drawing her knees up to her chest. I could do nothing for her then but watch and wait; and when she had recovered somewhat, help her down from the table this one last time.

For the governess, clearly, it had been a truly dreadful experience. That she was a courageous woman was beyond doubt. Pain can humble even the bravest among us, however, and that she endured was entirely due to strength of character, and of will.

I helped her to dress, for she was moving like a person bereft of wits, and then rang for Alice to assist her to her room.

'Thank you, sir,' was all she said to me before departing.

Her words were without irony, and her pained glance held no animosity. An altogether remarkable woman.

Chapter 14

'Well, Victoria?' I said. 'Do you have anything to say for yourself?'

Oversleeping is hardly a heinous crime, even though, under the influence of the sleeping draft in her milk, my red-haired ward had done a thoroughly good job of it.

'No, Uncle James,' she said meekly. 'I'm sorry, Uncle James.'

'I should hope you are,' I said, turning to Irene Hammond standing quietly by Victoria's side. 'How many strokes do you think, Mrs Hammond, for this slug-a-bed?'

In truth, the 'sin' deserved no more than a stern warning, but it was some weeks since the incident of the vase and I was keen to see Victoria naked and squirming prettily under the strap once more. I was eager too, I cannot deny, to explore her tantalus region, especially so since Mrs Hammond had suggested further developments might be possible.

I had debated whether it was appropriate to have the governess in attendance, with her own punishment of the previous day still fresh in her mind - and her bottom, no doubt. In the end I decided it was. Though I was confident I could manage on my own if needs be, having an assistant on hand was always useful. I was interested, too, to see how Irene Hammond composed herself. It is how we behave in times of stress that says who we truly are.

Mrs Hammond had seemed just a mite subdued as she led Victoria in, but it took a keen eye to notice it. She appeared somewhat surprised at my question, as though she had not expected to be consulted in the matter, but she answered promptly enough.

'One dozen, sir.'

We seemed to have developed an understanding, without ever having discussed the matter, that twelve was the minimum punishment to be awarded, no matter how trivial the offence. The classic 'six-of-the-best' had been relegated to the history books - and not before time, in my opinion. The cane is barely starting to warm up at twelve, let alone six.

'One dozen it is,' I declared. 'Victoria, you know what to do.'

She did, and she turned to her governess for help with the buttons. It occurred to me that dresses with buttons down the back are somewhat impractical for punishment sessions, necessitating that Mrs Hammond be on hand at all times, or that I perform the task myself. Neither option was particularly troublesome, indeed, the thought of undressing a young woman held considerable appeal. But still, some other arrangement might bear scrutiny. It ought to be possible to devise a special punishment costume of a more practical nature. It occurred to me also that such a costume might add a certain novelty value to the proceedings, and I resolved to speak privately with the governess on this matter.

For now, however, we were dependent upon the good woman's assistance, and she duly obliged.

It seemed to me, watching the process with keen interest, that getting Victoria out of her clothes took less time and less fuss than previously. It might be, of course, that this was no more than familiarity. Her previous punishment had been her very first, and therefore quite strange and frightening. The prospect of a beating might still be less than thrilling, but it was no longer an unknown.

When the last of her garments had been set aside, Victoria's hands again moved of their own volition to hide breasts and groin, and I expected Mrs Hammond to produce the ribbon as before. She did not, however, but instead spoke sharply to the girl, at which point Victoria dropped her hands guiltily to her sides.

I took my time, savouring afresh the sight of my ward in the nude, for truly Victoria was a most delightful specimen.

I decided to let Mrs Hammond deliver the twelve strokes, interested as I was to see how her own punishment of the previous day might affect her conduct.

'Mrs Hammond,' I said accordingly, 'would you please oblige me by doing the honours? Feel free to choose an implement from the cupboard.'

She went across and selected a paddle, slapping it against her palm to judge its fierceness. I saw Victoria flinch at the sound as she watched the governess out of the corner of her eye.

'Perhaps I could suggest, sir,' the governess said to me, 'that you would be more comfortable seated?'

It seemed she had some novelty in mind, and I complied gladly. I was all in favour of novelties and surprises - my grandfather had always been keen on 'ringing the changes', as he put it. I sat, and the governess brought Victoria up to stand before me; so close, in fact, that our feet were almost touching.

'Spread your legs, Victoria,' Mrs Hammond said. 'Wide, now - just as wide as you can manage.'

The girl did so, and I was treated to a close-up view of her cunny in all its glory. And what a sight it was, pink and inviting, showing tantalisingly through a neat nest of pale ginger hair.

To complete the stance the governess told my ward to put her hands upon my shoulders, then with everything apparently ready, Mrs Hammond took a step to one side.

'I want you to count the strokes, Victoria,' she said. 'Do you know what I mean by that?'

'No, Mrs Hammond,' came the whispered reply.

'After the first stroke you must say, "One, Uncle James". After the second stroke, "Two, Uncle James", and so on. Don't whisper, though, say it boldly. Do you understand?'

'Yes, Mrs Hammond.'

'Good. Then we'll begin, with your permission, sir.'

I nodded, and Irene Hammond raised the paddle. The blow was harder than I expected and Victoria gasped, her torso arching forward.

'One, Uncle James,' she said, her voice faltering already.

The paddle went up again, paused for a second, and then descended. Another forceful stroke, and this time Victoria yelped, her hips thrusting forward vigorously. It took her several seconds to gather herself enough to speak.

'Two, Uncle James.'

And so it went on. At each stroke Victoria's groin pushed at me, as though inviting exploration of its dark, moist recess. Her back was permanently arched as she instinctively tried to draw her buttocks away from the pain, so that her slit was mere inches away from my hands, presently resting upon my knees. I had an almost overwhelming urge to reach up and tickle it, though I resisted the temptation. It was a tolerably serious punishment that Mrs Hammond was handing out, and frivolity seemed out of place.

The last few strokes were duly delivered with no let up in vigour. Victoria's voice had been unsteady after just one or two, and by the end it was breaking spectacularly. Her eyes were full of tears, which tumbled freely down her cheeks.

Irene Hammond told Victoria to lie facedown across my knee. She did so, and her legs promptly opened of their own accord.

'The tantalus region, sir,' the governess said quietly. 'If you would be so good as to examine it now.'

I needed no second bidding. I laid my first finger along Victoria's slit as before, and began to rub up and down. Victoria moaned softly and her buttocks clenched; but whereas previously her legs had closed, requiring Mrs Hammond's intervention, now they opened wider. I glanced up at the governess in surprise, and she nodded as though something had just been confirmed to her.

'You should examine it thoroughly, sir,' she said. 'Most thoroughly.'

I took her at her word, and began to finger Victoria in earnest. I teased the soft folds of flesh, tickling and rubbing them by turns. My fingertip found her clitoris, and I stroked it gently but insistently. Victoria gave a soft wail and her hips began to move in sympathy with the intimate caress. She was hanging on to my leg for grim death, and trembling in my lap. Soon my fingers were wet with her female lubrication.

I had an urge to dip my finger into her there and then, I have to say, though I felt far from certain about this. To take her virginity was no small matter, even if it was my hand and not my cock I was proposing to take it with. Once taken it cannot be given back, no matter how much the girl may regret the loss. I looked yet again to Irene Hammond for guidance in this matter, relying on her commonsense to appraise her of my quandary. Our eyes met and held, then she shrugged. I took this to mean she was as uncertain as I, and the decision was back with me.

Victoria lay across my lap east to west - that is, her head to my left - and I worked her with my right hand. Then, without pausing in my diligent attentions to her clitoris, I reached with my left hand and put my middle finger to her vagina. Slowly, very slowly, I pushed it into her. Victoria gave a cry unlike her previous sounds, and I felt her stiffen. Irene Hammond reached out quickly to rest her hand on my arm, her face concerned. I nodded reluctantly and withdrew my finger. Victoria, it seemed, wasn't yet ready, and I would simply have to bide my time.

I continued the clitoral stimulation for several minutes more, to reassure the girl, but stopped short of bringing her to climax. This wasn't deliberate cruelty on my part, just further uncertainty as to what was appropriate. An orgasm might frighten and confuse her, and I wanted to take advice from Mrs Hammond before crossing that particular bridge.

I slowed my movements gradually, and finally came to a halt. I told Victoria to rise, delivering a single smack to her bright red bottom by way of emphasis. She got to her feet and looked at me, somehow managing to appear both sheepish and brazen at the same time.

Irene Hammond helped her to dress, again chattering away merrily to raise the girl's spirits. Personally I didn't think it necessary, for Victoria, I felt certain, was quite sure of herself by now.

They went out together, and Victoria hesitated at the door long enough to throw me one parting glance. It was a remarkably mature look for a girl her age, I thought, which spoke of unfinished business. Then they were gone.

I looked at my fingers, glistening with Victoria's juices, and smiled - unfinished business for now, perhaps... but not for too much longer.

Chapter 15

The first time I set eyes on Elizabeth, shortly after the accident that robbed her of her parents, I knew that one day I would spank her. And now that day, so eagerly anticipated, so painstakingly planned and worked for, had arrived.

As with her sisters before her, Elizabeth was instructed to remove her clothes, but it soon became apparent that things were not going to be that easy.

'I will not,' she said, in a quiet but determined voice. 'It is wicked and corrupt even to suggest such a thing.'

She was disturbed by the suggestion, clearly, but didn't appear unduly surprised. One of the others had obviously blabbed, and Elizabeth, forewarned, had been granted time to marshal her defences. She faced me resolutely, hands clasped before her, chin raised in defiance.

'You must do as your governess wishes, Elizabeth,' I said calmly. 'The consequences of disobedience are worse than you can possibly imagine.'

'I will not,' she repeated. 'I accept full responsibility for the loss of the package. I accept your judgment that I should be punished. You may strike me on the hand - I believe that is the customary practice. You may strike as many times as you wish and as hard as your conscience allows. But I will not reveal my person to you, and you will not strike any other part of me.'

I was, I have to say, very proud of her at that moment. Not once had she tried to disclaim responsibility for the theft of the package. Another might have blamed providence, or fate, not to mention the ragged man himself. Some would beg forgiveness, or at least leniency, but Elizabeth asked for neither. Her refusal to undress was not cowardice but moral fibre, pure and simple.

I could not let my admiration for her divert me from my course, however. Such an act of weakness would be poor tribute indeed to her courage and steadfastness.

'Elizabeth,' Mrs Hammond snapped, 'take off your clothes this instant.'

Elizabeth turned to her with a look of pure scorn. 'That tone may work with the kitchen staff, madam, and children, but it will not work with me. I have given you my answer. Do as you must.'

I looked at the pair of them standing there, two beautiful and spirited females at daggers drawn. Any minute now they would start pulling hair.

'Mrs Hammond, Elizabeth,' I said, 'I wish to tell you something.'

So intent were they on each other, I don't believe they even heard me. I rapped on the desk, and first one then the other turned to face me.

'I wished to spare you this,' I said, 'but I see now I have no choice. Mrs Hammond, Elizabeth... we are destitute.'

The pair of them regarded me blankly, not the least flicker of understanding on either face.

'Penniless,' I added, on the off chance the previous word was unknown to them. 'Bankrupt. Do you understand what I'm saying? We have no money.'

They understood right enough, but believing it was another matter. They were looking at me as if I'd just declared the three of us fairies from Dingle Dell. Any minute now they would be sending for Doctor McDuff.

'It's perfectly true,' I said. 'The estate has been in difficulties for many years. Poor management, I'm afraid, though it pains me to speak ill of the departed. The package that was stolen from you, Elizabeth, represented a last opportunity to recover our fortunes; a last throw of the dice, as it were. That is gone now, and most of our prospects with it.'

The blank looks were still in evidence, but I forged ahead regardless.

'I *had* entertained faint hopes that we might yet triumph; that by working together and supporting each other through the difficult times ahead, we might still succeed. But all I see about me is dissent and division. I therefore have no choice but to make whatever arrangements I can. Inevitably, the family will have to be split up. It is unfortunate, but unavoidable.'

That drew a response - from Elizabeth, at least. She stiffened and started to say something. I waited, but words seemed to fail her, so I nodded gravely and continued.

'You were easy to place, Elizabeth,' I said, 'with your charm and your talents. I have obtained a post for you as companion to an elderly lady in Bath. She wishes you to read to her twice daily from the Bible, and three times on Sunday. That, and pushing her wheelchair to the spa, will be your main function, so I'm given to believe.'

I delivered this speech in my most earnest and forthright manner. Elizabeth listened, appearing dazed and bewildered - and I thought I could detect also the first stirrings of fear.

'Your sisters were more of a problem, naturally,' I went on. 'I persevered, however, and now the owner of a coalmine in Huddersfield is expressing an interest in Victoria, though for what purpose I know not. I just hope it doesn't entail too many hours underground. As for Catherine, a farmer in County Cork has written to say he requires a governess for his children, of whom there are thirteen and still counting, apparently. An ideal position for young Cathy, I thought, given her adolescent mentality. She should have much in common with the brood, do you not think?'

Needless to say the whole thing was complete and utter tosh from start to finish. Any half-intelligent person would see through it in an instant, and I had no mind to deceive Elizabeth with such arrant nonsense. The beauty of the ploy lay in the fact that it didn't *matter* that it was nonsense - what mattered was that I had the power to do these things. I could dispose of my wards as I saw fit. I could scatter them across the face of the globe, even. I could sever the links between them so completely it would be most unlikely they would ever meet again in their whole lives.

I saw Elizabeth's expression change slowly as the full implications dawned on her. Her face became rigid and fear showed plainly in her eyes. Elizabeth loved her sisters dearly, and they her. To be separated from them was the worst thing she could possibly imagine.

That I had the power to do this was beyond dispute - the only question now was whether I had the will. And that was precisely what Elizabeth was attempting to divine, I knew, as she stared at me. Was the Uncle James she had come to know these past few months capable of such wilful cruelty? Could I be such a monster, to shatter the lives of three young women out of sheer spite?

Elizabeth looked at me, and I at her. The silence dragged on, seemingly for whole minutes, though in reality it was probably no more than ten or twenty seconds. Then Elizabeth's hands rose slowly, and she began to unbutton her dress.

My grandfather said something to me once on the subject of the female form that is as fresh in my mind today as all those years ago. I suppose I was eighteen or nineteen at the time, when the subject was of keen interest to me.

We were in his study at the time with Kitty, one of the housemaids, who was there to receive punishment. Kitty was a tall, well-built girl, a year or two older than I. She stood silent and fearful wearing just her cap, for my grandfather had made her remove everything else. He and I walked slowly around her, examining her closely, with my grandfather nodding in satisfaction.

'Look at this, Jamie,' he said, running his hand across her buttocks and down her flank, as though she were a thoroughbred. 'What wonderful creatures they are, eh, my boy?'

He gave her rump a hearty slap by way of approval, which drew a yelp from the unfortunate girl. I confessed that she was indeed a strikingly handsome young woman.

'The ways of the Almighty are mysterious to me,' my grandfather went on. 'He created heaven and earth in five days, did He not, and man on the sixth?'

'So our good vicar would have us believe, sir,' I said, my noncommittal answer the result of the serious doubts I was having at that time as to the veracity of the biblical account.

'Just so,' my grandfather said. 'And what a marvellous job He did when He made that first woman. Did you ever see a finer sight than this, Jamie?'

At this he grabbed Kitty's right breast and gave it an affectionate squeeze.

'Not to mention this,' he added, dropping his other hand to her groin and tickling her slit with a bony finger. Kitty trilled in alarm and lifted up onto her tiptoes.

'Magnificent stuff indeed!' my grandfather declared resoundingly. 'Quite magnificent!'

I was hard pressed not to smile at the sight of him - red-faced and blustering, his grey whiskers quivering with fervour - as he stood there feeling the maid.

'What I damn well *don't* understand,' he said, 'is why our Creator spent so little time on what's in here!' The bony finger rose to tap the girl on top of her head. I did smile then, but it was a smile of affection, for my grandfather, though he strenuously denied ever knowing a female with a mind, had a true appreciation of the female form in all its diversity. Short or tall, thin or fat, young or old, he loved each and every one of them. As proof of this I offer the observation that he was only too happy to thrash them all.

Of one thing I am sure - grandfather would have approved wholeheartedly of my ward Elizabeth. As she stood naked before me I thought her a Greek goddess come to life; from her skin, smooth and white as alabaster, to the perfect symmetry of her curves - surely the product of a master sculptor's labours. It was with sublime happiness that I contemplated her form; after all, it is not every day one gets to spank a goddess.

I turned to Irene Hammond, waiting patiently at the side. 'How many strokes, Mrs Hammond,' I asked, 'for this failure in duty?'

The governess pondered the matter briefly. 'For losing the package, one dozen, sir.'

For a moment I thought I must have misheard. A paltry one dozen? After all my scheming, all my conniving? It simply would not do, and I was about to advise her sharply to think again when she spoke up of her own accord.

'And for disobeying the order to undress, an additional three dozen.'

I was instantly mollified. Four dozen is a punishment one can get one's teeth into, certainly. It was also rather clever of her to apportion the strokes in this way. By allotting the greater part of the punishment to Elizabeth's disobedience, the governess was actively discouraging rebellious behaviour in future.

I decided once again to let Irene Hammond hand out the punishment, as this would give me an opportunity to observe Elizabeth more closely than would otherwise be possible. To see her face, for instance, at the precise instant the blows struck home.

'Please proceed, Mrs Hammond,' I said accordingly. 'The choice of implement and position I leave to you.'

She fetched the heavy tawse from the cupboard. For Elizabeth's first dozen the young woman was made to face away from me and touch her toes, affording me a perfect view of her delightful *derrière*. The strokes were of medium weight and placed with care, so that by the twelfth her entire bottom was blushing beautifully.

For her second dozen Elizabeth was obliged to go down on hands and knees, sideways on to me, facing to my left. My ward had remained silent up to this point, but these strokes were somewhat harder, each one drawing from her a gasp and causing her to jerk. This in turn made her breasts quiver in a most entrancing fashion, and I shook my head in wonder at this rare and delightful spectacle.

The next position was similar, except that Elizabeth faced to my right, and was required to lower her shoulders to the floor. These twelve were firmer still. Elizabeth's gasps turned to sobs, and her flinching was noticeably more pronounced. She was trembling as she awaited each stroke, eyes screwed tight shut, mouth half-open. Her fingers clutched at the rug, and I judged she was in some considerable pain.

For the final dozen Irene Hammond had Elizabeth stand facing me, straddle-legged, her hands on her hips. I had thus observed her from all sides; a satisfying symmetry that I felt sure was intentional.

The governess made a second trip to the cupboard to exchange tawse for cane, and I knew that this final twelve was to be rather special.

And I was not disappointed. The first stroke was delivered with gusto and Elizabeth let out a cry of dismay, her eyes opening wide in shock. Those that followed were no gentler, and soon tears were streaming down her cheeks. She remained in position, however, testament to her considerable will, though her back arched increasingly as the twelve were counted off, affording me an excellent view of her slit and dense, pelt-like bush.

The final stroke was a full-strength beauty that brought Elizabeth up onto her toes, howling, hands clasping her buttocks as if that might quench the fire.

'Stay as you are!' the governess snapped, and Elizabeth became still. Then Irene Hammond looked at me and gave a single nod.

I reached out and put my hand between Elizabeth's legs. There was no pretence, no talk of 'tantalus regions', or any such baloney. This was entirely as it seemed - a middle-aged man touching his young ward in the most intimate way imaginable, purely for his own pleasure.

Elizabeth gave a groan of dismay, and her eyes closed once more. I pinched her clitoris between thumb and forefinger - not hard, for it was not my intention to cause her pain, but sufficient to make her acutely aware of that sensitive nub.

'Elizabeth?' I said.

She did not respond. Her eyes remained shut fast, and I suspected she had taken her mind off to some remote place - a place, no doubt, where such degradations were unheard of; where young women were safe from lecherous, scheming guardians. A place, unfortunately for her but fortunately for me, that did not exist anywhere in the whole wide world.

'Elizabeth, look at me.'

She did so.

'Do you know what this is, this part of you I am touching now?'

'No, uncle,' she whispered.

'It is your clitoris. From the Greek, *kleitoris*, and not, as you might imagine, from the Latin.'

I glanced at Irene Hammond, and the governess smiled and blushed - unexpectedly and quite charmingly - no doubt remembering her own exploration in front of the fire.

I began to tease Elizabeth's clitoris, squeezing it gently and rolling it beneath the ball of my thumb.

'Must you do this, uncle?' my eldest ward asked suddenly, in an anguished voice.

It was the nearest she could come to pleading, probably. No matter - nothing she could possibly say would deter me from this course. 'Indeed I must,' I said. 'This, and much more. Turn around, my dear.'

She did so, though not without a look of deep misgiving. And she was quite right to suspect my motives, which were of the lowest sort imaginable.

I put my middle finger to my mouth, depositing saliva, then touched the tip to her anus and pushed it inside her. She gasped and went rigid, buttocks clenching tight as she rose onto her toes. I crooked my finger inside her and she murmured something, though I couldn't catch the words.

I reached around with my left hand and sought out her clitoris once more, rubbing that tiny organ whilst continuing to probe her rectum. To my great surprise and delight her hips began to move. It was no more than a subtle rocking at first, to be sure, but unmistakably coital. I continued to work her, and her movements became more pronounced. She let out a sigh, almost a moan.

For many minutes we continued in this way, with Elizabeth trembling constantly, her breathing shallow and rapid, and myself working her relentlessly. I sensed she was fighting her natural instincts, though she was not entirely successful in that regard.

Finally I desisted, and told Elizabeth she may put on her clothes. She did so, white-faced and tight-lipped. That she was angry was understandable, of course. I had stripped her, and beaten her, and degraded her, and it was only natural she should feel resentful. Worst of all, however, I had made her aware of her own lustful instincts; and for that, I thought, she would never forgive me.

Chapter 16

After a time it became evident that Victoria was deliberately 'sinning', and making sure she was found out, moreover. Since she did not appear to relish the frequent spankings this earned her, the conclusion was inevitable: what she actually craved was the stimulation that followed such punishment.

As may be imagined, I was only too happy to indulge the girl. Spankings were followed by ever-longer 'tantalus' sessions in a variety of positions. Facedown over my knee remained popular, though I also experimented with other poses, such as bending over and touching her toes, squatting on a table or chair, and - my personal favourite - sitting on my knee.

This latter position has much to commend it. To have a warm, soft, compliant female in your lap, her arms around your neck, sighing contentedly as your fingers bring her ever closer to fulfilment - this is an experience no man should deny himself. As a way of passing a pleasant hour or two it certainly beats Gin Rummy.

Whether Victoria had any personal preference as regards position I couldn't say, as she seemed to enjoy them all. The brazen little minx was utterly insatiable, and perfectly prepared to suffer a spanking in order to get her way. I did have a momentary pang of conscience that she might come to associate the two inextricably, and might never be able to achieve a climax unless she had been soundly spanked beforehand, but further consideration led me to conclude this was no bad thing. Floggers such as myself require victims, and Victoria was rapidly turning into the perfect specimen.

The manhandling she was receiving could have but one outcome, of course, as purely external contact led to the insertion of a fingertip, which led in turn to deeper probing. One day, encouraged by Victoria's moans of passion and the rapid coital thrusting of her hips, I thrust my finger deeper than ever. The girl suddenly shrieked, and clutched me as though stricken.

I was aghast at what I had done. Mrs Hammond was not there to advise me, as she had ceased attending these routine sessions of Victoria's some time before. Not knowing what to do, I simply held the girl close and murmured reassurances in her ear, telling her that this was normal, and that all women must experience it to be truly free. And probably that was as much as anyone could have done.

Unplanned and un-intentioned as it was, it certainly opened the door to more adventurous play, a fact of which Victoria and I took full advantage. Single finger penetration gave way to two, and then three - and still the girl seemed to want more. I stopped short of full sex, though I would be hard pressed to explain why. Perhaps it was the age difference between us, and the vague sense that sex with a female almost a third one's own age is somehow undignified; though that never stopped my grandfather - but then he was an exceptional man.

Victoria herself had no such qualms, I know, but she was a shameless hussy. I came to the conclusion there was nothing she wouldn't do for gratification, no stimulation she wouldn't try.

The opportunity to test out my theory came on the day of the May fair. I had already decided not to attend, as these village fêtes are not much to my liking, and I had work to do. Mrs Hammond and the girls had been looking forward to it most eagerly, however, and in a moment of weakness I decided the whole household must go. I therefore called Alice, Rose, Willy and Mrs Smith to the study, along with Foster, Phillips and Jack the stable boy, gave each of them a shilling, and told them all they could have the day off.

It was apparent from their expressions that they thought the master had taken leave of his senses, so I explained that everyone deserved a day in the sun occasionally, and that it hurt no one to eat and drink too much once in a while, and laugh and play games and generally have fun. Now they were *certain* I had gone mad, and looked to be on the point of overpowering me whilst someone ran for the doctor.

Finally, growling curses, I reached for the cane on my desk. This finally sent the lot of them scampering for safety, with looks of relief on their faces that the master was back to his old self once more.

The hour of departure arrived, as did the transport; the landau for Mrs Hammond and the girls and a farm wagon for the rest. I was to be all on my own in the house, but Mrs Smith had left me a plate of cold meats, pickles and cheese, so I knew I would not starve. At the very last moment Victoria announced that she had a sore throat, and didn't feel well enough to go. Her sisters looked dismayed, thinking the day out might be cancelled, and even Mrs Hammond seemed disappointed.

'You go on,' I said. 'I can look after Victoria.'

There were some remonstrations, but this was merely politeness and in the end the little convoy moved off in high spirits. I heard them singing all the way down the drive, with Irene Hammond's clear soprano soaring above the rest. It is astonishing what the promise of a day out can do.

Once the others had gone Victoria's sore throat seemed to cure itself miraculously, and it was then I began to suspect ulterior motives on her part. Sure enough, she came to the study and began to pester me as I worked, and I knew from the look in her eye and her exaggerated air of innocence that she was working towards some mischief that would earn her the thing she desired.

'Victoria,' I said, 'did you want something? If so, please ask. If not, kindly leave me in peace, as I have a great deal to do today.'

She shrugged, saying nothing.

'Do you want me to touch you?' I asked. 'Here?' I pointed to her groin. She seemed surprised by my candour, but nodded. I decided then and there that work would have to wait.

'Very well,' I said. 'Take your clothes off.'

She did so, with some assistance from myself, in record time. When she was naked I told her she must remain in this state for the rest of the day. Fortunately for Victoria the weather was warm and dry, otherwise her mock ailment might well have become all too real. I further explained that I would be about the whole house during the day, including the gardens and outbuildings, as I intended to conduct a full inspection while the staff were absent. Whenever and wherever I bumped into her, I told Victoria, I would feel her. Furthermore, I would use whatever objects fell to hand, providing they were of a suitable shape.

That was my declared intention, and that is precisely what transpired. Victoria flitted about the place like a naked, frisky little wood nymph. She was constantly under my feet, and paid the price accordingly.

In the hall I had her stand straddle-legged, her hands clasped behind her head, hips pushed as far forward as she could manage. I knelt down and fingered her enthusiastically for many minutes, deliberately stopping short of bringing her to climax - to Victoria's obvious chagrin. There were no suitably phallic objects close by, unfortunately, so I was not able to carry out my plan of probing more deeply, and had to leave matters there.

In the dining room it was a different matter. I told her to lie on her side on the dining table with her knees drawn up to her chest. I gave her a good fingering - from the rear, naturally - and followed this with a longer fifteen minute session in which I fucked her rapidly with one of the long, fluted candles from the mantelpiece. All in all, a most enjoyable session.

The potting shed gave me the opportunity to be more adventurous still. I sat my ward in a wheelbarrow with her legs draped over the handles, and gave her a thorough probing with - appropriately, I thought - the gardener's dibbler. This object proved ideally suited for the purpose, though I doubt the manufacturer had this particular use in mind, and I was able to administer a vigorous and highly energetic fuck. It had her gasping and squirming frantically as she desperately sought the fulfilment I continued to withhold.

In the study I had her kneel on my desk. As befits a place of such import, I made this a long session. I started by squeezing her lovely breasts and pinching her nipples to make her squeak. I rubbed her belly and slapped her bottom. Finally I fetched a particular lash from my special collection, one with a jade handle carved in the likeness of a penis. The reaming that followed had Victoria positively sobbing with delight - and sobbing with frustration when I terminated it prematurely.

But it was in the kitchen that I found the greatest potential for poking my ward. I had never fully appreciated it before, but the place is a veritable Aladdin's cave of phallic objects. Every utensil seemed to possess a handle shaped with sex in mind. There were also a number of vegetables that would serve: a carrot, or one of the smaller parsnips being the obvious choice. I was briefly tempted, I have to say, to use the rolling pin, and certainly Victoria, to judge from the greedy way she eyed the thing, was game to try it. In the end I decided it was simply too big, and settled instead for the wooden handle of a ladle.

In this encounter, as in those that preceded it, I denied Victoria her climax. Throughout the long day the girl had grown more and more frustrated as my fingering and fucking failed to give her that which she truly needed. This may seem an act of wilful cruelty on my part, but I had something special in mind.

'Tell me, Victoria,' I said, as I replaced the ladle on its hook, 'how are your sewing skills progressing these days? Is Mrs Hammond pleased with your work? I assume you can turn a neat hem, or whatever it is young ladies do.'

'My... sewing, Uncle James?' she said, blinking in bewilderment.

'Your sewing, yes. I take it your stitching is neat and tidy?'

'I would... I believe that it is. Our governess scolds Cathy all the time, but never me.'

'Good,' I said. 'In that case, I wish you make something up for me. It isn't very big, so it shouldn't take too long. Will you do that for me, Victoria?'

'Of course, uncle,' she said, clearly more confused than ever.

'Excellent. Needle and thread will be no problem, I assume, but do you have any ribbon? Two feet should be ample.' She asked what colour ribbon, and I said preferably black or brown, but that any colour would do at a pinch.

'We will also require a piece of coarse sacking, or something similar. Would you know where to lay your hands on material of that sort?'

She said that she wasn't sure, and I sent her off to the sewing room to look. She returned with her sewing bag and a length of black ribbon, but reported she could find no coarse material at all.

'Not to worry,' I said. 'I'm sure we can locate something in the stable.'

Victoria seemed just a little disconcerted at following me outside whilst totally naked, but I pointed out that, with the staff all away at the fair, it was unlikely she would have an audience - unless, that is, a family friend just happened to drop by, or some tenant farmer or delivery boy paid a call. She looked most anxious as we crossed the yard, skipping along furtively in my wake, her head turning this way and that as she tried to spot interlopers. The sharp stones on her bare feet soon proved a problem too, so naturally I walked quickly, forcing her to run to keep up.

Sadly, after all that, there was no suitable material in the stable and we had to extend our search, much to Victoria's dismay. The gardener's fruit store finally yielded up that which I needed - an old sack that smelled of sweet apples. We took it back to the house, and once inside Victoria could breathe easy again.

'What I want you to do,' I told her, when safely ensconced in the study once more, 'is make a sheath for my finger out of the sacking.' I held up the middle finger of my right hand. 'It needs two lengths of ribbon attaching, to tie around my wrist. That way it won't fall off. Can you manage that, do you think?'

I fully expected her to blush at this point, having divined my purpose, but she merely nodded and went to work. She cut off a small rectangular piece of sacking, wrapped it around my finger, and trimmed it to size. Then, with needle and thread, she began to join it along its length, forming a raised seam. That could be most useful, I realised, for providing extra stimulation.

Victoria worked steadily and meticulously, her stitching very neat and even, at least to my untutored eye. Then suddenly, with half of it done, she froze. She looked up at me wide-eyed, her mouth in a round O - and it took little insight to realise that she had finally realised to what use I would put the thing she was making.

'That's right,' I said, with a grin, 'it's for tickling your sweet little crack.'

She dropped her gaze quickly and carried on - except that now her cheeks were flushed and her hands unsteady. The neatness of her stitching, I noticed, took a definite turn for the worse, but I refrained from commenting on the fact. Neatness, after all, was not a prime requirement.

At last the sheath was finished, and I slipped it on my finger with the seam on the palm side. It was a perfect fit - snug, but not so tight that I could not bend my finger.

'A first class job,' I said. 'Now all that remains is to attach the ribbon.'

Victoria did so, securing it in place with half a dozen stitches. At my instruction she passed the two tails of the ribbon around my wrist and tied them in a bow. The finger sheath was thus held firmly in place.

'Perfect,' I said, inspecting the finished article. 'Excellent work, Victoria. Your governess would be proud of you.' I held up my sheathed finger, flexing it two or three times suggestively.

'Now then,' I said, 'any thoughts on how we might test it?'

I took Victoria into the library, as there was a particular armchair I had in mind. It was one of those capacious affairs in burgundy leather - the sort that looked as though it would seat a family of four in comfort. I sat Victoria down, spread her legs, and lifted them over the chair's padded arms. I drew up a footstool for myself, and sat down in front of her as closely as possible.

The poor girl was, I have to say, in a fever of anticipation at this point. Her cheeks were flushed, her breathing rapid, and there was a look in her eyes almost of desperation. And I was feeling not a little eager myself, I confess.

I began by dragging my sheathed fingertip lightly against her slit, teasing the folds of her inner labia. A minute or two of this saw the skin turning a deep shade of pink, at which point I focussed my attentions on her clitoris. Soon that tiny nub was flushing as prettily as Victoria herself. As you may imagine, my ward did not remain passive during all of this; indeed, she jerked and twitched constantly.

I next laid my sheathed finger against her slit. Using the thumb and forefinger of my left hand I pinched the folds of her outer labia, squeezing the soft flesh around the chafer so that my finger was partially enclosed. I then proceeded to slide it up and down. It was not easy to sustain this, as Victoria's juices were by now in full flow, and finger and thumb kept slipping, but I persevered as best I could for some few minutes.

Now it was time for deeper probing. I pushed my finger inside her and began to frig her. Victoria gave a hoarse sob and her hips began to jerk wildly. From time to time I withdrew and spread her lips to check the degree of inflammation. In this way I saw the neck of her vagina turn first a deep pink, then red.

I carried on relentlessly, and soon Victoria was moaning and writhing in the chair, driven by pain and pleasure in equal measure. Without ceasing to frig her I brought my left hand into play also, rubbing her clitoris. Her movements became almost frantic and her cries increased in intensity till she was positively wailing.

As the orgasm took her, her hips thrust upward out of the chair and she screamed. She held the pose, quivering, before slowly subsiding with a long, shuddering sigh.

I withdrew my finger, looking at her in wonder. Right to the end, when her cunny must surely be on fire, she did not close her legs. Truly she was an astonishing young woman.

Chapter 17

'Good Lord!' I exclaimed, upon reading a particular item in the morning mail, adding, 'Percy, you're an imbecile!'

The letter in question was an invitation for the coming week, and a very welcome one despite my opinion of the sender's intelligence. I considered the ramifications for several minutes, and then rang for Alice, for there was much to do.

'Ask Miss Elizabeth and Mrs Hammond to join me instantly,' I told her. 'Make sure you use that precise word - "instantly". I shall hold you personally responsible for any delay. Off you go now.'

She went, and I heard her footsteps running along the hall. There was no immediate need for the cane, however, as the other two joined me very soon thereafter.

'I've been invited to a festival at the Duke of Alberthorpe's place in Surrey,' I told them. 'I'll be leaving on Saturday, and staying the whole week. I need someone to accompany me, though I haven't yet decided who it shall be. Due to the arduous nature of the event, however, it will have to be one of you.'

'That sounds a little ominous, uncle,' Elizabeth said. 'May we ask what sort of festival this might be?'

'You may. Its official title is the Festival of Flogging and Fornication. The name speaks for itself, I think. Whoever comes with me can look forward to a considerable amount of both during the course of the week.'

'Considerable amount' was a serious understatement, if previous festivals were anything to go by. But I didn't mention that, as I didn't want to scare them to death.

Yet.

'A festival of... flogging, did you say?' Elizabeth said blankly, evidently thinking she must have misheard.

'And fornication,' I added. 'Otherwise known as FFF. They're supposed to be held every year, though it's been nearer two since the last one. I put the blame squarely on Percy's shoulders, myself. It was his turn to organise it this time around.'

Elizabeth looked thoroughly bemused. 'Is this some sort of a joke, uncle?'

'I've never been more serious in my life.'

'But surely...' she said, frowning, 'you can't possibly mean to subject one of *us* to... to something like that.'

'Well,' I said reasonably, 'who else? I can't possibly take Catherine, can I? She's far too immature. I did briefly consider Victoria, I'm sure she would cope with the fornication part admirably, but I do have a concern about the flogging. And, to be honest, she's still a little young. Alice can't go as she's needed here, unless one of you fancies rising at six in the morning to light fires and scrub floors and so forth. Also, I think Alice would be rather overwhelmed at having to face seven floggers simultaneously.'

'Seven?' Irene Hammond said in a faint, stunned voice.

'Quite so,' I said. 'Spankers Seven, we call ourselves. It's a sort of club, you understand. Each of us has to take a female along, to be flogged and fucked and so forth, and now you see why it has to be one of you. Rose would say something she shouldn't and shame me in front my friends, so she's out of the running; as is Mrs Smith, of course. I doubt she would enjoy the experience one little bit, and good cooks are so hard to find.'

They stared at me as though I were quite mad. Possibly I'd sprung it on them rather suddenly, but there was much to be done before departure, and so little time.

'Anyway,' I said, 'that's what it's all about. I think I can promise whoever goes with me a truly unique experience. I took Polly, my former maid-of-all-work, along to the last one at Jasper's old ruin of a place. When it was time to leave she positively begged to be allowed to walk the forty miles home, rather than sit on a coach seat for a day.'

I chuckled at the memory. It was one of the most enjoyable journeys I have ever taken, watching Polly's face as the coach bumped and rattled along.

Irene and Elizabeth were still staring at me, clearly appalled. The prospect of a week's holiday did not appear to thrill either of them.

'So the only question now,' I said, 'is, who shall it be? Irene...'

I sighted down my finger at her, and she stiffened and paled visibly. I tracked slowly across to my second potential victim.

'Or Elizabeth?'

She looked no happier. Indeed, her social position was such that this would be considerably harder on her, though she could always go incognito. Nigel, Lord

Newburn, always took Lady Newburn, who wore a mask for the entire week. Everyone knew who she was, of course, but we pretended not to, at least in public, thus preserving her dignity and reputation.

I swung my finger back and forth between them, keeping them in suspense, though I had already decided which of them it would be. They stared at the roving digit as though it were the barrel of a twelve-bore, and themselves a pair of hen pheasants.

My finger came to rest. 'Elizabeth!'

The dismay in her face was wondrous to behold - the poor girl looked positively stricken. Irene Hammond looked immensely relieved, of course, and turned to the younger woman, no doubt to offer comfort and consolation.

'Dear Elizabeth,' I said, 'you will be responsible in my absence. I'm counting on you to keep your sisters in line, and make sure the servants don't rob us. I shall expect a detailed report upon my return, mind you.'

They both froze. In slow motion they traded expressions. Now Irene Hammond was the one who looked like a prisoner in the dock watching the judge don his black cap. I turned to her, and nodded.

'Mrs Hammond,' I said, 'you, by a process of elimination, shall be the one to accompany me.'

We travelled on the same train as Humphrey and his companion, who was none other than Donnett, his trainee slave. She seemed as timid as ever, and I had serious doubts how well she would cope with a robust experience like FFF. Still, that was Humphrey's business. There were strict rules about interfering in another member's affairs.

It was a fine day, and Humphrey and I exchanged pleasant chitchat on the journey. I did notice that his eyes were mostly on Irene, however, and hers in turn were on young Donnett. Perhaps the governess shared my concerns, or maybe it was simply one female's curiosity about another, a trait they all seem to share. As for Donnett herself, she looked out of the window, or down at the floor. Just once she glanced up at me with her frightened-little-virgin look, and I smiled back encouragingly. She never did it again, so perhaps she interpreted my friendly smile as a lecherous leer.

It was late in the afternoon when we arrived at Crickforth station, and transferred to the coach Percy had laid on to take us up to the house. Thirty minutes later Percy's rambling place hove into view, looking much the same as the last time I'd seen it. A powdered footman, attended by a housemaid who took our hats and cloaks, opened the front door. Nothing so unusual in that, except that the maid wore cap, stockings and shoes, and not a stitch besides.

'Hullo,' Humphrey said, 'I seem to recognise those titties. Tess, isn't it?'

She bobbed, making the titties Humphrey so admired jiggle provocatively, and a faint flush rose to her cheeks. Watching an almost naked woman bob is a pastime I can recommend unreservedly.

Percy came to greet us, and took us through to the saloon. Nigel, Lord Newburn, was already there, standing by the fireplace with a brandy glass in one hand and a cigar in the other. Lady Newburn was sitting on the sofa by the window, masked as usual. She was wearing a most unusual outfit consisting of white corset, white silk bloomers that ended in a frill just above the knee, white silk stockings and dainty black lace-up ankle boots. Her mask was black, as was the long feather in her elegantly coiffured auburn hair. It was the corset, however, that caught my eye, and I strolled over and sat beside her just to get a closer look. It was tightly laced, so that her waist was excessively pinched, and at the top it was an inch shorter than decency allowed. Her pretty breasts nestled there, nipples peeping out tantalisingly.

'Evening, Belinda,' I murmured in her ear. 'Three guesses what I fancy nibbling on right now.'

'I dread to think,' she murmured back. 'And good evening to *you*, Jamie.'

'I'm afraid to say,' Percy announced to the assembly, 'that Michael will not be joining us. He has affairs to attend to that he insists simply cannot wait.'

'Thank God,' Belinda muttered quietly.

I glanced at her, but she had already turned away and was looking out of the window. I wondered why she should say such a thing. Everyone liked Michael, who had always been the life and soul of FFF.

'If you'd given us decent notice,' Humphrey pointed out, 'this wouldn't have happened. How can we be Spankers Seven, I ask you, when there are only six of us? Frankly, Percy, it just won't be the same without Michael.'

'Now don't remonstrate with me, there's a good fellow,' Percy drawled in his usual languorous tone. 'Nigel has already made his displeasure perfectly clear. We shall just have to settle for being Spankers Six instead. James, can I get you a drink? Humphrey, a whisky for you, sir?'

I declined but Humphrey accepted, and Nigel asked for a top-up. Percy rang for the maid. It was significant that he hadn't offered the ladies any refreshment. They were our 'slaves' for the next six days, and we, their masters, ordered their lives. We determined what they should or should not drink, and eat, and wear. We told them when to come and go, when to sit and when to stand.

Speaking of slaves, where the deuce was Mrs Hammond? She had wandered off, it seemed, despite my strict instruction that she was to remain close by me at all times.

'Hell and damnation!' I growled.

Belinda turned to me. 'Problems, Jamie?'

'I seem to have lost my slave,' I said. 'You didn't happen to notice a rather beautiful young woman with a stunning figure, did you? I can't imagine where she might be.'

'Not like you to misplace a pretty one,' Belinda said. 'I did notice a female answering your description in the doorway when you first arrived, but she declined to follow you into the room.'

'God!' I muttered. If I had to go looking for her I would never hear the end of it. To lose one's slave was bad enough, but losing her in the first two minutes would make me a laughing stock. On the other hand, I couldn't just sit here slave-less, could I? Humphrey still had Donnett, standing as close to him as she could possibly get - though I guessed this was more from fear than anything else. Nigel could at least see his wife, even if she wasn't by his side; Belinda was something of a law unto herself.

While I was deliberating on this quandary, the maid arrived to pour the drinks. She was wearing the same 'uniform' as Tess, who had greeted us upon our arrival; that is cap, stockings and shoes only. I didn't recognise this girl, and guessed she was a recent addition. The fact that she was blushing furiously, and trembling to boot, tended to bear this out.

'I say,' Nigel sang out, 'is this another new one, Percy? You must have more maids than the rest of us put together. Where do you find 'em all, that's what I want to know.'

'Aha, secrets of the trade, old man,' Percy replied. 'I've three new ones for you to try out, in fact. This is Jane. Say hello to the gentlemen, Jane.'

The girl bobbed, and her cheeks turned an even deeper shade of crimson. She went to pour the drinks, giving us the benefit of a rear view. She had a most delightful bottom and someone grunted approvingly, which nicely expressed all our views. I decided there and then I would definitely have to get young Jane alone sometime during the week. A bottom like that deserved my special attention.

'The prodigal slave, it would appear,' Belinda whispered in my ear, 'has returned.'

I turned. Mrs Hammond was standing in the doorway, looking around the room in a somewhat uncertain fashion. She saw me, smiled, and started towards me.

If she could only make it across the room without anyone noticing, I would be spared the humiliation I undoubtedly deserved. Since every man's attention was focussed on Jane's posterior at present, I thought I might just pull it off.

She'd covered half the distance when Percy, damn him, caught sight of her. He stared, and then turned to me with one eyebrow raised quizzically. There was only one thing for it, and that was to brazen it out.

'Irene!' I called out in a loud, petulant voice. 'Where in the devil's name have you been?'

Everyone turned to look at me, and then at Irene Hammond. She stopped dead in her tracks, her smile fading instantly. She started to say something but coherent words failed to materialise, and she simply stood there, looking lost.

'I asked where you've been,' I snapped. 'Might we expect an answer before the week is out, do you think?'

'I... I needed to be... excused, sir,' she stammered.

'Are you saying you wished to take a pee?'

'I... yes, sir.'

'In future you will ask permission, is that clear?'

'Yes, sir,' she murmured. 'Quite clear.'

'Good. I'm so glad.' I turned to our host. 'Percy, my things are still packed away. Might you have a cane I could borrow?'

'That's one thing there's no shortage of, old boy,' our host replied cheerfully. 'I keep one in every room, hanging by the door. Never know when it might come in handy, eh?'

Sure enough, I saw the cane on a hook beside the door. 'Fetch it to me,' I said to my wayward slave.

With all eyes on her, she did so. And so it fell to me to deliver the first flogging of this, the fourteenth FFF.

'Bend and present!' I snapped, and she bent forward from the waist, whipped up her skirts, and dropped her drawers all in a trice. If she had obeyed my earlier order to stay by me in half so diligent a fashion, I thought, she wouldn't be in this predicament.

Fast though she was, I think my own moves were faster, as six lively strokes were delivered in under three seconds.

'Cover!' I said.

She dragged her clothes into place and straightened up in one move. After a poor start we were now operating like a well-oiled machine. Teamwork - that's the key.

Chapter 18

The next member of the Seven to arrive was Jasper, accompanied as usual by Yvette, the housekeeper he brought back with him from Paris in eighty-six. Since Michael had bowed out, this left just Alex to join us. He did so soon after, accompanied by a tall, very striking young black woman. Her name, we learned, was Zuleika, and she was new to FFF; and new to England also, having arrived on these shores but three months before.

There were greetings and introductions all round, and then Percy led the party in to dinner. The slaves, as was the custom, were obliged to walk two paces behind their respective masters. They would not dine with us, but would take their nourishment later in rooms set aside for that purpose. For now they attended us, standing obediently behind our chairs, a very right and proper place for a slave to be.

During dinner, Percy announced that the format of this year's festival would be somewhat different. As host this was his privilege, though it was rarely invoked. Most of us were perfectly content with the usual arrangement - a cheerful hotchpotch of orgies and flogging frenzies.

Percy, it seemed, had other ideas, which he now proceeded to expound to us. First and foremost, he said, no one would be permitted to flog another man's slave.

'I say,' Nigel objected, 'this just won't do! First we're Spankers Six instead of Seven, and now you're telling us there's to be no flogging? I came for FFF, not FF, as did we all.'

'If you will allow me to finish, there's a dear fellow,' Percy drawled, 'I didn't say "no flogging". There'll be simply *oodles* of flogging, and no shortage of bottoms, I promise you. I've set on three new maids, in addition to those you've seen before.

From ten in the morning till six in the evening, their posteriors are all yours. You can thrash away to your heart's content.'

For a few moments there was silence as we all digested this information. Looking around at the faces of the others, I thought they looked mollified; with one possible exception - Humphrey.

'Disappointing, though,' my friend said quietly, glancing at Irene Hammond, 'not to be allowed to flog the other slaves.'

'Well, that's the way it is,' Percy said, 'and if you'll all keep quiet for just a minute, I'll explain why. On Thursday morning there is to be a flogging contest. Each man in turn will give a fifteen minute show using his own slave, and the one who gives the best performance will be declared Flogging Champion for eighteen ninety-two. I've commissioned a trophy especially for the occasion, which the silversmith promises will be ready in time. Now do you see why you can't flog them? It wouldn't be much of a show, would it, if they couldn't take a proper beating because their backsides were already raw.'

'A contest, eh?' Alex piped up. 'That sounds rather jolly.'

I confess, the idea appealed to me also. We'd never had anything of this sort at a festival before, and variety is the spice of life, as they say.

'We shall need a prize for the winner's slave, I think,' Percy continued, 'a little something to encourage 'em to put on a good show. If each of us were to contribute a nominal amount - ten guineas, say - it should do the trick, what?'

A sixty-guinea purse was no mean prize. I'd always believed Percy to be something of a skinflint, but now I was having to revise my opinion.

'As regards fornication,' our host said, in full flow now, 'I've made some changes there, too. Instead of the usual free-for-all, I'm implementing a roster. To start with, the bedrooms are all numbered. Humphrey, you're in number one, Jasper, you're two, James three, Nigel four, I'm in five, and Alex, you're in number six. Everyone's name is on the door, so you shouldn't get lost.'

'Worse than the damned army,' Nigel growled in my ear.

'Each slave will spend tonight with the next man on the list,' Jasper went on, 'so Humphrey's Donnett goes to Jasper, his Yvette goes to James, Irene to Nigel, and so on. Alex is last on the list - no offence, Alex; we just drew the names out of a bag - so he gets my Tess, and his own girl Zuleika goes to Humphrey. Tomorrow night they all rotate again, Donnett to James, Yvette to Nigel, and so forth. Wednesday will be the last night of this year's festival, and we'll round things off with the competition on Thursday morning. Any questions so far?'

'Saturday to Wednesday is five nights, if I'm counting aright,' Humphrey said.

'You are,' Percy said. 'I'd have made it six if Michael had joined us, but he hasn't, so five it is.'

'Five nights, six slaves?' Humphrey said. 'It doesn't add up.'

'What's the point travelling all this way just to bed your own slaves?' Percy said. 'You have all year to do that. A few days abstinence won't hurt any of you.'

'Speak for yourself,' Nigel muttered; and his wife Belinda leaned forward to plant a kiss on top of his head.

'Since all of you have some distance to travel,' Percy said, 'you're more than welcome to stay on an extra day and make an early start Friday morning - in which case you can tumble your own slave to your heart's content on Thursday night. Right, then, is everyone clear on what's happening?'

There was some general chuntering, but it was Alex who voiced our universal concern.

'Too damned complicated for me, old man,' he complained. 'You're not seriously expecting us to remember all this, are you?'

'No need to trouble yourselves on that score,' Percy said. 'I've had a chart made up so you can see who is supposed to be where, and when. It's pinned up in the hall. There are cards, too, in each of your rooms with the same information. No one should find themselves three-in-a-bed. Not unintentionally, at least.'

'Dream all this up yourself, did you, Percy?' Humphrey asked innocently.

I'd been wondering the same thing myself. Percy was the last person in the world I'd have thought capable of concocting such a scheme; and as for fornication rosters, names on doors, and 'appointment' cards in rooms...

'Of course... why shouldn't I?' Percy said in an offhand fashion, adding, 'Parker did lend a hand with some of the details.'

That explained a great deal. Parker was Percy's famous 'flogging butler', and I knew the man possessed a keen mind in addition to a powerful right arm. I had no doubt at all that this whole idea was his from start to finish.

'Anyway, that's it,' Percy said. 'Brandy and cigars, gentlemen? I suggest you send your slaves to see to the unpacking, and so forth.'

Several of us rose to our feet, and I took the opportunity to have a quick word with Irene Hammond in private.

'It seems you're to be spared the rod, Mrs Hammond,' I said, 'apart from the competition on Thursday. Not too disappointed, I hope?'

'Not in the least, sir,' she replied with conviction; and indeed, she appeared considerably relieved.

'The fornication still stands, however. You're with Nigel tonight, Percy said.'
'Yes, sir.'

She seemed less happy with this, but then I suppose the thought of having sex with five total strangers on five consecutive nights might be a little daunting.

'I'll be up to the room presently,' I said, 'and certainly before you leave to go to Nigel. Can you find your own way, or shall I ask Percy for a servant to guide you?'

'I think I can manage, sir. I'll look for the door with your name on it. I believe the duke said it was number three.'

'I believe he did,' I said. 'Very well, then, I'll see you in a little while.'

Some time later, having fortified ourselves with Percy's brandy, our small band said goodnight and retired to our separate rooms. In my absence Irene Hammond had unpacked my bags, and my things were neatly put away in drawers and cupboards. Every man, I decided, should have the opportunity to possess his very own slave. The standard of service from someone fearful of a cane across her bottom is impeccable.

Her own clothes, I noted, were still in her bag; and I thought I could guess why. Her next question confirmed it.

'H-how should I... should I dress, sir,' she stammered, 'when I... when...?' Nothing in her life had prepared her for a situation such as this. No one had ever instructed her in the correct attire for visiting a strange man's bedroom at night, all alone.

'Go as you are,' I said. 'Knowing Nigel - Lord Newburn, that is - I expect he'll want to watch you undress.'

'Yes, sir,' she murmured. She was sitting on the edge of the bed, hands clasped tightly in her lap, looking very nervous. All this was new and strange to her, of course. She had no idea what to expect, or what was expected of her.

'Don't be taken in by his crusty exterior,' I said. 'He's really a fine man, with a kindly heart. You have absolutely nothing to worry about, I promise you. He'll be very considerate and gentle.'

She nodded, but did not seem especially reassured by my words. Waiting, as always, was the hardest part. I knew she would feel better once her assignation was underway, for Nigel would soon put her at her ease.

'Go to him now, Mrs Hammond,' I said. 'Knock on the door and wait there till instructed to enter. His slave Belinda, the masked lady, may not yet have left the room.'

'Yes, sir. Thank you, sir.' She rose and went to the door, turned and gave me a brave little smile, and then she was gone.

Yvette, Jasper's companion, joined me a while later. She was looking a little dejected, I thought. Jasper's reputation as a flogger was almost as fearsome as Percy's butler's, and I wondered if Yvette was simply worn out by all of this. Whether too many thrashings, over too many months and years, had crushed her spirit.

At least there would be no punishment tonight, or indeed the next four nights, unless someone broke the rules - always possible, with an ill-disciplined lot like the Spankers.

I helped her off with her shift, and took her to bed. At first she lay inert, staring passively at the ceiling, presumably waiting for me to climb aboard and get it over with.

The last time I had bedded Yvette was at the festival of eighty-nine, at Alex's castle north of the border. My memory of that evening was somewhat hazy due to excessive consumption of a rather fine single malt whisky. At best, I suspect I performed poorly, and it is even possible - depressing though the thought might be - I failed to perform at all.

Perhaps Yvette assumed tonight would prove a similar debacle. If so, she was in for a (hopefully pleasant) surprise.

I began by putting my hands on her, stroking and caressing those regions guaranteed to arouse a woman's interest in the proceedings. Sure enough, she was soon wriggling and sighing in that adorable way they have, and murmuring in my ear.

'Oh, sir,' she pleaded, her Parisian accent truly delightful, 'you must not. Dear sir, no more, I beg of you!'

Why is it, I wonder, women quite often say one thing whilst meaning precisely the opposite? God knows, the virtue of always telling the truth was drilled into me by a succession of nannies and governesses, and I assume girls are taught the same thing. Are they not paying attention, do you think?

Whatever the reason, Yvette's voice continued to beg me to stop, whilst her clutching hands, gyrating hips, and thoroughly wet cunny sang an altogether different tune. Needless to say it was these latter 'voices' I chose to heed, and I rolled on top of her and skewered her with my cock.

No jockey ever mounted a filly more willingly, or rode a race more enthusiastically, than I did with Yvette that evening. I trotted her a mile or two, then picked up the pace and cantered her awhile, and finally, with the finishing line in sight, galloped her frantically home. Buck and toss in those final furlongs as she might, she could not unseat me, and with a wild cry from heaving mount and rider alike, we crossed the finishing line together.

Truly, these French fillies take some beating.

Chapter 19

The next morning I happily took up Percy's offer to thrash the maids - and a most delightful lot they were. Two or three hours passed in a happy blur of firm white buttocks and even whiter, tear-streaked faces.

Mrs Hammond, along with the other slaves, was ensconced in the drawing room, which was their 'prison' whenever we did not wish them with us.

One particular maid of Percy's - Tess - was not available to us, since she was to be his entry in the contest. A pity, as the sight of her jiggling breasts with their prominent little nipples had quite sparked my interest, and I had been looking forward keenly to warming her rear. So I had to console myself with the thought that she would be spending Tuesday night with me. Her bottom might be safe from my cane, but her nipples could not escape my teeth!

For recreation over and above the exercise of my right arm, I took to walking in the grounds. I asked Irene Hammond to accompany me on these excursions, party to give her a break from prison life, partly because I had resolved to let her out of my sight as little as possible. I had managed to 'lose' her once, and to do so a second time would certainly expose me to ridicule.

We were out later that first day, Sunday, strolling across the park to the sound of distant church bells. We were heading towards a folly that had caught the governess's eye when the sound of a horse coming up behind us at the trot made me look back. It was Percy on that big bay of his, and he touched crop to cap as he went by.

'A fine afternoon, James,' he said.

'It is indeed, Percy,' I replied. 'Most agreeable.'

Nothing so remarkable in that; except for his 'passenger'. One of the new maids, Lucy, was sitting across his lap, straddling both him and the horse. She was facing him, her arms tight about his chest, and she was stark naked. It took little imagination to deduce Percy's cock was inside her. A short way ahead he urged the horse into a canter, and they bounced away up the track with Lucy hanging on grimly, wailing in fear or discomfort or ecstasy, or possibly all three at once.

'Now there's a sight you don't see every day,' I muttered, as they disappeared behind a stand of trees.

Mrs Hammond smiled, though she seemed a little distracted. Something was troubling her; I knew her well enough now to recognise the signs. I remained silent, thinking she would broach the subject if she wished. Sure enough she turned to me, a thoughtful look in her eyes.

'Would you say we have a chance of winning the competition, sir?'

So that was it. She was after the sixty guineas. It was not avarice on her part, I felt sure, rather integrity. She was an honest woman, and being in debt caused her much distress. Even with the generous wage I paid her, it would take some time to clear the debts her late husband had left. A sixty-guinea windfall would help considerably.

'I don't know,' I answered truthfully. 'We're facing stiff competition. This is a most esteemed gathering of floggers, and we should not underestimate them.'

'I see,' she said. 'Am I foolish to entertain hopes, then?'

'Not foolish,' I said. 'We do have an ace up our sleeves.'

'Sir?'

'You, Mrs Hammond,' I said. 'You're the most beautiful woman here, and you possess the best figure. The sight of you naked will give us a clear head start over the rest.'

She blushed, though whether at the compliment or the thought of revealing herself to a roomful of strangers, I do not know.

'Thank you, sir,' she said, 'but I fear you flatter me. Zuleika and Donnett are both more comely than I. As to my figure, I know I'm too heavy by far.'

'Nonsense,' I retorted indignantly. 'What utter poppycock!' I spoke up instantly out of gallantry, but gave the matter a few moments thought. Certainly the black girl was very beautiful, and Donnett also in a different way. So was Belinda, beneath her mask - but were any of them more beautiful than Irene Hammond? Not in my opinion. As to their figures, not having seen Zuleika naked I couldn't say with certainty, but it seemed unlikely she could match Irene's spectacular curvaceousness. Highly unlikely. I glanced at the woman beside me, and all doubt withered and died.

'Nonsense,' I said again, very firmly.

She looked at me quickly, and her smile was reward enough.

That night, after Mrs Hammond had left to go to Percy, Humphrey's young companion Donnett tapped timidly at the door, then crept into my room.

'Hello, Donnett,' I said. 'I was about to pour myself a glass of Madeira. Would you care to join me?'

She made no answer, and would not look at me, but stood just inside the doorway shivering. I went to her and put my arm around her, drawing her towards the bed.

I was convinced now that my reckoning had been correct; Humphrey should never have brought her, for the festival and all it entailed was more than she could cope with.

I put her into bed, removed her shift, then undressed and climbed in beside her. Her head immediately dipped towards my cock, a sure sign that she had been well tutored.

'Wait,' I said. 'Just lay back and relax. I'll go first.'

I put my hand between her legs and fingered her, and she lay back as instructed and closed her eyes. She moaned as I brought her to climax, quivering as the sensation built in her. I put my arm about her shoulder and held her close as the orgasm took her, and held her after till she subsided, sighing, and her face in the moonlight from the window took on a dreamy look.

'Shall I suck you now, sir?' she asked drowsily.

Her willingness to service me was almost unbearably poignant. She seemed to have no will of her own, no thoughts in her head beyond those put there by others.

'Do you want to?' I asked. '*Really* want to, for yourself, I mean?'

'Why... yes sir, if you want me to.'

I wondered if she truly knew what she wanted. I doubted she could really desire a cock in her mouth right then, as sleepy as she was. God knows, she'd be tasting more than enough semen during the week, even without mine.

'Go to sleep,' I said, pulling the cover over both of us.

'Sir?'

'It's all right,' I said. 'Go to sleep, Donnett. That's an order.'

She did so, obedient in this as in everything.

I woke in the night to find Donnett trembling in my arms. She didn't feel chilled - indeed, we were snug as a pair of dormice under the covers - so I guessed she must have had a nightmare. Old fears, perhaps, returning to haunt her.

I slid my hand down to her cunny and stroked her there. She gave a little moan of desire, and her knees parted. I worked her slowly, intending to take a long time bringing her to climax. Probably the only time she was free of fear was on occasions like this, when in the grip of another, equally powerful emotion.

Sinners, the good Reverend Wilkins is fond of reminding us, must surely pay for their sins.

So, he insists, it is written.

As for me, I remain unconvinced - unless there truly is a life to follow. Forty-odd years' observation has taught me that, in this world at least, it is usually the innocent who do the paying.

Donnett, sad to say, was one of the innocent.

Monday morning was wet, but Spankers Seven spirits were high. Leaden skies held no fears for us. We had everything we needed for our amusement to hand, so there was no need to venture out into the rain.

As the clock struck ten we set off in pursuit of our quarry. By half past it was apparent it was not going to be quite that easy, for Percy's maids were nowhere to be seen.

'Not a one,' Alex complained as we passed in the hall. 'Not a sniff. Nigel managed to catch a straggler, I'm told, but he's hanging on to her.'

'I don't blame him,' I said. 'A bird in the hand, and all that.'

'Indeed,' Alex replied. 'Anyway, I think I'll brave the elements and try outside. They've got to be *somewhere*, haven't they?'

For my own part I wandered on down to the servants' corridor in search of prey. The only females in sight were the cook, kitchen maid and scullery maid, who had all been granted immunity. Percy had been adamant about this. If we were constantly harassing the kitchen staff, he said, there would be no food on the table. Since none of us relished this prospect, we had all promised solemnly to leave that particular trio in peace.

From there I went outside, but the inclement weather soon had me scurrying indoors again, where I spent a fruitless morning in search of the ever-elusive prey. It was, I have to say, a thoroughly frustrating experience.

Lunch was a cold buffet, and while we fortified ourselves I commiserated with Humphrey over our mutual lack of good fortune. Nigel, who'd reputedly had more success, joined us.

'Nigel,' I said, 'I heard you caught yourself a maid.'

'Young Jane, yes,' he said. 'Jasper kept nagging me to pass her on to him, so eventually I did.'

'With never a thought for your friends, you bounder,' Humphrey said. 'Why didn't you pass her on to us?'

'Sorry, old man,' Nigel said. 'You could always join the queue, I suppose. Percy's bagged her next, then Alex.'

'How about working together?' I suggested. 'Three heads being better than one, and all that.'

And so it proved to be, for within thirty minutes of resuming the search we landed a prize catch using a cunning ploy of Nigel's devising.

The three of us would enter a room, and one would immediately move to a corner and stand there quietly. The other two would then hold a conversation - in raised voices - along the following lines...

James: 'I'll wager someone's hiding in here.'

Nigel: 'I think you're right, old man. Don't worry, we'll root her out soon enough. Let's tear the place apart, search every nook and cranny.'

James: 'Good idea. But let's go back to the library first - I'm sure I heard a noise in there, and we forgot to look behind the curtains.'

Nigel: 'Right-o. We can search in here straight after. I pity the girl we get our hands on, Jamie. She's in for the thrashing of her life, and no mistake.'

And on that ominous note the two would depart, still discussing their victim's fate, their voices fading as they moved away.

It was a form of psychological warfare, of course, designed to unnerve any maid hiding within earshot. Once she believed the coast was clear, Nigel reasoned, she would make a run for it. Straight into the arms of Humphrey, who had waited behind for that very purpose.

The first two rooms drew a blank, but in the music room Nigel's ploy worked spectacularly well. As he and I walked away we heard a loud halloo from Humphrey, and we hurried back to find him standing guard over, not one, but two very unhappy-looking maids.

'Gentlemen,' he declared happily, 'our cup runneth over, does it not? Well done, Nigel; a masterly plan indeed.'

'Hear, hear,' I said. 'And as a reward, you shall decide the fate of these naughty young women. Whatever should we do with them, do you think?'

Nigel's answer was predictable, but thoroughly agreeable nevertheless.

The ensuing spankfest lasted the rest of the day.

Zuleika, as I had known she would, performed in a most spectacular fashion when I bedded her that same evening.

She started by offering to show me her speciality - though she cannot claim to have invented it, for it has a long and honourable tradition. She knelt over me, leaned forward, and took my cock into her impressive cleavage. She then squeezed her breasts tightly around my shaft and proceeded to move up and down - as you might imagine, an extremely stimulating experience.

I thought she would bring me to climax in this fashion but after perhaps five minutes she stopped, moved over me, and impaled herself on my cock. The next twenty minutes were memorable indeed. I have never known such an athletic, vigorous, demanding young woman.

That she was insatiable also, I soon discovered. I had been resting for a mere three or four minutes following my climax when she reached for my cock and began fondling it. I started to explain to her that it was too soon, that I couldn't possibly rise to the occasion yet, when my cock sent her a message of his own - and his was the more convincing, I have to say.

Soon we were at it again. I made a point of mounting her, rather than vice versa, though I had to wrestle her to the mattress to do so. She was remarkably strong and agile, and it took a nipple-twist to subdue her finally.

She woke me twice more during the night to demand that I service her. That I succeeded is entirely due to her abundant charms, skill, and persistence. I feel no shame in admitting she wore me out, utterly and completely.

Chapter 20

Straight after breakfast on Tuesday morning, having seen Mrs Hammond safely packed off to the drawing room, I made a point of seeking out Jane, the maid with the shapely bottom who had served us drinks on our arrival. I had been quite unable to get my hands on her the previous day as she was permanently engaged with one or other of my colleagues, much to my frustration. Today I was absolutely determined to be the early bird who caught the worm.

Following a tip from the butler I found her in the day nursery, ostensibly dusting. Since I cannot believe Percy requires his staff to dust inside the cupboards, 'hiding' seems a more apt description.

'Jane,' I cried, 'the very girl! Come along, my dear. Your *derrière* and this tawse have an urgent appointment, though you know it not.'

She came out, but with the utmost reluctance. Lifting her skirts and dropping her drawers (Percy's maids had abandoned the semi-nude 'uniform' after the first day) revealed the reason. Her buttocks resembled a painting done by an enthusiastic two-year-old, so spectacular was the bruising. I rubbed my hand over her abused flesh in amazement, and she winced. Two days of almost constant spanking had certainly taken their toll.

'You poor child!' I exclaimed. 'What have these monsters been doing to you?' I heard a sob, and saw that she was crying. When young women are feeling sorry for themselves, a little sympathy is often all it takes to open the floodgates.

'Come, dry your eyes,' I said, offering the handkerchief I always carried for just such emergencies. 'I promise it will be a light spanking only.'

'Beg pardon, sir,' she blurted out, encouraged perhaps by my seeming compassion, 'but I'd rather not be spanked at all.'

'I'm sure you wouldn't,' I said, 'but I think you're likely to be disappointed in that regard. Even if I let you off, those other rogues are sure to come seeking you out, aren't they? A beautiful bottom such as yours is just too good to resist.'

Her face crumpled, and her eyes, freshly dried, started to fill up once more. She really was in quite a state, and I was genuinely touched by her plight.

'I suppose,' I mused, as much to myself as to her, 'I could take you off somewhere. It might earn you an hour or two's reprieve, at least. Probably it's against the rules—'

'Oh please, sir,' she sobbed. 'Please take me away! I'll do anything, sir. Anything!'

And *that* was a most interesting thought, to be sure. Percy hadn't specifically prohibited us from tumbling his maids, though he hadn't said we could, either. Flog them, most certainly. Fuck them - well, why not indeed?

'Come, then,' I said. 'There's a summerhouse down by the lake; we can go there. Don't expect to get off scot-free, mind. One way or another you're in for a spanking. I missed you Sunday and Monday, and I'm damned if I'll miss you again today, you hear?'

Jane nodded, seemingly relieved in spite of my words. No doubt she saw a spanking from me as preferable to what she might expect from the others.

We went downstairs and were immediately confronted by Nigel, who was prowling the corridor like a tiger looking for his dinner.

'Jane, there you are!' he exclaimed as we made an appearance. 'I've been searching high and low for you. Have you finished with her, James? If so, I'll gladly take her off your hands.'

'Sorry, Nigel,' I said, 'I haven't even started yet. You'll just have to wait, I'm afraid.'

'Oh... right,' he said, looking a little glum. 'Wait how long, do you think?'

'As long as it takes,' I replied cheerfully. 'I've promised Jane here the thrashing of her young life. It could take hours, to be honest.'

Nigel sighed, and I turned and gave Jane a crafty wink. She was following the exchange with eyes the size of saucers.

'Perhaps you should find yourself a substitute, Nigel,' I suggested. 'I'd try the cellars if I were you. No shortage of hiding places down there, what?'

Nigel nodded and wandered off. Jane and I headed for the door once more, only to be pulled up short as we crossed the hall. 'James!' someone called out. 'I trust you're not thinking of absconding with that girl.'

It was Alex, coming out of the library, the cane in his hand making his intentions only too clear.

'Something along those lines,' I said. 'I wouldn't hang around waiting if I were you, Alex - we may be quite a while.'

'But I had plans for Jane myself.'

'Awfully sorry,' I said. 'Try again tomorrow.'

'Tomorrow?' he squawked. 'What the devil are you talking about - *tomorrow!* James, what's going on?'

I simply beamed at him, raising my hand in farewell; and Jane and I made our escape. We hurried down the front steps and out across the lawn, then on towards the lake before anyone else could stop us.

'Safe at last!' I declared, feeling somewhat like a felon who has found sanctuary in a cathedral.

Not that the summerhouse was an especially grand affair. It was an octagonal wooden building with windows on seven of the eight sides. It was sparsely furnished, with just a cast iron table and six chairs, painted white, several large terracotta pots with exotic-looking plants, and an empty birdcage hanging by a chain from the roof.

'Right,' I said. 'What's it to be first, I wonder - a spank or a feel?' Both were equally appealing to me, but Jane's expression left no doubt which she would prefer. I therefore sat on one of the chairs and patted my knee.

Jane looked uncertain and rather apprehensive. I hadn't specified whether she should sit on my knee or lay facedown, of course, and the distinction was a crucial one for someone who so dreaded a spanking. She looked about as happy as a nun at an orgy, in fact, and I couldn't resist smiling.

'It's all right, Jane,' I said. 'Come and sit.'

She came, and I steered her onto my lap, facing me, her legs astride my own. She winced as her buttocks touched my thighs, and I knew this was no act - her bottom truly was most tender. The spanking I'd promised her was shaping up to be little more than a token affair. Now, however, I had a different treat in mind.

'Let's have these titties out, shall we?' I said, then unbuttoned her dress and scooped her breasts out over the top of her corset. They were bigger than I remembered, and softer than is usual in one so young. This is in no way intended as criticism, I hasten to add. Much as I appreciate firm breasts, they do have one significant drawback - they don't jiggle half so well as soft ones.

And jiggle Jane's was what I did now, putting the tips of my fingers beneath them and flicking them rapidly up and down. As I did so a quite remarkable transformation overcame the young housemaid. Gone was the timid, anxious thing of just a moment before, and in her place was a panting, wanton creature with lustful eyes. Suddenly and without warning she took my head in her hands and kissed me full on the lips.

'Good God,' I said softly, when finally she released me.

We looked at each other, and it was as though a signal had passed. She jumped to her feet, as did I, and we undressed hastily. Naked as a newborn I sat down again, and Jane resumed her straddle position.

'Do it again, sir,' she begged. 'To my bosoms.'

Needless to say I was happy to oblige, jiggling her boobies enthusiastically. A few seconds of this and she made a most unladylike plea. 'Fuck me, sir! Fuck me!'

Without waiting for an answer she half rose, grabbed my cock as though fully intending to break it off, guided it to her cunny, and drove downwards, impaling herself.

Before I could catch my breath she was bouncing away fit to burst. The pounding of her buttocks against my thighs must surely have caused her considerable pain, but she gave no sign of wanting to stop. It was then I made a discovery of some significance, I think - cast iron chairs are astonishingly cold and hard when one is bare-arsed.

Not that I gave a fig at that moment, for I was caught up in our wild romp, babbling idiotic endearments like any love struck adolescent.

'My dear Jane! Oh, my sweet girl...!'

Jane was equally voluble, gasping, 'Oh, sir! Oh, sir! Oh, sir!' over and over again.

Mere pain made no impression on us, for we were in the grip of ecstasy, and needs must when the devil drives. In no time at all, it seemed, we were peaking, sharing a thundering climax. Jane let out a long, impassioned cry, and I grunted like a rutting boar as I drove deep into her. She clung to me, shuddering, and I hugged her. For those few precious seconds I would gladly have died for her.

We stayed like that, holding each other tight, till our bodies began to chill. I ran my hands down her spine, then over her buttocks. I stroked and kneaded them gently. Jane murmured, and a tremor ran through her.

Was I a brute even to think of spanking her after so delightful a coupling? Perhaps so - but think it I did. I pinched her bottom, not too hard, and she eased out of my arms and regarded me dolefully.

'Yes, sir,' she said, though I had uttered not a word. 'I'll try to be brave.'

I had left the tawse on the table, and she rose and searched it out among our scattered clothes, then brought it to me.

'A dozen, then,' I said, 'and not a single stroke more, I promise.' I told her the position I required, and she stepped up to the table once more and leaned forward, resting her forearms upon it. Her legs were together, her shoulders stooped, and her head bowed low.

I stood up and approached her. I rested my left hand on her back, feeling the smoothness of her skin. The incongruity of this was not lost on me. Just a few minutes before I was intent on giving her pleasure. Now I wished to give her pain. Was this weakness on my part, or strength?

'Are you ready, Jane?'

'Yes, sir.'

'Count the strokes, if you please.'

'Sir.' A faint whisper, barely heard.

I swung the tawse.

I intended light strokes, I swear - the very lightest - for my concern over the state of her bottom was real. It was the spanker in me who rebelled. A beautiful behind like Jane's deserves proper recognition, proper treatment. That she should suffer for it was regrettable - but then again, as one of Percy's maids, to suffer was her lot in life.

The tawse cracked across her multi-coloured buttocks and Jane cried out, her knees dipping. It was no light stroke. Five, perhaps six, on a scale of ten. 'Moderate', my grandfather would have called it.

'One, sir.'

Her voice was faltering on this very first stroke. Moderate it may have been, but her sensitised rump would register it as 'hard'. A second followed, the weight identical, Jane's reaction identical. Then more strokes, which she counted off, her unhappiness clear in her voice.

'Ten, sir.' She was sobbing openly now.

'Eleven, sir.'

And, at last, 'Twelve, sir.'

I told her to rise, whereupon she straightened and faced me, though she would not look me in the eye. We dressed in silence. We left the summerhouse and walked back across the park with not a word spoken. As we approached the house her step faltered. She turned to me then, and I saw the fear was back in her face. She wouldn't ask, but the silent appeal was unmistakable.

It goes without saying that sentimentality is a luxury no spanker can afford. I knew what I must do - and I knew no other member of Spankers Seven would give the matter a second thought. All of them, even kindly old Humphrey, would take Jane into the house and hand her over to the first man who asked for her. My duty, then, was clear.

I looked into her troubled eyes, remembering how they had changed when I played with her breasts. I remembered her gasps of pleasure, her breath warm against my neck, and the feel of her in my arms as she shuddered in her climax. Sentimentality, pure and simple. I cursed myself for a fool.

'Stay close to me,' I growled.

I took her arm and led her around the house to the servants' entrance at the rear. We entered, halting in the passageway. All was still and quiet. I steered her towards the back stair and we went up to my room without meeting another soul. Once inside, I closed and locked the door.

'Listen to me,' I said. 'Are you listening, Jane?'

She nodded, watching me as a puppy watches its new master - half eager, half fearful.

'You must stay here for the rest of the day. Lock the door behind me when I leave, then you won't be disturbed. I'll bring you something to eat and drink in a while. The flogging stops at six, so it will be safe to go back to the servants' hall. You mustn't tell a soul where you've been, you understand? Especially say nothing to Parker.'

'Yes, sir,' she whispered. 'Thank you, sir.'

'Don't thank me till it's over,' I said. 'You're not in the clear yet. Tomorrow you must come here while all the guests are at breakfast. Come up by the back stairs as we did just now, and make sure you're not seen.'

'Yes, sir. But my duties—'

'Hang your duties!' I said. 'No one else is worrying about duties - that's why you keep getting caught. Until the festival is over it's every woman for herself.'

'Yes, sir.'

'It may be more difficult tomorrow. People might try to trick you into telling where you've been hiding, or spy on you to see where you go. You'll have to be cleverer than them. Don't speak to anyone. Don't trust anyone. Can you do that, do you think?'

'I'll try, sir.'

'Good girl. As a last resort, if it all goes wrong and you get caught coming in here, tell them I ordered you to do it, all right?'

She nodded, her eyes filling with tears once more. Without a word she flung her arms about me and hugged me. There was no doubt about it - this was one housemaid who would be extremely glad when the week was over.

That night Irene Hammond went to Humphrey whilst Tess came to me. She had been Percy's companion at the last festival, and proved very popular in both the flogging and fornication stakes, encouraging Percy to choose her for his slave again this year.

Despite her previous experience, she hadn't yet overcome her natural shyness and blushed most prettily as she entered my room. I lost no time in getting her stripped off and into bed, where her reserve was soon dispelled. I sucked her nipples and flicked them with my tongue, which provoked squeals of delight. She was a cheerful little thing, Tess, with a pronounced tendency to giggle. In some girls this can prove irritating in the extreme; in Tess I found it simply enchanting. Soon we were romping away in fine style and giggles gave way to sighs, and sighs to moans.

The moaning, I'm happy to say, went on for some considerable time.

Chapter 21

At breakfast the next morning, Wednesday, Percy declared there was to be a maid hunt. As he made this announcement, the maid who was serving the tea started so violently she almost poured it in my lap.

'I apologise for the scarcity of backsides these past two days, gentlemen,' he said. 'My maids have grown rather cunning, it seems. Still, we can be more cunning, what?'

There were growls of assent all round. Spankers Seven are tenacious in adversity, and certainly not the sort to give up without a fight.

'We'll meet in the library at ten,' Percy said. 'I'll have men cordon off the house and gardens. Don't want the wenches escaping to the woods, do we?'

Needless to say, there was considerable excitement at the prospect. Men are hunters by instinct and inclination, and there is nothing quite like the thrill of the chase, hearing the terrified squeal of the quarry as she bolts from cover, and the howls of the pack as it closes in on her remorselessly. Wonderful stuff indeed.

At ten o'clock sharp we met as arranged. Needless to say, there was not a female in sight. Word had spread through the household, and they had gone to ground in nooks and cubbyholes - anywhere they thought they might escape the hunters.

Even our slaves were taking no chances. Though not, in theory, valid quarry, in the heat of the chase anything might happen.

Just as foxhounds will savage any small creature unfortunate enough to cross their path, so any female was at risk when the Spankers Seven pack was abroad. Belinda had gathered the others together in her room and locked and barricaded the door.

Broadly speaking, there are two strategies a maid can adopt to avoid capture - hiding, and fleeing. Some favour one approach, some the other; we call them sitters and runners respectively. Sitters find a hiding place and stay there, silent and still, hoping the hunt will pass them by. Runners, on the other hand, move about the house, trying to stay one step ahead of the pack.

Both strategies have advantages and disadvantages, and there had been a long-standing debate over which was the more effective. I personally believe that running is a better bet - and certainly it is vastly more stimulating for the hunters than rooting about in a broom closet and dragging out some petrified young woman. It remains a risky tactic, however, as this hunt was to demonstrate.

In high spirits we left the house by the front entrance and circled around to the gardens on the south side. The shrubbery by the pond looked promising but yielded nothing, despite a most thorough search. We drew a blank, too, in the formal gardens. Undaunted we moved on, and finally flushed a maid in the kitchen garden, catching just a glimpse of her as she dashed through a low arched gateway in the high wall. Jasper let out a whoop that would have done credit to a steam whistle, and we set off in pursuit. She was surprisingly quick on her feet, and quick-witted too, for she almost eluded us by doubling back through the orangery. But Nigel spotted her coming out and the chase was on again. While ever she stayed out in the open it was only a matter of time; and she must have realised this. With the pack leaders less than twenty paces away and closing, she ran squealing for the house. She dived into the kitchen door and somehow managed to give us the slip in the maze of rooms off the servants' corridor.

Disappointed, but resolute still in our quest, we quartered the entire ground floor, and then ascended the main staircase to search the first floor.

That was when we spied Lucy - last seen astride Percy and his horse - running along the landing. Unnerved by the clamour of the approaching pack she had decided to make a dash for it, but unfortunately for her she timed her break badly.

A great roar went up and Lucy shrieked with fright, picked up her skirts, and ran for her life. With the pack in close pursuit she sped through the first open door she came to, which just happened to be the master's bedroom. Since there was but one way in and out we cornered her there, and closed in for the kill...

'Stop!' Percy shouted. He was at the head of the pursuing mob and turned to face us, throwing up his arms. As one we fell silent.

'Catcher's privilege,' he said. 'I claim first whacks.'

'Not fair!' Jasper complained. 'I saw her first.' How he could even dream of making such a claim was beyond me, as we all saw her together, more or less. Percy, too, seemed unimpressed.

'We are in my home,' he said haughtily, 'and the wench is in my bedroom. She's my wench, if it comes to that.'

It was a convincing argument, and Jasper quickly conceded. It thus fell to Percy to strip the girl off, lay her facedown across his bed, and dispense the first half dozen.

Whilst awaiting our turn, the rest of us chatted about the hunt. Inevitably the perennial question arose - indoors, or outdoors? Opinion, as always, was divided. Personally, I favour outdoors, as they tend to last longer. Today we had sampled a little of each, which gave us the best of both worlds.

Jasper took over from Percy. Poor Lucy's wails of distress soon grew louder, and the conversation petered out as we all turned to watch. We would each give her half a dozen, after which we would take it in turns to mount her. If she was suitably enthusiastic she would then be free to go, but any sulking or pouting would be rewarded by another round of the cane, taking the total to six dozen.

No wonder maids, governesses, cooks and housekeepers alike turned pale and quaked in their shoes when the hunt was abroad. To fall prey to the Spankers Seven was not a prospect to relish.

That night, after dinner, Irene Hammond and I returned to our room and I described the hunt, and poor Lucy's fate. The governess made no comment, but she shivered, and no doubt thought herself fortunate to be behind a barricade on such a day.

Soon after there came a knock at the door. I assumed it was Belinda, and asked Mrs Hammond to let her in. She opened the door, then turned and looked at me uncertainly.

'It's Mr Jasper, sir,' she said.

If he was here for his bedmate he was a good fifteen minutes early - which was a nuisance, as I'd intended to have a quiet word with Irene before she left. I'd wanted to caution her not to expect the same courteous treatment from Jasper that she'd received from Nigel and Humphrey. Percy could be cruel at times, Alex too, but Jasper had the worst reputation of the lot. And now here the fellow was, denying me the chance to warn her in advance. It was most annoying.

'Jasper,' I said, as he pushed past Irene and came into the room, 'did you want something?' My tone was less cordial than it might have been, but it made no dent in Jasper's armour.

'I thought you might have a slave going spare, old man,' he said, rubbing his hands and grinning foolishly. 'One with big tits and a fine looking arse, preferably. Rather like this one, what?'

He ogled Irene Hammond lecherously. She, understandably, appeared somewhat taken aback. As for myself, I found his manner thoroughly offensive. He didn't know Irene well enough to use vulgar language in front of her, for one thing. Crudity for the sake of it is unbecoming in a gentleman.

'You're early,' I said coldly.

'A minute or two, perhaps,' he admitted. 'Yvette's gone off to Humphrey, so I'm just hanging about twiddling my thumbs.'

'All right,' I sighed, 'take her away. And remember, no thrashing.'

'Well, not a *proper* thrashing, of course,' he said.

'Not *any* sort of thrashing,' I said. 'They're Percy's rules, not mine.'

'Yes, well... that's Percy all over, isn't it? But just between ourselves, man to man as it were, we can bend the rules a little, can't we?'

'Can we?' I said doubtfully.

'Oh, come now,' he protested. 'No harm in a light spanking, is there? What's FFF if you can't even spank 'em, I say?'

Though it grieved me to admit it, I actually agreed with him on this. Novel though this particular festival undoubtedly was, I thought Percy had made a mistake in banning casual spanking of the slaves. It was one of the most enjoyable aspects of FFF, and I certainly missed the opportunity to tickle a few rear ends myself.

'A dozen, then,' I conceded grudgingly, 'and not a stroke more. And light ones, you hear? I'm putting you on your honour, mind.'

Jasper smirked. 'Now James, you know you can trust me.'

I said nothing, but I was almost certain I could not, in fact. Short of refusing to let Mrs Hammond go with him, however, there was little I could do. Once she was in his room she was out of my jurisdiction, and Jasper could pretty well do with her as he pleased.

Even so brief a conversation with Jasper had left me feeling irritable and out of sorts, and it was fortunate, therefore, that it was Belinda who would be spending the night with me. If anyone could restore my good humour, it was she.

Twenty minutes later there was still no sign of her, so I undressed and got into bed. No sooner had I done so when there came a knock at the door.

'Come in,' I said.

The door opened and Belinda, Lady Newburn, stood there, dressed in a long, sleeveless satin gown of pale gold. She slid into the room in a sinuous fashion, and I presumed she was impersonating a harem girl. She was also wearing, needless to say, another of her damn masks.

'You can take that thing off for a start,' I said.

'Your wish is my command, master,' she said. She reached down and took hold of the hem of her gown, and drew it up and off in one smooth sweep. She was naked beneath, and my caustic retort stuck in my throat as I took in her trim figure. For a woman her age - or any age, for that matter - she was in remarkably fine shape. Her waist was narrow, her breasts pear-shaped and utterly delightful, and her thighs just the right degree of plumpness. I could eat every last morsel of her - though I knew which parts I would start with, given a choice.

'I meant the mask,' I said, rather lamely.

'My mask?' she gasped, shrinking back in mock alarm. 'Sir, I cannot - for then you would learn my true identity.'

'Oh, for God's sake, Belinda,' I said irascibly, 'take the damn thing off and get into bed!'

The next hour was one of the most enjoyable I can ever remember. Belinda was a wonderful lover - warm, good humoured and unselfish. Her skills, particularly in fellatio, were unsurpassed. The only thing that spoiled it somewhat, were the noises emanating from Jasper's room. The sound of strap on bare flesh was quite distinct, and from Irene Hammond's cries I knew it was no token beating Jasper was subjecting her to. Neither did he limit himself to the dozen we'd agreed upon. It went on and on, and I made myself stop counting after thirty as I felt my mounting distraction was discourteous to my present companion.

'How old are you, Belinda?' I asked, as we lay side by side in the dark, our passion spent.

'Jamie,' she chided gently, 'it's most improper to ask a lady her age. Shame on you.'

'I could command it,' I said, 'master to slave.'

'Command away. I'm still not telling you.'

I grinned to myself. Belinda never changed. She was a strong-willed woman with a mind of her own. I pondered her motives yet again. Having observed her under the rod on numerous occasions - indeed, having spanked her myself a good few times - I was convinced Belinda was not one of those rare individuals who actually enjoy pain; which meant something else must be drawing her to these affairs year after year. Try as I might, however, I couldn't imagine what it might be.

'Forty-one,' she said unexpectedly.

'Really? I'd have put you at thirty-three at the outside.'

'Thank you, kind sir,' she said, in a tone that made it plain she knew I was flattering her. I was, but only a little. As I said, she was in remarkably good shape. I reminded myself just how good by running my hands over those parts of her within easy reach. This provoked a giggle, followed by a gasp as I located an especially sensitive spot.

As I fondled her, Irene Hammond, next door, began to groan. It was no groan of passion, of that I felt sure, yet the associated crack of the strap was absent. I hadn't heard that particular sound for some minutes, in fact, and I assumed Jasper's desire to thrash her was finally assuaged.

This new sound continued intermittently, rising in volume as the minutes passed, and took on a despairing quality.

'God,' I muttered, '*now* what's he doing to her?'

'His speciality, I suppose,' Belinda said.

'What's that?'

'Don't you know? I thought you men always bragged about your exploits.'

'Jasper and I have never been especially close. He'd never confide in me. So what's his speciality?'

'Now you know I can't answer that,' she said. 'It's a hundred strokes, remember, for any slave who tells tales about what goes on in private. Percy was quick to remind us all of that. He said that butler of his, Parker, would deliver them.'

Knowing Percy he would go through with it, too. I'd told Irene about it on the way there, warning her not to gossip, not even to the other slaves. A 'century' would be terrible indeed with Parker wielding the cane. The man's fearsome reputation was rightly deserved.

'It's buggery, as a matter of fact,' Belinda said, confounding me a second time by refusing to answer and then immediately changing her mind.

'Oh.'

'Don't say "Oh" like that - like it isn't anything much at all. Have you ever been buggered?'

'Not that I recall. Are you saying it's not much fun?'

'It all depends on who's doing it, and how considerate he's being. In Jasper's case, no, it's not fun at all. In fact, it hurts like the devil.'

As if to corroborate her statement, Mrs Hammond gave another long, agonised moan, and I found myself growing angry at Jasper, to the point where I even contemplated going in there and putting a stop to it. To do so, however, would result in my immediate expulsion from the Seven. There were strict rules about interference, and Percy and the rest would tolerate no behaviour of that sort. Whilst Irene Hammond was in Jasper's care, she was his to command.

At one point Belinda sighed. 'I take it she's not used to this sort of sex.'

'I wouldn't know,' I said. 'Not from me, at any rate.' That meant not at all, obviously - at least, not in the recent past. If her late husband had been a sodomite, Spikeman's enquiries had failed to uncover the fact.

'Poor woman,' Belinda said quietly, and then fell silent. I'd never quite stopped running my hands over her, and I continued to caress her breasts gently as we lay side by side in the dark.

'When Percy told us Michael wouldn't be joining us,' I said, 'you seemed almost pleased. Do you have something against the man? I always thought him the most convivial of fellows - or is there some dark secret I'm not aware of?'

'Fairly dark, I'd say. Michael likes to play games; painful games.'

I found her trust quite touching. One word from me to Percy would earn her probably the most agonising thirty minutes of her life. Nor was it carelessness on her part to confide in me thus. She knew exactly what she was doing, and exactly what she was risking if I chose to betray her. A thing, of course, I would never do.

'What kind of painful games, exactly?' I asked. 'Like Jasper, you mean?'

'Not exactly. You know about irrigators?'

'An enema man?' I said in surprise. 'I'd never have guessed. He never said anything to me about it.'

Some floggers of my acquaintance engage in such activity, and I've witnessed a few punishment enemas in my time. Though I'd never taken it any further, I'd always intended one day to obtain equipment of my own.

'It's not just enemas,' she said. 'He has ropes, straps, clips, and suchlike. Candles, needles - you know the sort of thing.'

So Michael was a devotee of restraint and torture too. That appealed to me also, in fact, but I wasn't about to admit as much to Belinda, as she seemed to find the whole idea distasteful. There were only three individuals in the whole world I counted as true friends, and Belinda was one of them, Nigel and Humphrey being the other two. Though caring what others think of one is undoubtedly a character flaw, I nevertheless wished to retain her good opinion of me.

The sounds of distress from the adjacent bedroom went on sporadically for a good two hours. Endurance, Belinda informed me, was another of Jasper's accomplishments.

Chapter 22

The final day of FFF dawned cool but clear. Breakfast was an unusually subdued affair, with little conversation and even less laughter. I imagine every man was thinking of what the next few hours might bring - glory or disappointment. Each of us, I had no doubt, was determined to win, for men are competitive creatures at heart.

At ten o'clock sharp Percy took us through to the ballroom, for it was there that the competition was to be held. Our slaves were in attendance, all looking somewhat anxious, I thought, with the notable exception of Belinda, who looked amused; or so I judged, as her lips - visible below her mask - were curved in a faint smile.

Her outfit caught my eye, as it was spectacular to say the least. She was dressed as a peacock, although a peahen would have been more appropriate, obviously, but the female bird lacks the male's flamboyant display. Her tight corset - blue, like a peacock's breast - was embroidered with sequins in a feather pattern. Her stockings and shoes were pale yellow. Her mask was most ingeniously crafted to resemble a peacock's head, complete with glossy black beak and blue tufted crown feathers. Most astonishing of all, however, was her tail. It was a full peacock fan in all its magnificence, sweeping across her back and shoulders. It radiated from a point level with her buttocks, and at first I assumed it was attached to her corset, but then saw that the garment in question did not extend down far enough. I could only conclude that Belinda's tail was somehow stuck up her bottom.

The other slaves were positively dowdy in comparison, apart from Zuleika, who had also taken some trouble to catch our eyes. She wore a harness of bright red leather that was little more than a grid-work of slender straps fastened at the intersections with silver studs. The straps circled her torso and limbs, squeezing her tightly, but leaving much voluptuous flesh exposed to the general gaze. Her breasts, bush and buttocks in particular were in plain sight.

In addition to the slaves, two of Percy's servants awaited us there, namely the butler, Parker, and a footman whose name I believe was Baxter.

Six couches had been arranged in a circle in the middle of the room, and just outside this ring was a table upon which presently rested a comprehensive range of flogging implements. I couldn't help but notice, however, that most of the other competitors carried a long slim case not dissimilar to my own. When faced with a critical, demanding task, it's better to stick to those familiar tools we know and trust.

The six of us seated ourselves, and I indicated to Irene that she should sit beside me. Donnett also sat, whereas the rest were made to stand behind their respective masters' couches. I doubted Belinda could sit even if she wished to, not without doing herself a mischief with that tail.

I was, I have to admit, a little nervous. Family pride was at stake, after all. I felt I would be letting my grandfather down if I should lose, for it was he more than anyone who made me what I am today.

'We shall now draw for running order,' Percy announced, signalling to Parker. The butler stepped forward with a black felt bag and took it from person to person, from which we all in turn extracted a token. Mine carried the number five, which presumably meant that Mrs Hammond and I would go next to last.

Percy took the one remaining token and we each called out our numbers. The order turned out to be Percy, then Nigel, Humphrey, Alex, myself, and finally Jasper.

Percy stood up and went to the centre of the circle, taking Tess with him. She was dressed once again in just cap, stockings and shoes, and appeared more nervous than I can ever recall seeing her. I wondered whether Percy had promised her special treatment should she fail to perform to his satisfaction. Our host could be a hard master indeed when the mood took him.

The footman, Baxter, had been assigned the task of timekeeper, and with a glance at his pocket watch he sounded a gong. Percy's fifteen minutes had started.

Our host nodded at Tess, who obviously had her instructions, for she proceeded to undo his trouser flies and take out his cock. She then leaned forward to bring her head level with that member and started to lick it, much as a cat washes its paws, with long, slow strokes of her tongue.

While she was so engaged Parker approached her, cane in hand, and commenced laying firm strokes across her buttocks. The involvement of a third party in this fashion was not wholly within the rules, but no one spoke up. Every man there respected Parker's skill, and enjoyed watching the 'flogging butler' at work, so it was most unlikely anyone would object.

Tess whimpered, but dare not cease her oral duties. 'Firm strokes' could soon change to 'hard strokes', and a hard stroke from Parker was a thing to be feared.

After perhaps five minutes of this Percy ordered a slight variation. 'Suck me now,' he commanded.

Tess immediately took his cock in her mouth and proceeded to suck him in a greedy fashion. Simultaneously, Parker ceased beating her, which showed extreme good sense on his part; flogging a woman whose teeth are in contact with your cock is a most risky venture.

While Tess was servicing him, Percy reached beneath her and pinched her nipples, squeezing them to make her squirm. She was not totally free from pain, therefore, though this must surely feel mild compared with the cane.

I was not surprised when, five minutes later, Percy ordered another change. Tess reverted to licking him, and Parker resumed caning her. These strokes were more forceful, and Tess struggled to maintain concentration on her allotted task. Parker watched her closely, rewarding any hesitation or unevenness in the action of her tongue with an especially hard stroke - which merely added to her difficulties, of course.

This final session saw out the remaining time. The gong sounded, bringing Percy's display to a close. There was a smattering of polite applause from the audience, who appeared to appreciate the show. I certainly found it enjoyable, and thought it a good start to the proceedings. Well done, Percy.

Nigel was on next, and once the gong sounded the first thing he did was remove Belinda's tail. As I had suspected, the peacock fan was attached to a plug in her bottom, and her sigh of relief as it came out brought a smile to a good few faces, including my own.

'Thank God for that,' she muttered. 'Now I know what the Christmas turkey feels like.'

With the tail out of the way Nigel proceeded to warm her bottom with a quirt. The short, braided leather whip was a particular favourite of his, and he soon had her dancing and yelping in a most entertaining fashion.

It is always a treat to watch Belinda take a whacking. She is very mobile, for one thing, and her titties bounce delightfully as she hops and skips about the floor. She is also extremely vocal. Belinda does not believe in suffering in silence, singing out in an uninhibited fashion, and prone to sharing her thoughts on the proceedings into the bargain.

Under normal circumstances, of course, most spankers would consider such antics undesirable, even unacceptable. I know that my grandfather would certainly have had something to say to Belinda about her behaviour. He always insisted that those under correction should remain as still and silent as possible. Twitching and jerking is inevitable, as are gasps and groans, but the penitent should certainly not shift from her allotted position, and comments such as Belinda was apt to make simply would not be tolerated.

Though I share his views on this, with Belinda it is somehow different. Whether out of affection for her or some other reason, behaviour that from others would have me in a rage, from Belinda just makes me smile.

The gong sounded, bringing Nigel's performance to a close. We all applauded, and Belinda made a curtsey to her appreciative audience.

'Thank you, kind sirs,' she said, and masked though she was, I could see she was smiling.

Now it was the turn of Humphrey and Donnett. 'Innocence lost' appeared to be Humphrey's theme, and I thought it an intriguing idea.

First he had Donnett strip naked, and the sight of her slender body, pale and vulnerable, set the scene, for she was the very image of innocence.

Humphrey nodded, and the show proper commenced. Donnett went to each man in turn, opened her knees, put her hands between her legs and spread her labia. Whilst maintaining this provocative, humiliating position, she received three strokes across her buttocks from Humphrey's tawse, before moving on to the next man.

The picture Humphrey was seeking to create, it seemed to me, was that of a virtuous young woman obliged to degrade herself, and in Donnett he had the perfect specimen. Her cheeks flushed scarlet as she stood before me, and her eyes looked anywhere except into my own. Each slap from the tawse drew forth a heartrending sob, and it was a perfectly delightful spectacle that was over all too quickly, unfortunately. Three strokes at a time were far too few for my liking.

Round and round she went, managing four full circuits before the gong brought a halt to her suffering, and she could scramble into her clothes once more and cover her shame.

Again we applauded. It was a clever idea of Humphrey's, certainly, and effective up to a point. The trouble was, every man had bedded Donnett during the week, so her innocence was thus compromised from the start, and the effect was a little diluted as a result.

Alex and Zuleika came forward next, and I knew I was not alone in expecting something rather special. It soon became apparent that we were not to be disappointed, for the black woman paraded before us, flaunting herself shamelessly. She strutted back and forth, cupping her large breasts and jiggling them in our faces. She rubbed her hands over her belly, thighs and groin in a most provocative fashion, moaning seductively as though thoroughly aroused by her own caresses.

After a few minutes of this, Alex, who had remained passively at the side till now, brought out a black lacquered box from a bag beside his couch. He opened the box and took out what appeared to be an item of jewellery - a heavy silver pendant, as large almost as a hen's egg, suspended on a fine silver chain no longer than a man's hand. He passed this to Zuleika, who proceeded to show it to each of the five other competitors in turn.

I was none the wiser, I have to say. The silver ovoid was engraved with an intricate pattern in a style unknown to me. To the other end of the short chain was attached a clip, also silver, fashioned in the manner of a crocodile's head... and then everything became clear. When Belinda had told me about Michael's 'games', she said he used clips. Alex and Zuleika, I deduced, were about to play the same sort of game.

The black girl had come to a halt directly in front of Percy, on my right. She offered him the pendant, which he took with a knowing smile. I glanced at my fellow competitors, and saw that Nigel and Jasper were also smiling. Only Humphrey appeared as baffled as I had been by these proceedings.

Zuleika cupped her left breast and plucked at her nipple, rubbing and flicking it rapidly. She then leaned towards Percy, holding her breast with both hands as though offering it him to suckle. He raised the pendant, fiddled with the clip, and fastened it to her nipple.

Zuleika gasped. For a moment or two she did not move. Then she slowly released her breast, and equally slowly stood up straight. The silver weight dragged at her nipple, distending her breast. Moving with some care she went to Nigel, on Percy's right. Alex handed her a second pendant, which she in turn gave to Nigel. Zuleika teased her right nipple to make it erect, and allowed Nigel to fasten the weight to it.

With both breasts now drooping under their load, the black woman moved on again, this time to Jasper. Alex produced a third pendant, and I saw that this one was of a somewhat different form. Larger than the previous two it somewhat resembled a short fat candle in shape.

Zuleika had no more nipples to offer, but I thought I could guess where this weight was going - and indeed she lifted her right leg and put her foot on the couch beside Jasper. He was directly opposite me in the circle and Zuleika's back was to me, masking my view. After a few moments she moved her foot to the floor, and sidled past Alex's couch to Humphrey, on my left.

This time I had a much better view. After handing Humphrey the fourth pendant she stepped up with her right foot as before. Her hands went to her groin and she teased her inner labia. Jasper's clip, I saw, was already attached on the right. Humphrey peered closely at it for a moment, frowning, and then his face cleared.

'Ah,' he murmured, in the tone of a man who has finally seen the light.

His clip was duly attached, and Zuleika continued on her way. And now it had come around to me.

Zuleika handed me my pendant - one of the smaller variety - and I had my first opportunity to examine it thoroughly. The weight, I discovered, was just that - a solid lump of silver - and surprisingly heavy for its size. The clip intrigued me more than a little. Fashioned, as I said, like the head of a crocodile, the lower jaw was hinged. Pressing in the appropriate place caused the jaws to open, revealing sharp little teeth. A small spring was most cunningly concealed inside the head, so that when I relaxed my grip the jaws snapped shut.

'Ah,' I said, precisely as Humphrey had done, curious as to what it would feel like having such a thing fastened to one's flesh. Without further ado I opened them and clipped it to the web of skin between the thumb and forefinger of my left hand. 'Ah!' I said again, though in a different tone. It hurt. The diminutive beast's teeth were surprisingly sharp, and his bite remarkably fierce. Once in place, however, the pain seemed to ease a little. Most curious.

I lifted my hand, and as the weight came on the chain the pain increased again. This explained Zuleika's caution when moving from man to man. Disturbing the weights, or causing them to swing, would no doubt be most unwise. I tested out this theory by doing precisely that. I swung the weight and the result was as predicted.

'Baxter,' Percy called out wearily, 'you'd better add a couple of minutes to the time. Mr Montague, it appears, wishes to conduct experiments.'

He was reminding me that the clock was ticking, but I was unrepentant for this was not mere idle curiosity. It is important to know these things, for how else can we judge what a slave can and cannot endure?

I removed the clip and made one final discovery - taking it off hurt just as much as putting it on. It was all most edifying; but the company was waiting, so I looked up at Zuleika.

'And where, my dear,' I enquired, 'would you like this one putting?'

With a smile she showed me, spreading her labia and flicking her clitoris. I was more than happy to oblige, and Zuleika stiffened as the jaws closed on that most sensitive of nubs, her breath hissing between her teeth.

Moving very carefully the black woman stepped to the centre of the circle and adopted a half-squat, her knees apart and slightly bent, her bottom sticking out. Alex came forward bearing a sort of miniature cat o' nine tails, the woven silk thongs knotted at intervals, with which he proceeded to lash his slave's buttocks vigorously. For reasons already mentioned, Zuleika tried to keep as still as possible under the onslaught, though inevitably her hips jerked somewhat, causing the weights to swing. Her cries of pain, though somewhat muted, were clearly heartfelt.

The build up to this flogging - Zuleika's strutting display, then the rigmarole with the clips - had taken so much time that the gong sounded before Alex had truly got into his stride. It was the only disappointing aspect of an otherwise excellent performance, and Zuleika was greeted with enthusiastic applause when she stepped forward, having removed the clips, to take a bow.

Chapter 23

Irene Hammond and I had discussed our 'show' at some length prior to the event, and agreed on what we would do.

She started by undressing. I had explained there was not a man alive who could fail to take pleasure from seeing her remove her clothes. I told her she should do this as slowly and provocatively as possible, teasing her audience and making them wait to see her charms.

This is easier said than done for someone who is not a professional performer, but Mrs Hammond made a very commendable showing, I thought. There was more than one grunt of appreciation from the assembled spankers, especially when she revealed her breasts, and again when the final garment was discarded and she stood naked before us. The bruising from the beating Jasper had given her was very pronounced, I noticed. Percy shot me a glance, frowning, but I merely shrugged. Now was clearly not the time to go into explanations.

This was the point at which I would make my contribution to the proceedings. I had previously taken the medium tawse from my carrying case, and I rose and approached the governess. She was standing in the centre of the circle, her arms by her sides. I went around her and slapped her smartly at the back of her right thigh. She barely flinched, though the stroke must have stung. Again I had advised her to show as little reaction as possible. Men such as these would be well able to judge how much it was hurting, and would appreciate restraint, I thought.

I struck her once on her poor buttocks, which certainly caused her to flinch, and once on her other thigh, then moved around and struck both thighs, high up, at the front. That drew an involuntary gasp from her lips, and she sucked in her belly.

'I'm getting tired,' I said. 'Why don't you ask these other gentlemen to lend a hand?' I gave her the tawse and returned to my seat, and Irene looked at the other five spankers in turn, finally approaching Alex.

'Would you kindly give me three strokes, sir, on my bottom?'

Though I said nothing, and gave no sign of disapproval, she was already deviating from the agreed plan. We had agreed she would ask for two strokes, not three. Since I knew the governess possessed an excellent memory, I assumed this change was deliberate, though I could only guess at the reason.

Alex smiled as he took the tawse from her hand. 'Nothing would give me greater pleasure, madam.'

Irene turned away from him and touched her toes. Alex rose, and swiped her across her buttocks.

'A little harder if you please, sir,' she said, though it had been no light stroke and must have hurt considerably. Alex duly obliged, and the next two were firmer still. The governess took them well, especially considering her bruised state. She then straightened and retrieved the tawse.

'Thank you kindly, sir,' she said.

Alex sat down again and Irene looked around, fixing her gaze on Humphrey. 'And you, sir? Could I trouble you for three?'

'No trouble at all, Irene, I assure you,' he said solemnly.

Again Irene presented her bottom, and Humphrey delivered the requested strokes. They were significantly lighter than Alex's last two, but his victim made no comment.

Next it was Jasper's turn. I half suspected some chicanery from him and my fears were soon confirmed. His first stroke cracked loudly against her flesh, and she let out a shuddering sob and stood up straight. She resumed her position commendably quickly, and Jasper struck her again. This second stroke was just as hard, as was the one that followed, and I scowled at him, though I doubt he cared or even noticed.

Understand me - I am not averse to dealing out hard strokes myself, but there is a time and place for everything. Irene was competing against others, and she should be allowed to compete on equal terms. Unnecessarily hard strokes could put her off her stride and spoil her performance - for that is what this was, after all. It was a show, for entertainment, not a punishment beating.

Irene moved on again, this time to Nigel. His three strokes, predictably, were easier. Next came our erstwhile host, Percy, who smiled wickedly as he took the tawse from her hand - and certainly made her feel it.

At this point I was supposed to take over once more and see out the remainder of the session. Irene and I had discussed and agreed upon (or so I thought) a number of unusual and provocative positions intended to titillate jaded spanker palates. Once again, however, she deviated from the script by ignoring me entirely and approaching Alex a second time.

I believed I understood why she was changing the plan in this way. Zuleika's performance was so remarkable that it would take something very special indeed to beat her. Irene Hammond had set her heart on that sixty-guinea purse, and was doing her damnedest to win.

'Could you oblige me with two more strokes, sir?' she said to Alex. 'Here, on my bosom.' She leaned forward and clasped her hands behind her back, her breasts offered invitingly.

'One stroke on each, or both together?' Alex asked.

'Whichever you prefer, sir.'

'Two on the left, then. Firm like before, I take it?'

'Yes, sir. Thank you, sir.'

Alex put his free hand on her shoulder and swung the tawse twice in quick succession, so that the two cracks could barely be separated. She jerked, for it would certainly hurt.

Changing the order she went next to Nigel, who gave her one stroke on each breast, as did Humphrey after him. All four were light strokes, but Percy, whom she next approached, put some force behind his, both to her left breast. Once again she flinched, and this time gasped also.

It was significant, I thought, that she left Jasper till last. Perhaps she was hoping the gong would sound and free her of the obligation to submit to his ministrations.

She handed Jasper the tawse, but he set it down on the couch beside him. Instead he reached up and began to knead her breasts, and Irene gasped, her shoulders lifting.

'A little tender, are they?' he enquired.

'A little, sir,' she admitted.

He nodded and continued to squeeze and prod her, watching her face all the while, and soon drew forth another gasp. 'Just here especially, it seems,' he mused, pressing the left side of her left breast, close by the nipple. 'Right-handed spankers you see, my dear. You get more power from that direction. And Alex and Percy each gave you two in this same place, didn't they?'

'Yes, sir.'

He was tormenting her, deliberately keeping her waiting, but this could easily prove counter-productive. The more time he spent talking the less there was for actual beating. Serve him right if the gong sounded and denied him the pleasure of strapping her.

'How long on the clock, Baxter?' Jasper sang out, almost as if he had been reading my mind.

'Three minutes remaining, sir,' the footman replied.

'Plenty of time, eh?' Jasper said, grinning at Irene. 'You might even get another round in, with luck.'

'One can but hope, sir.' Her voice faltered as she spoke, for Jasper was again exploring that same painful region at the side of her left breast. He nodded, oblivious to, or deliberately ignoring, the irony. Finally he released her, and picked up the tawse.

'Good,' he said. 'So then, I think I'll try two to the left also. You'd prefer them rather less hard than my previous three on your bottom, I suspect.'

'If you please, sir,' she whispered.

'Well, we'll see. I can't promise anything, you understand.' He put his left hand behind her head, and swung the tawse.

'Aaaahh!' she cried, and would have pulled back had he not been holding her. 'Aaaahhhh!'

If these strokes were less hard than before, then I certainly did not see it. Jasper, I decided, was an utter scoundrel.

He let her go and handed back the tawse. Irene thanked him in a decidedly unsteady voice, and then looked across at the long case clock in the corner of the room. She was now facing a difficult choice. She could carry on, or she could hand the tawse to me for a few token strokes, or she could simply stop altogether. The latter two, however, would be regarded as backing down, and that could only harm her cause.

I considered intervening, making the failure mine and not hers, but I knew this would fool no one. Percy and Alex in particular would be watching her keenly to see how bravely she coped with the situation. In the end I did nothing. This was Irene Hammond's show, and I thought it only right and proper to let the governess make the decision herself.

She decided to continue. She did glance briefly at Humphrey, but then approached Alex a third time. Maybe she thought that going straight to Humphrey or Nigel would also be seen as a sign of weakness. Alex delivered his two strokes as before, both to her left breast, though they were rather less forceful.

Humphrey was next, and it was immediately clear he thought this had gone quite far enough. He made no move to strike her, but peered at her breasts closely as though he had never seen a pair of tits before.

'I say,' he said, 'you're going to have the most astonishing bruise here, do you know that?' He pointed to, but did not touch, the painful area on her left breast. 'You ought to put a steak on it. Or does that only work with black eyes?'

It was obvious to everyone that Humphrey was deliberately wasting time. He hummed and hawed some more, then looked across to where Baxter stood by his gong. 'How much time have we left, Baxter?'

'Less than a minute, sir,' came the reply.

'A minute, eh? Better get a move on, I suppose.' He transferred the tawse to his left hand, and gave Irene two light strokes on her right breast. 'There you go, my dear,' he said. 'Trot off now to Lord Newburn. We wouldn't want him to miss his turn, would we?'

'No, sir,' she said, favouring Humphrey with a grateful smile, 'we wouldn't.'

Nigel played the same game, taking his time, and had barely delivered his strokes when the gong brought the session to a close, to Irene's obvious relief. Percy and Jasper were thus thwarted, thanks to Humphrey and to Nigel.

Irene picked up her clothes and started back towards me.

'A pity, though,' Jasper said, 'she didn't have time to finish the round. What say we allow her to continue?'

Irene Hammond froze, a stunned look on her face.

'Not fair,' Humphrey said quickly. 'Not fair to the others.'

'We could vote on it,' Jasper said, 'couldn't we, Percy?'

'I have no objection to a vote, certainly,' Percy said.

'I do,' Nigel put in, and Belinda, standing behind him, nodded vigorously.

'And in the case of a tie,' Jasper went on, ignoring the lot of them, 'our esteemed host, Percy, can cast the deciding vote.'

'Sounds reasonable enough to me,' Percy said. 'All those in favour of allowing Irene to complete the round?'

'Aye,' Jasper said.

'No,' Humphrey and Nigel said together.

'Yes,' Alex said.

'Aye from me,' Percy said. 'That leaves just you, James.'

They all turned to me, but the decision had already been taken. If I said no it would be tied at three apiece; in which case Percy would rule in favour. My vote was irrelevant. All I could do was make the best of a bad job.

'Most generous of you to make this offer, Jasper,' I said amiably. 'Very generous indeed. Naturally, I accept. I vote yes.'

Humphrey snorted in disbelief, but that was because he hadn't thought it through. Had Irene Hammond, I wondered? Did she believe I had deserted her in her hour of need? Her face showed only anxiety at the thought of further strokes, so I had no way of knowing.

Anxious or not, she had little choice but to face the two of them and take her medicine. She put down her bundle of clothes, moved in front of Percy, handed him the tawse, and assumed the position.

'Two to the left, you understand,' Percy said quietly.

'Sir.'

He smiled; and it seemed to me a smile of respect rather than derision. He got to his feet, leaned forward a little, and struck her breast, quite hard. She shot up straight and took a half-step back, though her hands remained behind her back.

'You shouldn't move,' Percy admonished, frowning. 'But then you know that, don't you?'

'Yes, sir,' she said. 'I'm sorry, sir.'

He nodded. 'If you move this time I shall repeat the stroke. Do you accept this?'

'Yes, sir.'

God, I thought; Percy and Jasper could make this last all night if they put their minds to it. I tried to remember the exact wording of the 'extra time' we had voted on, and was fairly sure that no actual time had been agreed. For certain, Baxter had not been told to sound his gong after a specified further period. Irene was simply required to finish the round - allow Percy and Jasper to deliver their two strokes apiece, no matter how long it might take.

'Very well,' Percy said. 'Present.'

Irene bent over and Percy struck her. I was fully expecting a sizzler, delivered with the clear intention of making her move, but Percy's stroke was no harder than before. It was by no means mild, however, and the governess jerked greatly and let out another tormented gasp. Would Percy class jerking as 'moving'? I was not the only one, I knew, hanging on his pronouncement.

'Well done,' he said, handing back the tawse.

I saw Irene's look of relief, but it was short-lived, for now she faced her greatest trial of all - someone who could not be trusted to act in any reasonable fashion whatsoever. It was with noticeable reluctance that she approached Jasper.

'Well well,' he said with a knowing smirk. 'Here we are again.' He took the offered tawse and once again set it down on the couch. And, once again, his hands went to her breasts - or rather, her left breast.

'Humphrey was right, I see,' he said thoughtfully. 'This looks very painful indeed.'

He pressed his thumb against the area in question, massaging the bruised tissue. Irene whined. He did it again, pressing firmly, and continued to knead her for a full half-minute more.

At last he seemed satisfied. He picked up the tawse and rose from the couch. 'Lean forward,' he said. 'Not all the way, just halfway.' Irene bent from the waist, and Jasper stopped her at the required position. 'No, arms up,' he said. 'Clasp your hands behind your head.' She complied, but I could see no reason for his wanting a change of stance, other than to demonstrate his mastery over her.

'I make you the same promise Percy did,' he said. 'If you move the stroke will be repeated. Do you understand?'

'Yes, sir.'

He was setting her an almost impossible task, of course, and everyone knew it. Humphrey was shaking his head in disgust. Alex watched with interest, as did his slave - indeed, Zuleika seemed to be thoroughly enjoying herself. Nigel looked on with a face like stone, and masked though she was, Belinda's feelings on all this were also clear. She looked angry enough to intervene, though what that might cost her I dreaded to think.

Jasper drew back his arm and I saw Irene close her eyes. He waited, however, with the seconds ticking by - and then he struck her.

It was a forceful blow, not absolutely full-strength but harder than she could possibly cope with in her present state. She cried out and straightened, stepping back.

'No good,' Jasper said. 'Let's try that one again.'

She did a little better the second time, straightening somewhat, but managing to keep her feet still at least.

Jasper shook his head. 'Again.'

Belinda muttered something and I glared at her by way of warning. Earning herself a thrashing would in no way help Irene.

The governess bent forward. Tears ran down her cheeks and dripped onto the carpet. Jasper's third stroke cracked across her poor breast and she let out a terrible wail, her shoulders lifting. I waited anxiously on his decision.

'Very well,' Jasper said, 'we'll count that one. One more to go.'

On the next her shoulders again rose, but no more than before, I thought.

'No,' Jasper said. 'Again.'

Belinda finally cracked. 'This is ridiculous,' she snapped. 'Are you going to put a stop to it, or will I?'

I wasn't sure to whom this was addressed, as she looked first at Nigel, then me, then back to Nigel. Perhaps she meant both of us.

'Nigel,' Percy said coldly, 'if you can't control your slave, then I will.'

Nigel nodded. 'Belinda, keep silent!' It was a measure of his discomposure that he positively barked at her. Not that it made an iota of difference, for Belinda had the bit well and truly between her teeth.

'I shall do no such thing,' she retorted hotly. 'This is a travesty. How in God's name is the poor girl—'

'Belinda!' Nigel snapped.

'Two dozen for you, madam,' Percy said angrily, 'when this is over!'

'That's your answer for everything, isn't it?' Belinda fired back. 'It's pathetic!'

'Four dozen! I will not tolerate such behaviour, not even from you, do you hear?' Belinda sneered and opened her mouth to retort.

'Not another word, madam, or by God I swear it will be six! I advise you to think very carefully before you speak.'

His words finally got through to her, for she clamped her jaw shut and just stood there, fuming. An embarrassed silence followed. We'd had the odd angry word at festivals in the past, but nothing on a par with this.

Finally Nigel cleared his throat. 'Gentlemen, ladies - I suggest we continue with the proceedings.' He seemed somewhat put out, but at least he was making an effort. Since it was his wife who had provoked the altercation, perhaps he felt it was his duty to make the peace.

'Just so,' Percy said. 'Jasper, I believe we await your final stroke.'

Was I imagining it, or was there a slight emphasis on the word 'final'? Perhaps Jasper was being instructed to bring this particular phase to a close. If so, it was not before time. Some might blame Belinda for the fracas, but I knew who the real culprit was.

Jasper had said not a word during the exchange, and he said nothing now. He simply stared at Irene Hammond, slapped the tawse against his palm, and gave a single curt nod.

Irene nodded also, her tongue licking her lips. She leaned forward and clasped her hands behind her head. Jasper stepped up to her and grabbed a fistful of her hair.

She gasped, her face twisting with pain, and her hands clutched at his wrist. He swung the tawse and fetched her a tremendous crack on her breast.

Had he not been holding her hair she would most certainly have moved. As it was, she screamed and tried to pull free. He held her fast and kept her there a second or two till she became still. Only then did he release her and hand back the tawse, bowing as he did so, and return at last to his seat.

Mrs Hammond's ordeal, it seemed, was finally over.

Jasper did not remain seated for long, however, as he was the sixth and final competitor. Once the governess had sorted out her clothes - slipping on her undergarments for decency's sake - and returned to take her place beside me, Jasper led Yvette to the middle of the circle and told her to strip. When she was naked the show, such as it was, began.

Not even his closest friends, I thought, could describe Jasper's performance as imaginative or entertaining.

As for me, who certainly did not count myself amongst them, it was positively crude. He simply subjected Yvette to a long, severe caning. Was he taking out his temper on her, I wondered? Did he think to impress us with the sheer brutality of the display? Or hadn't he given the matter much thought at all? I suspected the latter, but I may be biased.

Whatever the reason it was a poor showing, and a disappointing end to what had been a stimulating and engaging, if not particularly harmonious, event.

Percy took the floor once more, and explained how the voting would work. Each of us, he said, would be given a card bearing the names of the six competitors. All we had to do was underline the name of our choice, and put the card into Parker's black bag.

'I hardly need tell you,' Percy added, 'no one is allowed to vote for himself. Is everyone clear, then, on what they must do?'

We replied that we were, and Parker duly handed out cards and pens.

There were only two in contention, for my money - Alex and myself. By rights the cards should have carried the names of the slaves, since they were the real performers, but Percy had arranged matters otherwise.

Zuleika's performance had been the more novel, I thought, and highly entertaining to boot. Irene's, on the other hand, had been an astonishingly brave show and most enthralling to watch. In fact there was little to choose between them. It was a difficult decision for others, perhaps, but not for me. Since I wasn't allowed to vote for myself the choice was easy. I underlined Alex's name, and dropped the card into the bag.

When all the cards had been returned the butler took himself off to one side and counted the votes. He then came back and murmured in Percy's ear. Percy nodded, and turned to the audience.

'Gentlemen,' he said, 'we have a tie. With three votes each, Alexander McFeash and James Montague.'

There was loud applause and everyone stood up and started talking at once. Humphrey walked over and patted my shoulder. Alex was smiling, and I went up to him and shook hands.

'Better tell that silversmith of yours to make a second trophy, Percy old fellow,' Humphrey sang out.

'Gentlemen!' Percy shouted above the hubbub. 'Gentlemen, your attention please!'

One by one we fell silent and turned to look at him.

'Gentlemen, this eventuality was anticipated,' he said. 'So we have prepared a tiebreaker.'

That certainly got everyone's attention. The competition, it seemed, was far from over.

Chapter 24

'Since Alex and James have been judged equal,' Percy said, 'they will take no further part in the proceedings. Their slaves will each give the other a dozen strokes, in any fashion they choose, and the four of us will vote on who gives the best display of flogging.'

This was good news, surely? An experienced spanker such as Irene would have an enormous advantage over a novice. Not that I was familiar with Zuleika's history - she might have flogged her way from Addis Ababa to London, for all I knew. But there was one obvious danger, and I decided to tackle it head on.

'I do have one condition,' I said. 'My slave's breasts are not to be beaten. Zuleika must promise not to touch them, even. Is this acceptable?' I looked at Alex as I asked the question, and he shrugged.

'No objection here,' he said, turning to Zuleika.

'I will not touch your slave's teats,' the black woman said softly.

I looked at Percy and nodded. 'We are agreed, then,' he said. 'Excellent. The contestants will now draw for position.'

Parker brought forth his bag once more, and Irene and Zuleika each took out a token. Irene was again fortunate in the draw, in that she would perform last.

Everyone settled back in their seats, and the mood in the room was one of pleasurable anticipation. Even Belinda appeared to have calmed down, and now regarded the two protagonists with interest.

Zuleika led Irene to the centre of the circle, and looked her up and down. She seemed less than impressed at what she saw, and tugged at Irene's undergarments almost with scorn.

'Take off these rags,' she said contemptuously.

I assumed she was attempting to intimidate her challenger by deriding her garb in this way. The ploy was unsuccessful, however, for the governess appeared quite calm as she removed her things.

'Lie down on the floor,' Zuleika said, 'and spread your legs.'

Irene lay down as instructed. Zuleika kneeled between her parted thighs and stared at her breasts. 'Indeed, you have fine big teats,' she said, 'for a white lady.'

I watched her closely, ready to intervene if she tried to handle them, but she made no such move.

'It is sad,' she went on, 'that I am not allowed to touch them. You, however, are free to do so - and I tell you to stretch them. Do it now.'

'Stretch... my breasts?' Irene said uncertainly.

'Take hold of your nipples,' Zuleika said impatiently. 'Pinch them hard, like this.' The black girl demonstrated by taking her own nipples between thumb and forefinger, and Irene mimicked her. 'Now pull,' Zuleika said. 'Pull them up. Stretch them up.'

Again she demonstrated, pulling on her nipples to distend her breasts. Possibly Irene could have refused, as this was an infringement of the spirit of my agreement with Alex, if not the word. She did not, however, but pulled her own nipples as Zuleika had done. Her breasts assumed a pagoda-like shape, and someone, Humphrey, I think, muttered in approval. Zuleika seemed less happy with the results.

'You think that is stretching them?' she said scornfully. 'Pull harder, bitch woman, or I will have Parker pull them for you. He made no promises, did he?'

I would not have allowed that, needless to say; nor was it a serious threat on her part. Zuleika was merely attempting to browbeat her rival. In fact, despite Zuleika's derisive dismissal of her efforts, I could see that Irene was making a genuine attempt to do as ordered. And it was evidently causing her considerable pain, possibly from the strapping, possibly since nipples are sensitive, and do not appreciate being pinched and tugged in this fashion.

Zuleika now released her own breasts, put her hands on Irene's parted thighs, just above the knee, and then ran them slowly up to her groin. She fingered Irene's labia, seeking out her clitoris. There was a question in my mind as to whether all this was strictly within the rules, but of one thing I was certain - not a man there was about to challenge it.

'In the place where I was born,' Zuleika said, 'it is the custom for the clitoris to be cut off. The old women of the village do it, with a piece of broken glass, when girls reach the age to be married.'

She dragged her fingernail across Irene Hammond's clitoris mimicking the slicing action. The governess flinched.

'They did this to my friend, Udela,' Zuleika added. 'Her screams were most terrible to hear. They wanted to do it to me also, but I fought them, and the next day I ran away from the village. I left my homeland and ran all the way to this beautiful green country of yours.' She glanced up at Alex, favouring him with a sly smile. He chuckled and shook his head, as if at some secret shared.

'If you were my slave,' Zuleika said, turning her attention to Irene once more, 'I would do this to you, slowly, so that you would know great pain.'

Irene shivered and Zuleika laughed softly. She looked up again, and now it was my turn to come under the mocking gaze of those dark eyes. It takes more than looks to intimidate a Montague, however, even a look from a beautiful black witch, and I merely smiled.

'But I am not your master,' she said. 'I am a mere slave, like you. Still, it may be that I can arrange for a little pain, just a little, to give you a taste of what Udela was forced to endure.'

She rose and went to the black lacquered box, returning with one of the silver egg pendants. She knelt down as before and fastened the clip to Irene's clitoris. The governess whined and reached to her groin, but Zuleika anticipated this and caught her wrists, and the two of them struggled briefly.

'He has a harsh bite, does he not,' Zuleika said, 'my little silver friend? He comes from my country too, this crocodile, as you name him.'

Irene soon ceased struggling, and lay there panting, her eyes shut tight.

'Up!' Zuleika commanded. 'Get up, now!' She rose and pulled on Irene's wrists, the governess started to rise, and the pendant, which lay on her belly, slid down between her legs.

'Aahhh!' she gasped. 'Wait...'

The pendant had clearly jerked the chain, causing the clip to tug on her clitoris, but Zuleika had little sympathy for her rival's predicament and hauled on her arms. 'Up!' she repeated, dragging Irene to her feet.

The governess rose, and as the weight came clear of the floor she let out a shriek.

Her knees sagged and it seemed as though she would sink back to the floor, but Zuleika was having none of that and forced the governess to her feet, pulling her to where Alex was sitting. Within a step or two Irene's knee caught the weight, and set it swinging. She whined once more and hobbled rather than walked.

'Stand facing my master,' the black girl commanded. 'Adopt the monkey position.'

Irene shook her head. 'I don't... the monkey position?'

'As I did, fool!' Zuleika snapped. 'Spread your legs and bend your knees. Do you know nothing?'

Irene Hammond adopted the half-squat stance. It was a most degrading position, and despite all her other problems the governess flushed scarlet.

'Stretch your teats,' Zuleika commanded once more, and Irene did so. Zuleika asked for a cane, and Percy handed her one. She positioned herself behind Irene Hammond and struck her twice on her buttocks. These were hard strokes, as Irene's cry testified. Her hips jerked and this set the weight swinging once again, compounding her misery.

Zuleika gave her no time to reflect on this, for she took her arm again and led her across the circle to Percy, sitting opposite. The bow-legged shuffle the governess was obliged to adopt caused her further humiliation, if such a thing were possible. The Spankers seemed to find it most entertaining, however, and first Percy and then Nigel had an opportunity to witness both Irene's shame and her pain at close quarters.

Zuleika led her on again. I knew Irene's buttocks would be burning cruelly by now, but she did not ask permission to rub - she must have known Zuleika would refuse. The governess had little option, therefore, but to grit her teeth and carry on as best she could.

Humphrey and Jasper followed Percy; and then it was my turn.

I don't know if Zuleika left me till last intentionally, but I thought it likely. As Irene's 'master', I had a special relationship with her, and for her to be humbled in front of me would be especially demeaning.

Once more the governess was made to adopt the 'monkey position' and stretch her breasts; and Zuleika duly delivered the final two strokes. These were, without a doubt, the hardest of the lot and Irene cried out loudly - a most heartrending sound. Her knees straightened as she took the strokes so that she ended up on her toes, straining upwards. But take them she did, and at last it was over - or almost so. Zuleika had still to remove the clip, and remembering how much that had hurt when I conducted my 'experiment', I did not envy Irene Hammond the experience.

It was done in the end, though, and the governess could finally, truly, relax.

Zuleika's performance, I had to admit, was an extraordinary one - stylish, imaginative, and most important of all, supremely entertaining. I doubted whether any man in the room could better it. I knew that I, personally, could not, and though I did not underestimate Irene Hammond's expertise in this field, I judged that she too had met her match. The sixty guineas would go to Zuleika and the title to Alex. It would be churlish to begrudge either of them their well earned victory, though it was only human to feel disappointment, and to wish it could have been otherwise.

If Irene Hammond was dismayed by her opponent's performance, it didn't show in her face. She appeared quite calm as she led Zuleika towards me. The black woman was wearing a sly smile, as though the prize was already in her hand.

'Lay across my master's knee,' the governess said. 'Face to his left.' Zuleika obediently draped herself over my lap, her belly pressing on my thighs. 'Open your legs,' Mrs Hammond commanded, and again Zuleika complied without hesitation.

'Would you be so good as to hold her, sir?' Mrs Hammond asked of me. 'Here...' She took my left hand and guided it to Zuleika's left breast, which I dutifully grasped. 'And here...' The governess directed my right hand to the black woman's groin, and I looked up at her, not sure precisely what she wished of me. By way of explanation she took hold of Zuleika's labia and stretched it.

'Kindly pinch hold here, sir,' the governess said. 'You will need to nip hard, as she will most certainly jump when I strike.'

An invitation to nip a beautiful woman's vulva is not something that comes along every day, and I lost no time in complying. Zuleika grunted.

'Are you pinching hard, sir?' the governess enquired.

'Yes I am.'

'And your left hand, sir? Do you have a firm grip there also?'

'Oh, indeed,' I assured her. 'Any firmer and we'll have to ask Parker to fetch a pail for the milk.' There were chuckles from several of the attendees, but Zuleika did not join in. The fact that I was squeezing breast and labia as though my very life depended on it may have had something to do with it.

'Thank you, sir,' the governess said. 'Then with your permission, we will begin. A single stroke only, at this time.'

She took a half step back, raised her arm, and delivered a mighty swipe across Zuleika's buttocks. Predictably the black woman squawked and recoiled on my lap. My grip proved sufficient to the task, however, and she didn't rise far.

'Thank you, sir,' Irene said. 'Your assistance is much appreciated. Up, you black trollop - do you think to lie there all day?'

This last question was underscored by a slap of the tawse across Zuleika's shoulder. I released her, and she stood up.

'No mean feat,' Belinda confided to her husband in a whisper that could be heard clear across the room, 'getting Jamie to let go of a shapely bubbie.'

'You ought to know, my dear,' Nigel retorted dryly.

Irene led a noticeably less exuberant Zuleika to Humphrey, on my left, and lay her across his lap in turn. He needed no invitation to take hold of her as I had done, nor any instruction, having my example to follow. The single stroke was repeated, and from the viewpoint of spectator, rather than participant, I could see the effort Mrs Hammond put into the blow. No wonder poor Zuleika warbled.

The circuit continued, and eventually they came around to me once more.

'Please take hold as before, sir,' Irene said.

'Gladly,' I said. 'Though perhaps not *precisely* as before. With your permission, madam, I would like to try a more localised grip.'

With my left and right hands respectively, I sought out Zuleika's nipple and clitoris. 'A nub hold, to be precise,' I added, pinching them between thumb and forefinger. Zuleika wriggled and squeaked in surprise; and every man there laughed.

'Trust you, James,' Jasper chortled. 'Bravo!'

I glanced up at Irene Hammond, and she acknowledged my small contribution with a smile. I winked to let her know there was more to come, and pressed hard with both thumbnails against the nubs in question. Zuleika squealed as though hot needles had been driven into her tender flesh, and tried to get up.

'Down!' Irene Hammond barked. 'Stay down, wretch!' She grabbed the back of Zuleika's neck and forced her head down. 'Keep still, you miserable creature, or I swear you'll start over again, rules or no rules!'

There was undeniable power and authority in her voice, and when she released Zuleika a few moments later the black woman remained still, though she trembled in my lap, whimpering softly.

'And bravo Irene,' Percy said quietly.

'Hear, hear,' Nigel concurred.

It was a repeat of the previous round. Irene Hammond delivered another of her scorchers, Zuleika wailed, and the pair of them moved on. I noticed that every man bar one chose to adopt the 'nub hold'; Alex declined, out of loyalty to his slave. Jasper, grinning evilly, drew a positive shriek from the poor girl as he nipped her clitoris - presumably his nails were extra long and sharp.

'Perhaps,' Irene suggested sweetly, 'you should have let the old women cut it off while you had the chance.'

Zuleika had no answer, or perhaps her mind was on other matters, such as the fire raging in her rear end, which Irene further fuelled with another sizzling stroke, and then they moved on to Nigel, and finally to Percy.

With the second circuit complete, Zuleika could rise and dry her cheeks and return to her master, considerably more subdued, I noticed, than when she started.

I thought we could not have wished for better performances, for both had been splendid. Zuleika's was again the more novel, in my opinion; her humiliation of Irene Hammond beautifully executed. The sight of the governess standing straddle-legged, clitoris clipped and distended, stretching her breasts, was an image that would stay with me forever.

Mrs Hammond, on the other hand, allowed each one of us to take an active part in Zuleika's punishment - and in a most unusual and stimulating fashion. Another memory I would treasure was the feel of Zuleika's breast in my hand, and the way she squirmed when I nipped her nubs.

On the face of it there was little to choose between them. There was one final factor, however, that just might tip the balance. In the aftermath of her flogging, Zuleika's buttocks exhibited a single raised band barely wider than the tawse that was used on her. Every one of the twelve strokes had landed in precisely the same position. This was no easy thing, and veteran spankers would appreciate the skill involved.

On the other hand, for all Zuleika's flair and imagination her actual technique left something to be desired. The strokes had been decidedly wayward, as evidenced by the weals on Irene Hammond's rear. Some were high, almost on her lower back, whilst others adorned her upper thighs. Direction and strength also showed considerable variation, and the overall impression, I have to say, was one of poor control.

While we were waiting for the vote I told Irene she should dress. She did so, taking care when covering her breasts to touch the left one as little as possible.

'Gentlemen, we have a winner,' Percy declared solemnly. 'As eighteen ninety-two flogging champion - or perhaps I should say "champions", in view of her contribution in the tie-breaker - I give you...'

He paused, and looked at the cards once more, and if I didn't know better I'd swear the rascal was toying with Alex and me.

'I give you - James Montague and Irene!'

There was a loud burst of applause, and cries of 'Well done!' and similar from the assembly. Even Alex was grinning, appearing not to resent my triumph, though no doubt he was disappointed, as I would have been in his place.

I stepped forward and took a bow, trying to look suitably modest in victory. Indeed, the success had little enough to do with me, and I insisted the real winner step forward to receive her accolade. Irene curtseyed, looking just as pleased as I felt.

The trophy was presented, to Irene, at my insistence, and what a marvellous thing it was indeed - a pair of figures beautifully crafted in solid silver, mounted on a polished marble pedestal. And if the diminutive maid touching her toes, skirts up and drawers down, looked somewhat like Tess, and the man wielding the cane more than a little like Percy, I did not begrudge our host that.

Servants then arrived bearing trays of drinks and snacks, and the party started to break up into separate groups. Nigel and Belinda joined Irene and me, and Nigel shook my hand warmly.

'Congratulations, Jamie,' Belinda said, beaming. 'Though I think it's Irene who deserves—'

'Nigel,' Percy called out, 'a word with your slave, if you would be so kind.'

Belinda froze and the smile vanished. She turned to face Percy.

'I believe we have unfinished business, madam,' he said coolly.

I'd been so taken up with the contest I'd almost forgotten about Belinda's transgression. Percy's next words quite shattered my good mood, and robbed the victory of its sweetness.

'I promised you four dozen, I recall,' he said.

'Yes, sir,' she replied meekly. 'I'm very sorry, sir. My behaviour was inexcusable.' Her contrition seemed genuine enough, though one could never be totally sure of anything with Belinda.

'I must say, Percy,' Nigel chipped in, 'four dozen seems harsh to me. She spoke out in the heat of the moment, nothing more.'

Though it was loyal of Nigel to come to his wife's aid in this fashion, it would have been wiser to keep silent. Percy, as event host, had responsibility for maintaining order among the slaves, and had been entirely within his rights in disciplining Belinda. Nigel's intervention appeared to challenge Percy's authority, though I'm sure that was the last thing on Nigel's mind.

Percy was not pleased; that much was clear. He stiffened and looked down his nose at Nigel.

'Yet she spoke,' he said, 'and spoke again, despite repeated warnings from both of us.' Every person in the room, it seemed, was hanging on Percy's pronouncement. 'The four dozen stand,' he said.

Belinda dropped her gaze, and Nigel turned away from us.

'Parker,' Percy said, 'you will bend this lady over a chair and give her four dozen strokes with a heavy cane on her bare buttocks. Have Baxter hold her wrists. I want fully severe strokes, mind. Make sure she feels each and every one of them.'

He cast his glance over the rest of us. 'Should any of you gentlemen wish to witness the punishment, you are more than welcome to stay.'

'Yes indeed, old man!' Jasper enthused.

'I will,' Alex added.

'And I,' Nigel said quietly.

I had no desire to see Belinda humiliated in this way, and indicated to Irene that we were leaving. Humphrey and Donnett also came away.

As we four left the room Jasper came hurrying after us, calling out my name. Since he was the last person in the world with whom I wished to converse at that moment, I pretended not to hear and walked on. The fellow actually had the temerity to put his hand on my shoulder, and I turned and gave him my coldest look.

'Jamie, old fellow,' he said, as though we were lifelong friends, 'ever considered selling this governess of yours?'

The question took the wind right out of my sails, so unexpected was it. Trust Jasper to come up with something so outrageous. Humphrey smiled and seized the chance to slip away with his companion, leaving Irene and myself alone with Jasper.

'*Selling* her?' I said. 'Never in a million years—'

'I'll give you three thousand guineas for her,' Jasper cut in.

I stared at him in astonishment. Spankers Seven members occasionally traded servants, but the sums involved were generally in the hundreds. Though we called them 'slaves', they were not slaves in any true sense, to be bought and sold like cattle. It was more in the way of a transfer of labour from one employer to another, and a corresponding transfer of cash in the opposite direction to cover the cost of obtaining a replacement. I could think of no occasion when the sum had reached a thousand, even; and as for three...

'Three *thousand?*' I said. 'Is this some sort of jest? If so, I quite fail to see—'

'I'm perfectly serious,' he said, interrupting me once again. 'Never more so, in fact.'

I was about to tell him to go to blazes when I happened to glance at Mrs Hammond. Her face had turned deathly pale and bore an expression of utter consternation. And that, of course, put an entirely different complexion on things.

'I see,' I said slowly. 'Three thousand guineas - that's a great deal of money, isn't it? A *great* deal. I'm tempted, Jasper, I have to say.' I heard a hiss as Irene sucked in her breath, but I ploughed on regardless. 'If I do sell her to you,' I said, glancing at the governess, her expression an absolute picture, 'what then? You have no wife, no children. What on earth would you *do* with a governess, Jasper?'

'Oh, there's no need to concern yourself on that score, old man,' he said. 'I can think of a good many things. Yes indeed - a *good* many things.'

He stared at Irene Hammond like a fox eyeing a chicken, and had the effrontery to raise his hand as though to touch her breast - her left breast, I noted. At that moment there came the sound of cane striking flesh, followed by a most terrible cry from Belinda. Jasper's head whipped round, dismay written all over his face.

'It seems you're missing the show,' I said. The cane struck again and Belinda's tortured cry was even louder than before.

'Your answer?' Jasper said.

I took hold of Irene's arm and drew her away from him. 'Regretfully, I shall have to decline,' I said. 'Mrs Hammond is a jewel beyond price. Good day to you, Jasper.'

I turned and led her away. She was trembling with fright and I began to regret tormenting her in such a way. Mischievousness is natural in a boy, but is less excusable in a grown man. I really must learn to curb these adolescent impulses - though Irene's face, I have to say, had been truly wondrous to behold.

'Four thousand!' Jasper shouted after me.

I felt the governess stiffen, and squeezed her arm reassuringly. 'Good day, Jasper,' I sang out, without looking back.

We crossed the hall and mounted the stairs. By the time we reached the sanctuary of our room I could no longer hear the sounds of punishment from the ballroom.

Bedding Irene that night was exceptionally satisfying, I have to say. Her breasts were too sore to be fondled, so I was denied that pleasure, and her buttocks most painful also. I was careful, therefore, to select positions that afforded her the minimum discomfort.

Afterwards we lay together, Irene's head on my chest, and my arm around her shoulder.

'May I ask you a question, sir?' she asked.

'Of course,' I said. 'And you may address me as James when we're alone.' In view of everything we had shared, the familiarity did not seem out of place. I was confident also she would not attempt to take advantage of it.

'James, then,' she said. 'My question is this. After the competition, when Mr Jasper offered to buy me, you intended all along to turn him down, did you not?'

'I did.'

'But you pretended to consider it... why? Just to torture me?'

'Well,' I said, 'perhaps "torture" is putting it a little strongly. Let's just say I have a somewhat warped sense of humour.'

She was silent for perhaps a whole minute, as though digesting this. Then a strange statement followed. 'I gather you don't believe in heaven and hell.'

'Quite correct,' I said, puzzled by this new direction. 'I don't, in fact.'

'That's fortunate.' I heard the smile in her voice, and thought I could guess what she was driving at.

'You're saying I'm destined for the fiery pit in the afterlife? Or would be, if I believed in an afterlife.'

'For terrorising me beyond belief?' she said. 'Almost certainly.'

I had no doubts that she was right. If wilful cruelty is a passport to hell - and if indeed there is a hell - there's little doubt where I am bound. Considering everything I put her through, it's a miracle Irene stayed with me. Jasper wasn't alone, I supposed, in wishing to take her off my hands.

'Would you prefer some other master?' I asked, almost casually, but as soon as the words were out the strangest thing happened. I suddenly realised that her answer was of the utmost importance to me. I didn't want to be without her, ever.

'No, sir,' she said, and I could breathe again.

'James,' I said automatically.

'James. I am most happy in your employment. Of all the men here you're the only one who considers my pleasure and my needs just as much as his own.'

'Ah,' I said. 'Bed.'

'In bed, certainly. I reach my climax every time we make love. Since we arrived here I have reached it with only one of the others.'

'Humphrey,' I said, knowing it was he, but not knowing how I knew.

She declined to answer, and she was right not to do so. It was most indelicate of me even to ask. 'In bed,' she said, 'but out of it, too. You grant me free rein in the disciplining of two young men. You trust me not only in the schooling of your wards, but also in the choice of a new cook. You allow me to assist with the punishment of the girls. In Elizabeth's case, you even asked me to administer her strokes, when I know that is a duty you are most eager to discharge in person. In short, James, you treat me as an equal; and for that I am more grateful than you can ever know.'

I was rather taken aback by her words, truth to tell, for I had never thought of it in those terms. I wasn't even sure I merited her good opinion, as these things she credited me with had happened more by accident than design. Perhaps it was guilt at this undeserved praise that made me play devil's advocate.

'I also beat you,' I pointed out.

'You have,' she said, 'twice, prior to the festival. The first time I fully deserved it. The second I am less sure about. I half suspect a subterfuge, though I cannot imagine how it was arranged. I think probably I shall never know the truth of it.'

One thing was certain - she would never hear it from me. And since Rose was unlikely to speak up, Irene would just have to learn to live with the incertitude.

'You don't resent being beaten?' I asked.

'Resent it?' she said. 'No, I don't resent it. How can I hold it against you, when you're simply doing that which I enjoy doing myself?' That did seem, I have to say, inordinately fair-minded of her.

'I don't enjoy being beaten,' she went on thoughtfully. 'I tell myself if I am diligent and hardworking I may never have to endure another, but I suspect I am being overly optimistic. I do pray I never have to experience another five dozen, however.'

Part of me, the maudlin part, wanted to promise her she would never have to suffer again; but another part, the more realistic, cynical part, told me I was being a sentimental fool. At some point in the future I would wish to spank her again. Indeed, just thinking about the possibility made me want to spank her right then. She would commit some error, or I would concoct one, and that would be all the excuse I would need to tell her to bend. I held my tongue, therefore, and made no promises I could not keep.

Chapter 25

The following morning, as we were making ready to depart, I enquired of Nigel whether it might be possible to have a quick word with Belinda, as she hadn't attended him at breakfast. He seemed withdrawn and uncommunicative, which was most unlike him, and all he would say was that his wife was 'indisposed'. I knew then it was as I'd feared - Belinda's punishment had been terrible indeed. Possibly it would be some days before she was able to travel, but there was nothing I could do to help so I simply asked him to pass on to Belinda my respects, and my wish for a speedy recovery.

'Much appreciated, James,' he said quietly. 'Perhaps you could visit us in a few months' time - Humphrey too. It'll be just like old times, won't it? Just the four of us, together.'

I thanked him, and said that sounded most agreeable. The coach arrived to take Humphrey, Donnett, Irene and me to the station, and I shook hands with Nigel and climbed aboard. Percy, Alex and Jasper came out to see us off, and my last glimpse from the coach window showed the three of them waving, and Nigel also, standing a little apart from the rest.

The train journey home was uneventful. Humphrey and I chatted about the events of the past few days, and agreed that this year's festival, though certainly different, had been a success.

'It lacked one thing only,' Humphrey declared, turning to Mrs Hammond with a smile, 'and that was the chance to put dear Irene through her paces.'

Given that she had shared his bed, his use of her first name was acceptable, I supposed. Certainly she did not seem to mind, for her own smile held a certain warmth, even affection.

'Forgive me, sir,' she replied, 'but I seem to recall otherwise. Just yesterday, in fact - during a certain competition?'

Humphrey gave a snort of pretended derision. 'Oh poo, a few strokes only! I meant a *real* session, five or six dozen at least, with a chance to lay 'em on good and hard!'

Of one thing I was confident - Humphrey had never laid on 'good and hard' in his entire life. It was evident that Irene knew this, or guessed it, for her eyes positively twinkled with humour as she replied.

'Indeed, sir, that does sound most appealing. My bottom is positively distraught at the loss.'

The hussy was actually flirting with him! Perhaps I shouldn't have been surprised, for Humphrey always did have a way with the ladies. What was surprising, however, was my own reaction. If I didn't know better, I would say I was jealous. Ridiculous, of course - yet I was pleased when we reached Beckton Measby station, and Humphrey and Donnett left the train. Oddly enough, though I now had Irene Hammond all to myself, we completed the remainder of our journey in silence.

Safely ensconced in my study once more, I sent for Elizabeth and demanded a full report on everything that had occurred during my absence. Her answer was that nothing whatsoever had happened; certainly nothing out of the ordinary.

'That's reassuring,' I said, 'if perhaps a little dull. And tell me, how many punishments have you administered during the week?'

'As many as were necessary, uncle,' she replied. 'None.'

'*None?*' I echoed. 'You must tell me the secret of your success, my dear. Getting staff to perform satisfactorily without flogging them is no easy matter. Although perhaps we'd better make sure everything *is* satisfactory before handing out any laurels, eh? Kindly accompany me on a tour of inspection.'

The two of us went from room to room, and as I suspected, the house was in a pitifully neglected state. Dust was in evidence on furniture and picture frames, carpets were in need of a good brushing, and as for the silver, I doubt it had been polished since the day I left.

'What do you expect, uncle?' Elizabeth said calmly when I pointed all this out to her. 'There's far too much work for two maids and one hall-boy. A house this size needs three times that number.'

This was overt criticism of my management of household affairs, a thing I was not prepared to countenance. 'I will not have my methods questioned, Elizabeth,' I said coldly. 'I shall punish Alice and Rose for slovenly work, and I expect Mrs Hammond will make her displeasure with Willy equally plain.'

She stiffened. 'The servants are not to blame,' she said, in a tone as icy as my own. 'They were acting under my instructions. If you are determined to punish someone, then let it be me.'

I laughed without humour. 'Oh rest assured, Elizabeth, you won't be spared. Though their punishment will be harsh indeed, for failing in your duty yours will be crueller by far.'

We returned to the study, and having made the decision to punish Alice and Rose, I advised Elizabeth she would remain and witness their castigation. To judge from her expression she viewed the prospect with dismay, even alarm.

'I would rather wait outside, uncle,' she said faintly.

'I do not doubt it,' I said. 'Nevertheless, you will do as I say. By your own admission, the responsibility for their error is yours. It is only right and proper you should observe the consequence of your actions.'

I tugged on both bell-pulls to summon Alice and Rose simultaneously, and while we waited for them I went to the cupboard and took out the heavy cane. Elizabeth watched in silence, angry with me still, I knew, but more than a little apprehensive into the bargain.

The two maids duly arrived. They must have guessed what was in store for them, for they looked none too happy as they stood before me. Even Rose's customary impertinence was noticeable by its absence.

'I am most dissatisfied with the state of this house,' I said to them. 'It is clear to me you have both been slacking in my absence, and for that there is but one remedy.' As I was speaking I noticed they both glanced at Elizabeth. If they were looking to her to save them, they were in for a disappointment.

I had them bring a chair apiece out to the middle of the room, place them side by side, and stand facing them. I then told them to bend over and place their hands on the seats, whereupon I raised their skirts and lowered their drawers in the usual manner. The two maids waited side by side, buttocks bared for whatever I chose to inflict upon them. I contemplated this happy scene for a moment or two before announcing their fate.

'Two dozen each,' I said, 'and you have Miss Elizabeth to thank that it is so few. She took the blame upon herself, and pleaded for clemency on your behalf; otherwise it would have been four dozen.'

Since it was Elizabeth's misguided liberalism that got them into this mess in the first place, I didn't think they would be too enamoured of her, but at least I had done my best to set the record straight. It would be unfair to lead them to think their mistress, having condoned their misdeeds, had callously abandoned them to their fate.

I flexed the cane and eyed the unfortunate girl closest to me, namely Rose. I drew back my arm and whipped the cane across her buttocks. She gave a shriek of pain and stood up straight; then shot me a fearful glance and quickly assumed the position once more, pulling her skirts hastily up about her waist.

Her reaction was perhaps understandable. In the past, with the principle of escalation in mind, I had invariably started out relatively modestly. Not so today, however. Every single stroke was to be a hard one.

'Yes indeed,' I snapped. 'You will remain bent over, unless you wish me to reconsider the two dozen.'

The room was deadly silent, and Rose trembled as she awaited the onslaught. Alice, waiting her turn, trembled even more.

I swung the cane and struck Rose a second time, and then a few seconds later, a third. The force was no greater or less than the first, but she was expecting it now and was able to control her reaction. She still let out a most pitiful cry and jerked as though branded, but her grip on the chair seat remained firm, and she did not rise from her allotted position.

I paused after the third, and stepped forward to bring myself in line with Alice. She whimpered, and her legs shook dreadfully. A punishee of no small experience herself, she knew from Rose's reaction just how bad this would be.

I did not disappoint her, delivering the three strokes with gusto. Now Alice generally took her punishments in virtual silence, a firm stroke drawing from her lips a gasp or faint hiss at most, but these strokes were considerably harder than normal and poor Alice wailed just as loudly as Rose before her, gripping the seat so hard her knuckles showed white.

With Alice's three delivered it was back to the older girl once more; and so it went on, with me moving back and forth between the pair of them, delivering the cruel strokes three at a time.

I paused somewhat longer after the first dozen. They would be expecting a change of position, of course; but instead I had them remain there while I surveyed the damage. Their pale buttocks carried virtually identical marks, for I had been as even-handed as possible, favouring neither one nor the other. The weals were deep red, tinged with purple. The skin was not broken, but I judged it had been a close thing.

'One dozen gone,' I said, 'one dozen still to go.'

I positioned myself behind Rose once more, glancing at Elizabeth to see how she was bearing up. Her face was very pale; so deathly white, in fact, that I feared she might swoon. Watching a punishment can be trying indeed for those of a sensitive nature, and this, the first she had ever witnessed, was clearly having a profound effect on Elizabeth - not forgetting that her own punishment was still to come. Since fussing over her was out of the question, I could do little but carry on and hope she remained upright.

The next set was harder on the two maids. I am not without compassion, and I pitied them during their trial, but easing up now was out of the question. Call it a matter of principle, call it respect for my grandfather's spirit... call it what you will; I simply could not do it. I had promised Elizabeth that Alice and Rose would receive a severe punishment, and I was honour-bound to deliver one.

And deliver it I did - in threes, as before - each fierce stroke drawing the most wretched cry from the recipient. I had a concern that Alice in particular might not have the will to see it through to the end, but surprisingly it was Rose who broke first. On the eighth stroke of the second set, with just four remaining, she stood up and clutched her bottom.

'Down!' I roared. 'Get back down! An additional six strokes for both of you!' She looked at me, and Alice turned her tear-streaked face to me also. I had never seen such abject misery in my life, and I hastily amended my decision. 'Unless you bend over this very instant, that is,' I growled, trying not to make it sound like an afterthought.

Rose quickly resumed her position. The last few strokes were truly dreadful for both of them, but finally it was over and they could stand up, and pull up their drawers slowly and with great care, and straighten their skirts, and wipe their faces with their handkerchiefs.

Often at this point I would deliver some suitably stern reprise, but I felt on this occasion the cane had spoken far more eloquently than I ever could, so I kept it brief.

'You may now go to your rooms,' I said. 'You are excused duties for the remainder of the day.' I realise that I was sending conflicting messages, in that I had just punished them for slackness and was now giving them the day off. Practical considerations ruled, however. I thought it unlikely they could manage much more than to lay facedown on their beds for the next few hours.

They bobbed and walked stiffly from the room, and as they departed I did wonder briefly whether I had been too hard on them. They were acting upon Elizabeth's instructions, after all, and following orders is all any servant can be expected to do. But anyone with a brain in her head would know what my response was likely to be. If they couldn't see that, then they deserved the two dozen for rank stupidity.

With the two maids out of the way I turned my attention to the chief defaulter. 'Elizabeth,' I said, 'I trust that was a salutary lesson, for you as well as those two unfortunate young women.'

'Indeed,' she replied, so softly I strained to hear it. Her face was as pale as before, but the swoon I feared had not materialised. I should never have doubted her, for Elizabeth was made of sterner stuff than that.

'I think,' I said, 'I shall have you naked before I pronounce sentence.'

Elizabeth gave me a look, but seemed disinclined to argue the point - which was most wise of her, considering her present situation. She started to unbutton her dress, a task I was obliged to finish for her. She shrugged off the garment and cast it to the floor

'I promised you that your punishment would be crueller by far than theirs,' I said, struggling somewhat with the lacing on her corset. 'Do you recall my words?'

'Yes, uncle.' Once divested of that recalcitrant item, she was able to manage the rest for herself. Shoes and undergarments followed dress and corset to the floor. Her stockings came off last of all, and she stood up straight. I allowed my eyes to track slowly over her, taking in her magnificence. The temptation to order her onto the couch was - as any man with eyes in his head and blood in his veins would understand - almost irresistible, but I managed to control my urges.

I flexed the cane and examined it closely for signs of distress, for a cane that breaks during use can skewer the penitent with sharp splinters. Satisfied, I swished it through the air and saw Elizabeth flinch at the sound. She had tasted the cane before, of course, at Irene Hammond's hand. Four dozen strokes in total, though for the first three the governess had used a tawse. That final dozen though, with the cane, would have given her some notion of what Rose and Alice had just endured.

I swished the cane again, to torment her.

'What might a punishment crueller by far than two dozen entail?' I asked. 'Four dozen? Five? Six dozen, even?'

She dropped her gaze, and said not a word. I waited, watching her face, wondering if she would break down. It would be only human to burst into tears and beg for forgiveness. Many would. Somehow I knew Elizabeth would not.

The seconds ticked slowly by. Elizabeth remained still, with just the twitch of a muscle in her cheek to betray her nervousness. And still she did not speak.

'Very well,' I said. 'Consider yourself punished, Elizabeth. I trust you will never again fail me in this way.'

For a moment she did not respond, then she looked up quickly, hope written across her beautiful face.

'Watching others suffer whilst waiting for punishment oneself can be cruel indeed, can it not?'

She nodded slowly. 'It can.' A shiver ran through her, and she began to fidget. Now that the dreadful threat was past, reaction had set in. She would find it difficult to keep her hands still unless she could find something to occupy them, which was an interesting thought, to be sure. The word 'masturbation' was probably unknown to her, but that was easily remedied.

'You are duly grateful, I trust, to be spared the rod?' I said.

'More than you know, uncle,' she said feelingly.

I walked over to the cabinet and picked up a brandy glass, then carried it to the couch and sat down. I unbuttoned my trousers and took out a rod of a very different kind.

'Then come over here, Elizabeth,' I said, 'and show me just *how* grateful.'

Chapter 26

Passing Rose in the hall one evening, still busy at her work at the end of a long day, I couldn't help but notice how weary she looked. Though I had admonished Elizabeth for challenging me on this selfsame subject, I knew she was right. Absorbed as I had been with other matters, I had let the question of additional staff drift for too long, and I resolved to do something about it forthwith.

Though my concern over Rose and Alice's well-being was genuine, it was not my sole motive. Extra maids meant extra bottoms to spank, which was never a bad thing. As my grandfather used to say: 'You can never have too much land, too much money, or too many female bums to thrash.' In this, as in so many things, he was perfectly correct.

Finding suitable girls, it has to be said, was never going to be easy. That they should be honest, industrious and presentable went without saying, but - and this was the difficult part - they must also be prepared to take a beating. It was not absolutely essential that they take it in good spirit, but take one they must.

In this matter of 'new blood', I felt I had already exhausted all the likely possibilities in the immediate area, and resolved therefore to look further afield. Once again I turned to the ever-reliable Charlie Spikeman, that veritable human bloodhound, to sniff out a maid or two who might fit the bill. I wrote to him on the matter, not expecting a reply for at least a month. Imagine my surprise, therefore, when a response came just a week later - and a most unusual response at that.

I was in the library at the time, searching out a book on crime and punishment in ancient times, when Mrs Hammond entered. She was bearing a letter, and looking not a little discomposed.

'I'm sorry to trouble you, sir,' she said, 'but there are two women at the servants' entrance with a handcart, who wish to speak with you. They say they've been sent by a Mr Spikeman, and they asked me to give you this.' She handed me the letter. It was addressed to me in a hand I knew as well as my own.

'It's from Spikeman, sure enough,' I said, and opened the letter.

Mr Montague sir,

Forgive my boldness in sending these two girls to you, but an opportunity arose which I did not think wise to pass up. If I have taken too much upon myself, I expect I shall be hearing from you on the matter, but I hope and trust this is not the case.

My enquiries indicate Molly and Mary Tavistock are trustworthy girls and good workers. Mr Keens, their previous master, says he will send a letter with them to explain what is what.

As to that other topic of particular interest to your good self, from what I hear you will not be disappointed, though I am certain you are a better judge in these matters than I.

Yr obedient servant
Charles Spikeman

'I see,' I said, though I wasn't entirely sure that I did. 'I suppose you'd better send them in.'

Molly and Mary Tavistock, as I found out a few moments later, were twins - and identical twins into the bargain. They were robustly built girls of medium height, square-jawed, with plain, strong features. Their attire, I have to say, did not show them to best advantage. Their cheap brown coats were almost threadbare, their boots covered in mud, and their somewhat battered black bonnets looked, not to put too fine a point on it, as if they had been slept in.

They stood before me, watching me with a peculiar intensity that I found a little disturbing, I have to say. Each held a letter clutched tightly in her hand.

'Which one are you?' I asked the one on my right. 'Molly, or Mary?'

'Mary, sir,' she replied.

'And what's that you're holding, Mary?'

She glanced at her sister before speaking. 'A letter, sir.' There was no hint of irony in her voice as she passed it to me, and I formed an instant opinion that Mary

- and by inference, Molly also - was not the sharpest of young women.

The envelope was unsealed, and I opened it and took out a single sheet of paper. In a fine bold hand the writer assured me that the Tavistock sisters Molly and Mary were honest, hard working and reliable, and went on to recommend them unreservedly to any individual or family wanting two dependable maids. He signed himself W. Keens esquire, a name that meant nothing to me.

It was a straightforward enough character reference then, which I slipped back into its envelope and returned to its owner. Her sister Molly handed me her letter in turn. This one was sealed, and addressed to me personally in the same hand. I broke the seal and read on.

My dear sir,

A mutual friend, Lord Mannisham, has advised me that you and I share similar views on the need to maintain strict discipline within a household, so I judge I may speak with you man to man in this matter.

It is with deep regret that I am obliged to discharge Molly and Mary. I am recently married, and their demeanour in general, and manner of speech in particular, are driving my new wife to distraction. Though they are certainly a most unusual pair, I hope that you may learn to tolerate their foibles as I have. I have tried for three years to persuade them to act less strangely, but no amount of flogging seems to make any difference.

Should you decide not to retain them, I beg you to see them well placed if it is at all within your power. They are good girls at heart, though a little simple, and I fear their trusting, not to say naïve, natures would lead to their downfall should they be cast adrift.

I do hope everything turns out well, as I have grown quite fond of the two of them over the years ~ a thing I never expected to hear myself admit.

Yours faithfully
William Keens

P.S. I cannot tell the pair of them apart, even now, and the risk of a miscarriage of justice ~ punishing one girl for the other's mistakes ~ has always seemed unduly high. For this reason I always punished them both, no matter who was at fault ~ an arrangement they appear not to resent in the least. You may wish to consider adopting a similar stratagem.

I put down the letter and regarded the pair of them.

'Well then,' I said, 'I understand you're seeking employment as maids. Are you housemaids? Kitchen maids? Scullery maids?'

'Anythink, sir,' Molly said, her face breaking into a broad grin for reasons that eluded me completely.

'We don't mind,' Mary added, her expression matching that of her sister precisely.

The grins, I decided, were more disturbing even than the stares. Remembering

136

William Keens' letter, I put it down to a lack of wit, and pressed on doggedly.

'When would you be able to start?' I asked.

'Right this minute sir, thank you sir.'

'Our bags is outside, in the handcart.'

'The handcart?' I said, remembering that Irene Hammond had made mention of such a thing.

'Yes, sir,' Molly said. 'The handcart what we brought our things in, sir.'

'From Peterborough, sir. It's a good cart, but one wheel has a squeak.'

'Fair drives you mad, it does, but it's better than carrying the bags on your back.'

Their ping-pong manner of speaking was making me dizzy, and I felt some sympathy with the new Mrs Keens' inability to cope. I also wondered if I'd understood them correctly. Were they really trying to tell me they had pushed this squeaking handcart all the way from Peterborough? Surely not - it was a good ninety miles if it was a yard.

Further questioning revealed that this was precisely what they'd done. It had taken them three days, sleeping under the cart at night by the roadside, and my judgment on the bonnets had been more accurate than I suspected. Not the most usual method of travel, I have to say. On the positive side, it removed any possible concerns over their stamina, even if it did cast serious doubts on their sanity.

I decided to set them on anyway, for a three-month trial period. They were, without a doubt, the strangest two women I had ever met, but if William Keens could cope, then so could I. And, to be frank, the thought of spanking identical twins held considerable appeal, opening up as it did all manner of possibilities in my mind.

I gave them my decision, and their grins reappeared as they thanked me. I sent for Irene Hammond and asked her to see them settled in. With a doubtful glance in my direction, she led the pair away.

The next morning I was woken by the sound of someone singing lustily just outside my bedroom door. It was a good strong voice, but at seven o'clock in the morning that was not the point.

I put on my dressing gown and went out into the passage. One of the Tavistock sisters was on her hands and knees scrubbing the floor, and she looked up at me and smiled.

'Good morning, sir.'

'No,' I snapped, 'it is not! I will not have any singing in this house, do you hear? And most certainly not at this ungodly hour. Report to my study at ten, and we'll see if we can't get you singing a different tune.'

I went back into my room, only remembering Keens' recommendation at the last moment. 'And bring your sister along with you!'

The pair of them stood before me in the study, looking not the least sheepish or contrite. Mrs Hammond had worked wonders with them, I have to say, for they were smartly turned out in crisp new print dresses and clean white caps - their morning uniform.

I told them they were not in Peterborough now, and that in this house we insisted on decorum at all times. This met with blank looks, and I was obliged to explain what the word meant. After that I sentenced them to a dozen apiece, a paltry figure, I know, but it was their first offence, and the rules had not yet been made clear to them. I then fetched the medium tawse from my day collection.

'Which one of you was singing outside my room this morning?' I enquired.

'Me, sir.'

'Molly, is it?'

'Yes, sir.'

'Right then,' I said. 'You can go first.'

'Will you be punishing us yourself, sir?' she enquired.

'Why, who else?' I said, somewhat perplexed by the question.

'Our previous master used to have us do it, sir.'

'He said it was better that working up a lather,' Mary added.

They seemed perfectly serious about this, and my first reaction was to dismiss the idea as nonsensical, but then I reconsidered. Why not, indeed? It would be different, at least, and it might prove entertaining.

'Very well,' I said. 'But be warned - if this is a trick to get off lightly it won't work. If I think you're holding back you'll get a further dozen each from me, is that understood?'

I handed the tawse to Mary, and sat down to watch.

'I usually start, sir,' Molly said, taking the tawse from her sister's hand.

Mary gave it up without protest, and indeed, she looked rather relieved. With sudden insight I realised Molly was the dominant twin, and thinking back, I decided she was the one who always spoke first in any exchange, with Mary chipping in to lend support. If I was right it should be relatively easy to keep track of who was who, at least when they were together.

They were watching me, presumably waiting for me to tell them to begin. I nodded, and the performance commenced.

'Let's be having a look at you then, Miss Roly-Poly,' Molly snapped. 'Get those things off, and be quick about it!'

The transformation was startling, not to say uncanny. Molly's posture, mannerisms and even her voice had changed in an instant. It was like watching an accomplished actor slip effortlessly into a new role.

'Get a move on, slowcoach, I haven't got all day!'

Mary stripped hurriedly, casting anxious glances at her sister all the while. Molly paced back and forth, slapping the tawse against her palm.

'Come on, pudding,' she said, in a voice deep as any man's, 'get those dumplings out.'

Mary discarded her under-things and stood before us, naked and trembling. Her figure was a little heavier than I expected. Her breasts were plump, not overly large, with dark, prominent nipples. Her legs were sturdy and her hips wide, and her bush dark and thick.

Without a word Molly began to strike her sister, hitting her thighs, buttocks, back, ribs, and breasts almost indiscriminately. The blows landed with an impressive meaty crack and Mary howled and hopped about, trying to cover up. Protecting one area only exposed another, however, and Molly continued to swipe her mercilessly for a full minute or more. I soon lost count, but it was far in excess of the allocated twelve strokes. Finally Molly paused and stood back.

'Right, old girl, let's see you touch your toes.'

Mary did as commanded, and I realised that this had been no more than a warm-up, and that the punishment proper was now about to start.

Molly swung the tawse and delivered a tremendous whack to her sister's rear. It was a mighty stroke, using the full power of Molly's arm, and the unfortunate victim let out a yelp and shot bolt upright.

'What, jump up, would you?' Molly barked. 'Do that again and you'll get some more! And cease that racket this instant, you hear?'

Mary settled back into position, and was promptly subjected to another scorcher, and a third, and a fourth. She continued to leap about and sing out loudly as the fearsome blows landed, and sister Molly continued to snarl and threaten extra strokes for her wayward behaviour. She was as good as her word, for in the end it was eighteen strokes precisely that the unfortunate Mary drew - and felt each and every one of them keenly, I'm sure.

When the final stroke had been duly delivered, they changed places. The transition from flogger to penitent - and vice-versa - was effected in a trice, and proved another of those uncanny experiences. Molly handed the tawse to her sister and they swapped positions, and swapped personalities also. Mary became the snarling bully, and Molly the wailing victim.

The whole performance was repeated exactly, down to the last detail. During both the warm-up session and the beating that followed, including the six additional strokes, Mary used precisely the same words - so far as I could remember - at precisely the same point in the proceedings. Even the pattern of strokes was exactly as I recalled. In fact, the only difference I could see was that, this time around, both chastiser and sufferer were naked.

When the eighteenth stroke had fallen Mary handed the tawse back to me, and they stood side by side before me. Molly rubbed her buttocks briefly, the only indication from either of them that they had just endured a particularly harsh beating.

They stood quietly, regarding me expectantly. The whole affair left me speechless, so I simply told them they could return to their duties - at which point their faces fell.

'Aren't we to get our treat, sir?' Molly enquired plaintively.

'Treat?' I said. 'What sort of treat?'

'You know, our special treat... here.' She pointed to her groin.

'We always get a treat, sir,' Mary confirmed solemnly.

'And I give you this treat how, exactly?'

'Why, sir, with your hands, of course,' Molly said, and by way of demonstration she held out her hands, extended both middle fingers, and proceeded to make wriggling movements. I found it unexpectedly comic, and had to suppress a smile.

'Or sometimes with your cock, sir,' Mary said.

Molly nodded. 'Or sometimes the wooden cock.'

'Ah, yes,' I said. 'I think I understand. And yes indeed, you shall have your treat. You deserve a treat, the pair of you, for a fine display.'

I put my arms out, extending my middle fingers as Molly had done, and as one the Tavistock girls stepped forward, opened their knees, and lowered themselves onto my hands. I slipped my fingers into their cunnies, provoking simultaneous gasps, and considering what had gone before I was fully expecting a synchronised display, but this did not materialise. Each sister's movements, though broadly similar in form, were all her own.

Whilst in their squatting stances they proceeded to rotate their hips, or rock them back and forth, or raise and lower them, or perform combinations of any and all of these. I tried to complement their movements with movements of my own - no mean feat, considering they were performing independently. It required total concentration and a fair degree of manual dexterity to boot.

As with most things, practice makes perfect, and after a while I was feeling sufficiently confident to bring my thumbs into play. I rubbed each sister's clitoris, drawing forth sighs of delight and quickened gyrations. Vigorous manipulation brought the pair of them rapidly to climax, which they achieved at precisely the same instant.

I found this oddly reassuring, I confess. I was already thinking of them as two halves of the same whole, I suppose, and this commonality of action seemed the most natural thing in the world.

They clung to each other in the immediate aftermath, trapping my hands between them. Eyes shut tight, they sighed and whimpered in a truly engaging fashion, and I flexed my fingers, still inside their cunnies, to make them wriggle.

We three disengaged at last, and they both thanked me solemnly. I thanked them in turn, adding that - though it had been a most splendid show - I might wish to beat them myself, sometimes.

'Of course, sir.'

'Whatever you like, sir.'

I dismissed them, and they gathered up their clothes, put them on - chattering to each other all the while as though I had suddenly become invisible - and left.

When the sound of their voices had died away I poured myself a brandy and collapsed on the couch to recuperate. The whole experience had been exhausting, slightly terrifying, but without a doubt, highly entertaining. All in all, Molly and Mary were a wonderful find and a valuable addition to the household.

All I had to do now was teach them to be quiet in the mornings.

Chapter 27

In the days that followed the twins' arrival, the behaviour of everyone in the household, both above and below stairs, was exemplary, leaving me with no excuse to hand out a thrashing. This sorry state of affairs was bound to end sometime, of course, but lack of exercise was making me vexatious, so I decided to accelerate matters by arranging another of my 'incidents'.

I chose Catherine as the target. It had been a while since our first and only session, and I was keen to set eyes on her slender loveliness once more. I therefore sought out her exercise book - at a time when my wards were otherwise engaged - opened it up, and poured ink upon the page. It was a crude stratagem, but effective nonetheless. I made Irene Hammond aware of my actions, thus ensuring that the offending blot was quickly discovered. A simple 'sin' such as this would earn the girl no more than a dozen, but twelve was better than nothing.

At the appointed time on the appointed day, there came a knock on the study door.

'Enter.' It was not Cathy who came into the room, however, but the eldest of the three sisters.

'Elizabeth,' I said in surprise, 'is something amiss? I was expecting Cathy.'

'She won't be coming,' Elizabeth said. 'I told her to stay in her room. I intend to take her place.'

Her manner was brusque, almost antagonistic, as though she expected an argument and was bracing herself for the ensuing contest of wills. But I did not become angry, for this was a new and intriguing development. From our previous sessions I was certain Elizabeth did not enjoy being beaten, and I therefore assumed her request was made out of genuine concern for her sister. Much as I enjoyed watching Elizabeth present her beautiful bottom for punishment, however, I wasn't about to give up the opportunity to discipline the youngest of my wards. So I leaned back in my chair and gave her a long, thoughtful look.

'A most interesting proposition,' I said. 'I do feel compelled to ask, though - what's in it for me?'

'Why...' she said, somewhat nonplussed, 'you get to punish me instead.'

'But I have that already,' I pointed out. 'I can punish you any time I wish. Even if your behaviour is impeccable, I can always invent some excuse, as I'm sure you must realise by now.'

I had decided to be perfectly frank with her, you see. I wanted the two of us to have no secrets, no illusions. For once I was in full agreement with Reverend Wilkins - honesty is the best policy.

'Yes,' she conceded reluctantly. 'But you can also do... those other things.'

Aha, I thought. Now we're getting to the heart of it. 'These "other things" you speak of,' I said, 'I can also do to you whenever I wish, can't I? Squeeze your titties; tickle your cunny; poke my finger up your bottom - anything I want, in fact.'

My deliberate vulgarity was all part of our new open and honest relationship, and the fact that it brought the most charming flush to her cheeks was purely a bonus.

'Speak up, Elizabeth,' I said, when she failed to reply. 'Can I or can't I do these things to you?'

'You can, uncle,' she said coldly, and although she hadn't said as much, I felt it was the sexual aspects that were troubling her the most. She might indeed wish for Cathy to be spared the rod, but it was the thought of her sister having to submit to my gross fondling that was the real reason for Elizabeth's concern.

In fact she needn't have worried, as I had no intention of fondling Catherine. Mrs Hammond had advised that the girl was still not yet ready, so for the time being at least such pleasures were denied me. I wasn't about to admit as much to Elizabeth, however, as it seemed likely I might profit from the situation. So I leaned forward and looked her straight in the eye.

'Understand me, Elizabeth,' I said. 'I will never relinquish the right to spank your sister. I am utterly resolved on this, and you should put all such thoughts from your mind. Furthermore, Catherine will continue to take her punishments in any way I see fit - including naked, if I so choose - and I will continue to select the implements, the positions, and the severity of the punishment as I deem appropriate. However...'

I left the word hanging. Elizabeth waited, clearly having some difficulty keeping her temper in check.

'However,' I repeated, 'we may be able to reach an understanding on the "other things". I *may* be willing to pledge, for the time being at least, not to touch her in any way that you would consider improper. But you have to offer me something in exchange, something I don't possess already. To repeat my original question - what's in it for me?'

She saw the problem immediately, of course. I never had any doubts about Elizabeth's intelligence, though this self-sacrificing devotion to frivolous Catherine did make me wonder about her commonsense. She frowned, and I could see she was thinking furiously. I waited patiently.

'You could do other things to me,' she said at last. 'We could... go further.'

'Indeed we could,' I said. 'Indeed we *shall*. I've planned all along to do precisely that - in my own good time. No, I need something else from you. Something different.'

We then had a second pause, complete with furrowed female brow and look of intense concentration.

'I could... invent things,' Elizabeth declared carefully. 'Things you could do to me.'

'What sort of things?'

And there, of course, she had a problem. She was an innocent in these matters. She had no idea what might tickle the fancy of a corrupt, lecherous, wicked man-of-the-world such as myself. She was no more capable of inventing her own humiliations than of donning a farrier's apron and shoeing horses. I resolved to help her over her dilemma, however, for it was an intriguing idea that deserved

142

nurturing.

I went to the bookcase that houses my private collection, and selected two rare and rather valuable volumes, one entitled *The Diary of a Slave - Ursula's Story, and the other The Book of Earthly Pleasures*. I handed these to Elizabeth.

'A little light reading,' I said, 'which may prove instructive. The smaller book, *Ursula's Story*, describes the degradations this remarkable young woman was obliged to endure. The other has numerous illustrations, each with a short description of the activity in question. Keep them as long as you wish. If you have any questions I would be more than happy to answer them. For you, Elizabeth, my door is always open.'

She thanked me and left, with two volumes of wickedness clutched to her innocent breast.

Something did occur to me regarding this new development with Elizabeth. Not once in our conversation had she mentioned her other sister. Could it be she knew Victoria was already a 'lost cause', as it were? Perhaps it was precisely because she didn't want Cathy to stray down the same path that Elizabeth sacrificed herself.

Whatever the truth of it, I looked forward to our next meeting with eager anticipation.

I didn't have long to wait, for the very next day Elizabeth came to see me. She was a quick reader, obviously.

'Most instructive, uncle,' she said, as she handed the books back to me.

'Did you find them entertaining, my dear?' I enquired.

'More puzzling than entertaining, in fact. Why do you suppose the people in the *Earthly Pleasures* photographs should be so unhappy, when the author goes to great pains to assure us sexual union is such a joyous activity?'

'Unhappy? What makes you think that?'

'Well, none of them are smiling, are they? Indeed, they all look decidedly glum. Do you not find that strange?'

I knew what she was driving at. She was trying to trap me into admitting there was little joy in sexual activity for its own sake. Probably her argument would develop into an outright condemnation of fornication and an affirmation of the joy of physical union within marriage.

'Camera shy, I expect,' I said, refusing to take the bait. 'But I'm glad you found the books instructive. Can I take it then that you have a proposal for me?'

'You may. I propose to play a piece of music of your choosing. For each false note I play, I will afterwards receive one stroke. As to the hardness of that stroke, and all other related matters, I leave that to you, uncle.'

'An interesting idea,' I admitted, 'but I see one major drawback: your playing is too accomplished, Elizabeth. I can't remember the last time I heard a wrong note from those clever fingers of yours.'

It was true. Unlike Victoria, who played only tolerably well, and Catherine, who played very badly indeed, Elizabeth was most adept.

'I hadn't finished,' she said. 'During the recital, I will be naked.'

I had an instant mental picture of Elizabeth seated at the pianoforte, her beautiful hair done up in an elegant coil, wearing nothing but her mother's string of pearls. It was an entrancing thought, and for a moment I was tempted, but then I shook my head. Even with the distraction her nakedness would undoubtedly cause her, I could still expect a near-perfect rendition.

'I'm sorry, my dear,' I said, 'but I need more.'

'Oh, there's more, uncle. You will be seated on the piano stool, and I will be seated on your lap.'

This was *certainly* an appealing idea, and I started to say as much; but then I noticed her expression. She was watching me with a mixture of amusement and contempt, and I realised there was still more to come. She was mocking me, feeding me a morsel at a time, undoubtedly relishing my puzzlement. But what else might she be suggesting? So far we had Elizabeth playing the piano, naked, and seated on my lap... oh, but surely not...?

'Well done, uncle,' she said. 'I was sure you would get there in the end. While I'm playing, your "throbbing manhood", as Ursula seems fond of calling it, will be inside me. In my bottom, to be precise.'

I was, to put it mildly, thunderstruck. For someone as unworldly as Elizabeth to concoct such a scheme was utterly astonishing, and in so short a time! My grandfather always maintained that nothing good ever came from books. Though I had and have the most enormous respect for him, in this he was quite wrong - and Elizabeth was living proof.

'Well done yourself, my dear,' I said. 'I accept your proposal. It is evident to me now, if indeed I ever doubted it, that you have hidden depths - depths, it seems, I shall shortly be plumbing.'

I was happy to see she had the grace to blush at this point. Ursula's revelations may have broadened her mind quite dramatically, but she was still an innocent at heart.

'Tell me,' I said, 'what shall we name it, this new game you've invented?'

'Name it, uncle?'

'Indeed. Every game needs a name, doesn't it? Where would tiddlywinks be if someone hadn't called it "tiddlywinks"? Or chess, or Beggar-my-Neighbour?'

'Indeed,' she said, looking at me a little uncertainly.

'What about Buggery in B-flat?' I suggested. 'Or Sodomy Sonata?'

'Ah, yes,' she said, as the light dawned. 'I see what you mean.'

'I have it,' I said. 'Anal Aria.'

Elizabeth scowled at me. 'Shame on you, Uncle James; now you're just being cruel. You know I have no voice for singing. This is to be an instrumental piece, as I believe I made plain at the start.'

It was remarkable. One could not hope to meet a more intelligent, level-headed young lady, but still she possessed that flawed female logic. She was happily offering herself for buggery one second, then taking umbrage over my implied suggestion she might have to sing the next. Make what sense of that you can.

'Oh, you'll sing, Elizabeth,' I assured her. 'An instrumental piece it may be, but you'll certainly sing, I promise you that.'

Now that it was settled I was understandably keen to press ahead with the Rectal Recital, as we eventually decided to call it, and we agreed that it should take place that very evening.

Irene Hammond was also invited, as we would need her to count the false notes and mark these on the score. Elizabeth was not entirely happy at this (from her reaction when I suggested it, I suspected some slight animosity between the two of them) but understood the need. I therefore sent for the governess and appraised her of the situation. She took the news remarkably calmly, I thought, with just a slight raising of the eyebrows to betray her surprise. The woman had enviable self-control.

'This evening you say, sir?' she said.

'Indeed,' I said. 'Nine o'clock sharp. I would ask both of you please to be punctual. Late arrivals at a concert are such a bore.'

At the appointed time the three of us assembled in the music room.

'You are clear on what is required of you, Mrs Hammond?' I said. 'Your task is to count the wrong notes. Keep score on the score, as it were.'

The pun tickled my fancy, and I confess I laughed out loud. Irene Hammond allowed herself a slight smile, but Elizabeth quite failed to see the humour in it. In fact, now that the moment of truth was almost upon her, she seemed decidedly subdued. Never mind; she would soon perk up once the recital was underway, I had no doubt about that.

I nodded to my ward, and she began to undress. After lowering the piano stool as far as it would go, I sat down, unfastened my trousers, and took out my 'throbbing manhood'. I'd had the foresight to obtain a small packet of butter from Mrs Smith, and I proceeded to lubricate said organ in preparation for breaching Elizabeth's back passage.

Irene Hammond placed the score on the music rest and waited, pen in hand. We both turned to Elizabeth, naked now, but seemingly ambivalent all of a sudden about the whole affair.

'Elizabeth,' I said, patting my knee, 'please be seated.'

She did not move. Her mouth opened, and for one terrible moment I thought she was going to call the whole thing off. But whatever she was about to say remained unspoken. She closed her mouth, took a deep breath, and walked stiffly over to me.

She looked down at my erect cock with a mixture of fear and fascination. I put my hands on her hips and steered her into position, facing the keyboard, her legs straddling my own.

'Come down, now,' I coaxed. 'Gently... gently...'

She bent her knees and lowered herself onto my lap. With one hand I guided my cock between her buttocks, and touched the tip to her anus. She came to a halt, pivoting there on my cock.

'Sit,' I commanded firmly.

She sat... and cried out, her whole body stiffening. I think she would have risen but I had both hands on her waist once more, and held her down.

'Heaven help me,' she groaned.

It was some time since I'd read *Diary of a Slave*, and I was somewhat hazy on the details, but I suspected Ursula had failed to point out that the human anus is by nature tight, and the insertion of a cock is therefore painful, especially to the uninitiated.

'Try to relax,' I said. 'Not easy, I know, but it will help.'

We stayed like that for some minutes, and Elizabeth did indeed seem to find a degree of relief. As for myself, the sensation of being inside the beautiful young lady was incomparable, and though the last thing I wanted was to hurry the experience, I thought we should make a start.

'Please proceed when you feel ready, Elizabeth,' I said.

'Yes, uncle,' she gasped sweetly, then placed her fingers on the keys and the Rectal Recital commenced.

I had chosen - or, more precisely, Irene Hammond had chosen - a piece by Beethoven, Elizabeth's favourite composer. I play no instrument myself, nor can I read music, so I had no way of judging how difficult a piece it was. Certainly, however, there were many, many notes on each page, and plenty of potential, therefore, to find wrong ones.

Elizabeth was doing exceptionally well at the halfway point, Mrs Hammond marking just two false notes on the score, right at the start of the piece. As may be imagined, I was growing increasingly frustrated at the way things were working out, and more from bad temper than by design I tried to distract my ward, and found that by judicious tensing of buttock, thigh and calf muscles, I could bounce her slightly on my lap. I was instantly rewarded with three more wrong notes, and I realised I had hit upon the answer. I bounced her faster, and Elizabeth's playing took a significant turn for the worse, with Irene Hammond's pen scattering ticks across the sheet. Perhaps it was panic on Elizabeth's part at seeing the strokes mount up, or maybe the growing ache in her rectum distracted her, but things deteriorated rapidly from that point onwards.

But bouncing her soon proved extremely tiring, and my leg muscles began to protest violently at the unaccustomed exercise. Elizabeth was almost at the end of the piece, however, so I drove myself on, and as the final note sounded we both slumped forward, gasping. Truly, for performer and audience alike, good music can be both physically and emotionally draining.

Following the Rectal Recital the household has settled into a most satisfactory routine. Rarely a day passes without some female or other having to bare her buttocks and submit to my most diligent attentions.

I try to ensure that both Elizabeth and Catherine are disciplined two or three times a month at least. Any less, I find, and Elizabeth tends to become difficult and Cathy surly. It is usually necessary to arrange some incident to justify thrashing them, though Cathy has occasionally been known to err all by herself. With Irene Hammond's help, of course, orchestrating incidents of this sort is simplicity itself.

Victoria's punishments remain much more frequent - two or three times a week, generally - for reasons that have been sufficiently well explained, I think. Our 'tantalus' sessions grew ever bolder following the May Day incident, until, inevitably, I ended up mounting her - an experience Victoria is eager to repeat at every possible opportunity. The age difference, I am happy to say, has proved not to be an obstacle after all.

As to the staff, corporal punishment figures significantly in their lives also. In Mrs Smith's case, I decided Irene Hammond and myself would share the responsibility for maintaining discipline. Though most honest and earnest in her endeavours, the cook has an uncanny knack for getting things wrong. She seems to me a woman permanently dogged by ill luck - the incident with the eggs being only the first of many such calamities, as it transpired - so that Mrs Hammond and I are frequently obliged to send for her. The cook's broad buttocks and plump thighs, one observes, are rarely free of stripes.

Molly and Mary Tavistock's exceeding strangeness did diminish somewhat in time, as I grew more used to their ways. Their behaviour remains unconventional to say the least, however, and I find it necessary to warm their backsides - or have them do it for me - on a regular basis. They are, I note, just as greedy as Victoria when it comes to their 'treats'.

Eccentricity aside, the twins have proved themselves very hardworking and willing, so that Rose and Alice have been able to shed a good deal of their workload - to their obvious relief, and to the benefit of their health. Alice remains as anxious as ever, and as fearful of the cane - which is unfortunate for her, as she seems by nature destined to taste the thing often. Rose has mellowed a little, and is less inclined to disrespectful behaviour, so that punishments for her have become a tolerably rare event. I do make sure to service her regularly, however, knowing she would soon seek pastures new if I did not.

Irene Hammond's own prediction that she was not done with punishments was soon shown to be entirely accurate. From time to time the urge to lay a few stripes across that perfect posterior proves irresistible, and I find some reason to call her to my study. A brisk dozen or two is generally enough to exorcise the demon, after which an altogether different urge overtakes me. Bedding my beautiful governess remains one of the chief delights of my life.

With no dearth of bottoms to spank and young women to mount, fate could not have been kinder to me. As I would be the first to admit, I am indeed a most fortunate man.